Dead Between the Lines

Center Point
Large Print

Also by Denise Swanson and available from
Center Point Large Print:

Devereaux's Dime Store Mysteries:
  Nickeled-and-Dimed to Death

Scumble River Mysteries:
  Murder of the Cat's Meow
  Murder of a Bookstore Babe

**This Large Print Book carries the
Seal of Approval of N.A.V.H.**

Dead Between the Lines

A Devereaux's Dime Store Mystery

DENISE SWANSON

CENTER POINT LARGE PRINT
THORNDIKE, MAINE

This Center Point Large Print edition is published in the year
2014 by arrangement with NAL Signet,
a member of Penguin Group (USA) LLC,
a Penguin Random House Company.

The text of this Large Print edition is unabridged.
In other aspects, this book may vary
from the original edition.
Printed in the United States of America
on permanent paper.
Set in 16-point Times New Roman type.

ISBN: 978-1-62899-111-6

Library of Congress Cataloging-in-Publication Data

Swanson, Denise.
Dead between the lines : a Devereaux's dime store mystery /
   Denise Swanson. — Center Point Large Print edition.
pages ; cm.
Summary: "Opening an old-fashioned five-and-dime shop in her small
Missouri hometown has been a great change for Devereaux 'Dev'
Sinclair. But when she hosts a reading group there, she learns that bad
writing can mean life or death"—Provided by publisher.
ISBN 978-1-62899-111-6 (library binding : alk. paper)
1. Stores, Retail—Fiction. 2. Businesswomen—Fiction.
   3. Murder—Investigation—Fiction. 4. Large type books. I. Title.
PS3619.W36D43 2012
813'.6—dc23

2014008478

To the real Stepping Out Book Club.
You gals rock!
Thank you for the inspiration.

Dead Between
the Lines

Chapter 1

Well, this was awkward. In my head, I could hear my grandmother, Birdie, yelling, "Devereaux Ann Sinclair, what have you gotten yourself into this time?" Ann wasn't my real middle name, but little details like that never stood in Gran's way when she was truly ticked off at me.

I slid a cautious glance to my left. My shop, Devereaux's Dime Store and Gift Baskets, boasted three soda-fountain stools, and two of them were occupied by men who had recently kissed me silly. In the antique Bradley & Hubbard cast-iron mirror hanging behind the counter, I could see them sitting shoulder to shoulder, glaring at each other. The gilt cherub on top of the glass smirked back at them.

Being the coward that I am, I ignored the two rivals for my affection and forced my poor weekend clerk, Xylia Locke, to deal with them while I stayed firmly behind my beloved 1920s brass cash register, ringing up the purchases of the last few, lingering customers. As I bagged Mr. Williams's Lucky Tiger liquid cream shave, I wondered what my straight-laced employee thought of the two smoldering men in front of her, or, for that matter, what her opinion was of my less than orderly life. Xylia was majoring in business administration at the local junior college, and she hated it when life—especially the emotional part—got muddled, chaotic, or messy.

Xylia liked her world to be neat and tidy. She was a woman who never appeared in public in anything but perfectly tailored slacks and sweater sets in muted colors. In fact, when I had first hired her, she'd offered to take a pay cut in exchange for not having to wear a sweatshirt with the store logo embroidered on the front. I'd been a little insulted that she didn't want to have my name across her chest, but I'd swallowed my pride and agreed to her proposal.

Even the small amount of money I saved on her salary was a godsend to my cash-starved bottom line. Because while quitting my consulting job at Stramp Investments and buying the dime store had reduced my round-trip commute from two hours to fifteen minutes, and cut the time I spent at work almost in half, it had also shrunk my income from six figures to nearly poverty level. So even if it bruised my ego a bit that Xylia didn't like my sweatshirt design, any way that I could keep my books in the black was okay with me.

The change in career path, aspirations, and lifestyle had all been worth it, because it had enabled me to spend extra time with my grandmother. When Birdie's doctor had informed me that Gran needed me to be around more due to her memory issues, I knew it was my turn to help her. How could I do anything less, since she had been the one who had taken me in and loved me when I had nowhere else to go and no one else who cared?

I had just turned sixteen when my father went to prison for manslaughter and possession of a controlled substance. My mother, unable to handle the shame, loss of income, and reduced social status, had dropped me on my grandmother's front porch with a fifty-dollar bill and a couple of suitcases containing all that was left of my previous life. Having disposed of her burden, Mom then headed to California to start over, leaving my grandmother and me to face the town's condemnation by ourselves.

"Ms. Sinclair?" Xylia slipped from behind the soda fountain and scurried over to me as I flicked off the neon OPEN sign. It was Friday and we closed at six o'clock.

"Yes?" I had given up trying to persuade her to call me Dev or even Devereaux. She claimed it didn't show the degree of respect an employee should have for her superior. Sometimes I wondered what century Xylia thought we were living in. While I loved vintage collectibles and antiques, I had no desire to bring back the formal manners and rigid customs of days gone by.

"What about them?" Xylia glanced uneasily

between the men and the locked door. "Are they staying?"

"Apparently." They obviously had no intention of budging from their perches. Having swiveled around to face the store, they had crossed their arms in identical gestures of stubborn defiance, and were now glaring alternately at me and at each other. Their silence was unnerving, and if looks could kill, both guys would be dead and I'd be fatally wounded.

"But we have to get ready for the book club." Xylia fingered the tiny heart-shaped birthmark on her cheek, something she did only in times of extreme stress. "They aren't members."

"It'll be fine." Throughout Xylia's shift, I'd noticed that she had been even more tightly wound than usual. Now I realized that she must be nervous about hosting her club's meeting. It had been her idea to have it at the dime store, and she probably felt responsible for the event's outcome.

"We won't have enough chairs." Her voice rose. "Mr. Quistgaard was very specific in his requirements. He'll leave if anyone is standing. Everything will be ruined."

"We'll work it out," I assured her. "Do you know Mr. Quistgaard?" Seating for everyone seemed an odd condition for an author to have, especially one who wasn't a big name. If J. K. Rowling or Nora Roberts wanted everyone sitting, you'd damn well better have everyone off their feet, but Lance Quistgaard? Not so much. "Did you select his book for your club?"

"Our president, Mrs. Zeigler, engages all our speakers." Xylia backed away from me, bumping into the APRIL SHOWERS BRINGS MAY FLOWERS display. "Usually through their Web sites."

"I see." I bent to replace an overturned red clay pot on a bag of mulch.

"Let me do that." Xylia nudged me out of the way and moved the small Victorian iron patio table a fraction of an inch to the left, then straightened the two matching chairs. "I've been meaning to fix this all afternoon." She adjusted the shepherd's hook plant hanger holding a basket of yellow and purple pansies a smidgen to the right.

Did I mention that my clerk was a little OCD?

As I leaned against the gas grill that the hardware store had loaned me for my display, I said, "Did you enjoy this month's book?"

"Uh." Xylia bit her lip. "I'm sure I will once I understand the poems better."

One of the men at the soda fountain cleared his throat, and Xylia flinched at the sound. She grimaced, then put her hand on my arm and pleaded, "Do something before they spoil the whole evening."

"Don't worry." I turned away so she couldn't see me roll my eyes. "They'll be gone before the author arrives." I was fairly certain neither of the men currently scrutinizing me was interested in attending a poetry reading.

"But wh—"

"I'll handle it." I cut her off before she could hyperventilate. "My Supergirl cape is at the dry cleaner, so you'll just have to take my word for it, but I promise they'll leave before you're finished setting up."

Xylia opened her mouth to protest, but closed it when I frowned and ordered, "Go start getting the crafting alcove ready for your group."

With one last worried peek over her shoulder, Xylia headed toward the back room, where the folding tables and chairs were stored.

The minute she was out of sight, both men shot off their seats and stomped toward me. Taking a deep breath, I focused on the one who, by elbowing his competition, then cutting his opponent off at the pass, got to me first. Tall, dark, and devastating, Deputy U.S. Marshal Jake Del Vecchio had blown back into town an hour ago, plainly expecting us to pick up where we had left off, and just as plainly unhappy to find another guy warming *his* stool at *my* soda fountain.

I had met Jake when he was recuperating from a line-of-duty injury at his granduncle's ranch. He had helped me clear my name when I was accused of murdering my old boyfriend's fiancée. Then a month ago, after being declared fit for duty, he'd returned to St. Louis, and except for a brief visit and make-out session a few weeks ago, that was the last I'd seen of him.

Now, as he cupped my cheek, his words sent a sizzle down my spine. "I've been dreaming about doing this the entire time I was gone."

He leaned in for a kiss, but with his mouth inches from mine, I stepped back, and his hand dropped to his side. It had been hard to pull away. The electricity between us was enough to light up most of North America. But I knew that if I let our lips touch, I'd lose all my willpower to resist, and I couldn't allow that to happen.

In the meantime, the guy who had been sitting next to Jake had reached my side. Sleek, elegant, and aristocratic, Dr. Noah Underwood had been my high school boyfriend. Because both our mothers were pregnant at the same time, we claimed to have known each other since the womb. The Underwoods and the Sinclairs were two of the five founding families of Shadow Bend, Missouri, our hometown, which meant that while growing up we were constantly thrown together at parties, charity events, and community functions. So when Noah and I hit adolescence, it had seemed inevitable that we would become sweethearts.

For a while, we were inseparable. During that time, Noah was the most important person in my life, and I thought I was the most important one in his. Sadly, I'd been mistaken. When we started dating, the Sinclairs and the Underwoods were social equals. But after my father's disgrace, the Sinclairs became the town pariahs and Noah dropped me like a lit match, before his reputation could go up in the same flames that had consumed my family's good name.

According to Noah, he'd had a noble reason for breaking off with me. However, even though he'd proven there was still a spark between us, I wasn't sure I believed his version of past events. And I definitely didn't trust that he wouldn't dump me or betray me again if a similar situation were to occur.

Moving with an inherent grace, Noah put both hands on my shoulders and spun me so that I was facing him. That I now had my back to Jake was probably just a bonus. Once Noah was sure he had my attention—he was a methodical kind of guy—he put his lips to my ear and whispered, "Get rid of Deputy Dawg. I've got a surprise planned for you."

"What?" His warm breath tickling my neck sent a bibbidi-bobbidi-boo message to my girl parts. Both of these guys could melt my panties right off my hips. "Were we supposed to get together tonight?" I knew we didn't have plans because that wasn't something I would have forgotten, but I wanted to hear his explanation.

"No." Noah's head dipped closer. "I thought it would be fun to be spontaneous."

"Possibly." I finally got control of myself and

leaned away from him. "Except I have a club meeting here at seven, and Gran is expecting me home after that."

"Take your hands off her, Frat Boy." Jake muscled his way in between us.

I moved so that I was facing both guys, but when they crowded forward, I realized that I had let them corner me. My back was against solid shelves, so I couldn't retreat, and the men had cut off any possible forward escape route.

"Hold it, fellas." I crossed my arms. "Let's maintain a little personal space here, shall we?"

Jake cocked a dark brow and gave me a badass grin but he didn't budge, and Noah, despite looking a little sheepish, didn't give an inch, either. Frustrated, I put a hand on each of their chests and shoved. Even though Jake was brawnier, Noah had a lean strength, so it was like pushing against twin statues.

Lowering my gaze to their crotches, I threatened, "Don't make me go for the family jewels."

Jake raised his hands. "Fine." He tipped his head toward Noah. "But are you really dating this bozo?"

Noah narrowed his slate gray eyes, shouldered his way in front of Jake, and said to me, "After not hearing from this jerk for weeks, you're not thinking of seeing him again, are you?"

Well, hell! This was truly a hot mess. I *so* didn't want to have this conversation with either of them right this minute. Mostly because I had no idea what to say. Both men were gorgeous in utterly different ways. Mysterious versus familiar. Strikingly masculine versus classically handsome. A German shepherd versus a Russian wolfhound.

However, both had significant drawbacks as well. While the sexual chemistry between Jake and me was off the charts, he lived in St. Louis, a good five hours away. There was also the trouble-some detail that he worked closely—very closely—with his ex-wife, who happened to be his team leader and thus his boss. In fact, his most recent assignment had required that they pretend to be boyfriend and girlfriend.

So, Noah had the advantage of availability, but I had a painful history with him. Jake had a clean slate, but complications.

Neither guy was a sure thing, nor was either one an obvious choice. With all that in mind, as well as the knowledge of my many previous romantic missteps, I figured that dating either man would probably be a lesson in candy-coated misery.

What I should do was convince them that we could all be friends and keep both relationships platonic. Of course, I rarely did what I should. Still, I had to do something before they killed each other or shed someone else's blood, namely mine. I'd detested being a suspect in a murder case, but I was pretty damn sure I'd hate being a victim even more.

Chapter 2

It had taken all my schmoozing skills to persuade Jake and Noah to leave without me. In the end, I'd had to promise to go out with each guy alone. Jake had insisted on Saturday night, and Noah had settled for Sunday afternoon. To be honest, I was curious as to why they'd both turned up at the dime store within minutes of each other, since I hadn't had a date with either one of them, and I figured it would be easier to get the truth if I talked to them separately.

Now, as I greeted the members of the Stepping Out Book Club, I put my man problems aside and concentrated on charming the attendees. They were all commenting on how nice the weather was for early May, and I agreed, subtly pointing out my gardening display as they passed.

This was the first time they had met in my store, and I hoped the group would decide to use my place on a regular basis. When Xylia had approached me about having their meeting at the dime store, I was a little hesitant. I loved hosting the various craft groups, but most of them met during the day, and I didn't want another evening commitment that would mean spending more time away from Gran. I couldn't afford to hire extra help, so if the store was open, I had to be there.

However, after Xylia had outlined the arguments in favor of her proposition, I'd had to admit it was a good deal. The club had agreed to order this month's selection from me, which meant eighteen copies—one member already owned the book—of *Ode to a Small Midwestern Town* at twenty-five bucks a pop, which gave me a profit of a hundred and eighty dollars. I had also insisted that they had to clean up afterward and pay me to provide the refreshments.

I was charging the members fifteen clams each for the wine, cheese, and crackers that had cost me less than a C note and taken only half an hour to set up. This little shindig would net me nearly four Benjamins for two hours of my time. It was as close to the salary I'd been making as an investment consultant as I'd gotten since buying the store.

A familiar voice snapped me out of my greedy reverie. "Devereaux!"

"Yes, ma'am." I involuntarily straightened my spine, then pasted a smile over my startled expression. Mrs. Ziegler, the book club president, was standing on the threshold of the dime store's open door, her face twisted into an impatient frown. Evidently, I was blocking her path, and judging from the tapping of her impeccably shined black pumps, I had been doing so for quite some time.

She had been the principal of the high school for as long as I could remember, and although everyone called her Mrs. Ziegler, no one could recall a Mr. Ziegler. Not that anyone had the nerve to question her about him.

I stepped out of her way and she swept past me, stopping near the glass-front candy case. For a nanosecond, I thought she wanted to purchase a delectable piece of vanilla-caramel-praline fudge or the candy of the month, a lavender lemonade truffle. Instead, she smiled and said, "Thank you for allowing us to meet in your store."

"You're very welcome." I admired Mrs. Zeigler, but in a scared, she-might-humiliate-me kind of way. She was always immaculately dressed, usually in a well-tailored skirt and pristine blouse. And neither heat nor rain seemed to affect her perfectly smooth black chignon. When I'd been in school, I'd half believed she was a robot or some other nonhuman life form.

"But . . ." Mrs. Zeigler waved her index finger back and forth in front of my nose. "Fifteen dollars for refreshments is outrageous. If we come back here, the cost will have to be much, much lower. Understood?"

"While I'm honored you chose my store . . ." I automatically started to refuse to negotiate, since spending more hours away from Gran would only be worthwhile if I could make a huge profit. But I stuttered to a stop when I realized that ticking off one of Shadow Bend's most influential citizens would not be a good idea.

"Yes?" Mrs. Zeigler crossed her arms. "So you'll lower the price?"

Thinking fast, I said, "I could do that if I served pastry and coffee."

"Hmm." Mrs. Zeigler pursed her mouth. "No. That won't do at all. I doubt many of our members would be happy without their alcohol."

"My only other option would be to serve less expensive wine and cheeses." There was no way I was making less on the arrangement, so something else had to give. "I could do a jug red and white, with grocery store cheddar, Colby, and pepper jack for ten dollars per person."

"It's a deal." Mrs. Zeigler adjusted her purse strap to sit more securely on her shoulder. "By the way." She pointed to my worktable where I, thankfully, had gathered the retro-themed materials for Mr. Anders's retirement party basket and not the sexy paraphernalia for the country club's Girls Night Out raffle. "Good job on those Easter baskets you made for the Athletic Booster Club's fund-raiser."

"Thank you." I glanced discreetly at the vintage Ingraham schoolhouse regulator hanging on the wall behind the cash register. It was already a few minutes after seven. If I didn't get this show on the road, I'd be here all night. "I heard the boosters made enough to buy new uniforms for all the teams and the cheer squad."

"Yes, they did." Mrs. Zeigler pressed her lips together, creating a parenthesis of wrinkles around her mouth and a deep valley between her dark eyebrows. "But the latter had to be returned. The cheerleading coach's judgment left much to be desired."

"What a shame." The clock was ticking and Gran was expecting me no later than nine thirty. If I didn't move things along, she'd give my share of the pizza to her cat. "We've got chairs and tables set up in the craft corner." I gestured toward the rear of the store. "I believe everyone but your speaker is here, and I'll bring him to you as soon as he arrives."

"Very good." Mrs. Zeigler nodded and headed toward the alcove.

Phew! I slumped against the wall. I always felt as if I was standing up for my master's degree's final oral exam when I spoke with Mrs. Zeigler.

"Devereaux!"

I snapped to attention. Mrs. Zeigler had turned back toward me and was tapping her foot again.

My shoulders tense and expecting the worst, I said cautiously, "Yes?"

"After everyone leaves tonight, please remind me that I want to place a basket order," she instructed. "I don't want to forget."

"Okay." I stretched out the word, wondering why she didn't just call or come into the store during my regular business hours.

"At the end of this month, my spouse and I will have been together for thirty years." She winked at me. "We're going away for the weekend and I want to bring one of your 'special' creations with us as an anniversary surprise."

I inhaled so abruptly that I choked. When my eyes stopped watering, Mrs. Zeigler was gone. Had the school principal, the Terror of Shadow Bend High, really just told me she wanted to order an erotic basket? More to the point, could I make her one she'd like?

Nearly half an hour later, while I was still contemplating the fact that Mrs. Zeigler did indeed have a husband, and apparently a love life, the guest of honor finally showed up. There hadn't been much information about him on his Web site, and what was there hadn't been all that flattering, making him seem supercilious and elitist. It always amazed me that on the Internet, where people could be anything they wanted to be, they so often chose to be stupid.

I'd been surprised that there hadn't been an author photo anywhere online or even in his book, a collection of poetry from a small press, but Lance Quistgaard was exactly as I had imagined. Actually, he was perhaps a tad better-looking.

He was tall and lean, dressed in a charcoal gray

suit and black silk turtleneck. His dark hair was brushed straight back to reveal a dramatic widow's peak, and on his cheeks was a day's worth of stubble that stood out starkly against his pale skin. He looked like an idealized Hollywood version of a poet. Or possibly a vampire. Maybe that's why he was so late. The sun had set only a few minutes ago, so maybe he'd just risen from his coffin.

Laughing at my wild imagination, I stepped forward and said, "Mr. Quistgaard, I presume?" When he inclined his head, I held out my hand. "Welcome. I'm Devereaux Sinclair, the owner of the dime store."

He stared silently at me for a long moment. His eyes were so black that I couldn't make out a pupil. At last, he said, "With your less than slim figure, you should never wear a sweatshirt. It adds pounds to your frame. Actually, women should always dress in fitted apparel with appropriate foundation garments. Most men do not want to see jiggling flesh."

"I didn't realize you were a fashion expert as well as a writer." It took almost all of my willpower to keep from smacking the arrogant jerk, and the rest of my self-control to stop myself from tugging at the offending article of clothing. "Now let me show you to where the people who care about your opinion are gathered."

"No need to get testy." He raised a brow. "All women need a little discipline."

Oh. My. God! I would so have to "accidently" spill red wine on this pervert. Too bad I didn't have any hot coffee to pour on his crotch. Biting my tongue, I led him to the crafting alcove, introduced him to Mrs. Zeigler, and retreated before I gave in to the impulse to beat the crap out of him. Some people really ask for a high five. With a fist. To the chin.

I would definitely not be carrying Quistgaard's hardcover in my store or ever use it as the one perfect book that I placed in the center of all my baskets as my trademark. Speaking of which, after making sure the front door was locked, I headed toward the old kitchen table I used as a workbench to continue assembling the retirement basket I had begun that afternoon.

The basket part of my business was much more profitable than the dime store. I was selling my creativity more than the actual bits and pieces, so the markup was terrific. Because of that, I squeezed working on them into any spare moment I had, and the book-club meeting was an ideal time to fill several orders.

I set the alert app on my cell phone for forty-five minutes and let my muse fly free. I was humming Alicia Keys's "Girl on Fire" when the alarm sounded and I came crashing out of my fantasy world. Pleased with my productivity—two finished baskets and a good start on a third one—I cleaned up my workbench and went into the storeroom to get the refreshments.

The wine and glasses were already arranged on a cart. I retrieved the cheese platter from the mini fridge and took the plastic wrap from the tray of crackers, then wheeled the food and drink into the craft area. As soon as I stepped into the alcove, I noticed that Quistgaard was backed up nearly all the way to the wall, and it was clear that he wasn't happy with the way the Q and A was going.

While I placed the refreshments on the table in the rear, I looked over his audience. The club members appeared to be an eclectic group that was fairly evenly divided in gender, age, and socioeconomic standing. I knew at least half of the attendees by name and recognized the others from having seen them around town. Many were active in other organizations that I hosted, and it was interesting to see the expressions on their faces as Quistgaard spoke.

Only one or two of the younger members seemed captivated by the poet. The rest of the participants were frowning at Quistgaard's answers to their queries. I wondered if his offensive attitude toward women had been apparent in his poetry or if there was another reason for the attendees' animosity. I hadn't read his book, and, after meeting him, I didn't intend to.

I was filling the last of the wineglasses when the local pawnshop owner, Addison Campbell, raised a beefy arm. Addie was a massive guy with multiple tattoos—some of which were rumored to be in places most guys would never allow a needle. When he had joined the knitting group that met in my store, I had been astonished to see a man with tats, earrings, and a shaved head drive up on his Harley. He'd shocked me again when I'd seen his name on the book-club membership list.

Someday I would have to quit prejudging people, but I didn't see that happening anytime soon. Even though I knew it was wrong, I wasn't evolved enough to make myself stop doing it. As Poppy Kincaid, one of my best friends, would say, she and I are works in progress, and, unfortunately, we aren't making much headway.

When Quistgaard acknowledged Addie, my attention returned to the drama unfolding in front of me and I listened closely as the pawnshop owner's gravelly voice rumbled from his barrel-shaped chest. "It seems to me that many of your poems dis small-town life. I thought you were local. Are you originally from the city?"

"My private life isn't up for discussion." Quistgaard attempted to turn away from Addie, but the brawny merchant shot to his feet.

"I'm not asking about your private life." Addie's acne-scarred face was furrowed in a menacing glare. "My question was, Do you have any personal experience to back up your contempt?"

"And I said, I'm not answering it." Quistgaard

folded his arms. "It's obvious that a Neanderthal like you would never understand my life or my poetry. Why are you even here?"

Addie growled, then closed his eyes, and his lips moved silently. I wondered if he was counting to ten or maybe reciting the serenity prayer. He'd told me he was seeing a counselor for anger-management issues, but other than taking up knitting, I didn't know how the life coach had advised Addie to handle his rage.

I was relieved when Addie, still breathing heavily, stomped out of the craft alcove, muttering that mosquitoes have lots of buzz until you smack them. Better the pawnshop owner leave early than beat Quistgaard to a bloody pulp—even if the man deserved it.

Quistgaard smiled in triumph, then nodded to Kiara Howard, the event coordinator for the country club, and asked, "Do you have a question, little lady?"

The striking African-American woman hadn't raised her hand, but she didn't hesitate. "My name is Ms. Howard, not little lady, and, actually, I'd like to hear what you have to say about Addie's observation that your writing appears to disdain rural communities. Your poems seem to totally disparage our values and beliefs."

Quistgaard narrowed his eyes and snapped, "You are correct." He folded in half the sheaf of papers he held and stuffed them into the pocket of his suit jacket. "Small towns are full of hypocrites who claim to have high moral standards, but when no one is looking, they act differently."

"That's a gross generalization," objected Yale Gordon, a thirtysomething physician's assistant. "Is that your personal experience? Or perhaps you've studied the subject and have proof to back it up."

"A bard doesn't need proof." Quistgaard's tone grew even more condescending.

When he ignored the raised hand of Veronica "Ronni" Ksiazak, the owner of the local B & B, she stood up and stated, "Your opinion of women and their place in society is also quite evident in your writing."

"Yes, it is." Quistgaard stared at her. "And nothing I've experienced here tonight has changed my mind about either women or small towns."

"And nothing you've had to say here tonight has changed my mind about you." Ronni raised her chin. "I'm just sorry I wasted my money buying your book."

"It always comes down to money with women like you," Quistgaard said with a sneer. "Any author worth his salt doesn't sell his talent for mere money. He writes for the sake of the art, not for cash. I'm not a genre hack." His lips twisted; then he said almost to himself, "Money is a necessary evil, but how that money is earned is what adds to an artist's prestige. Any other procurement of income should remain unspoken."

Ronni looked over at Mrs. Zeigler and asked, "Why *did* we choose him?"

"Mr. Quistgaard sent me a letter saying that he was a local author and requested to speak to our club." Mrs. Zeigler turned her gaze to the poet. "The sample of your poetry that you sent was quite different from what appears in your book. Why is that, Mr. Quistgaard?"

"I don't know what you mean." Quistgaard brushed past Mrs. Zeigler, grabbed a glass of wine from the table, and mocked, "As a poet, I address various topics. Surely you didn't expect all my poems to be about puppies and rainbows."

"Perhaps not," Mrs. Zeigler replied, joining him in front of the refreshments. "But shouldn't your writing be strong enough that even if the reader doesn't agree with your point of view, he or she finds the work compelling enough to overlook any objections?"

The rest of the group had risen to their feet, gathered around the duo, and were avidly watching the exchange between them.

"Are you saying my writing isn't gripping?" Quistgaard chugged his chardonnay, grabbed the bottle from my hand, and poured himself another glassful. "It's clear from all the inane questions, you people have no concept of great poetry. I should never have come here. I thought

I'd finally found readers who would discern my talent now that I'd written something on which I could proudly put my name."

He opened his mouth to continue, but snapped it shut when a man who looked familiar but whom I couldn't place scowled at him, then got up and walked away.

"This clearly isn't a group that can appreciate my brilliance." Quistgaard took another swig of wine, swallowed, and said, "But I still expect my honorarium." He held out his palm, muttering something about this being the last time he'd ever need to beg for money.

"Certainly." Mrs. Zeigler placed an envelope in his hand. She didn't appear at all flustered by his diatribe. "I'm sorry you feel we disrespected your work. We certainly didn't mean to offend you, but the purpose of our club is to discuss both what we like and what we don't like, as well as to try to understand what we've read."

Sniffing loudly, Quistgaard clanked his glass down on the table and strode out of the alcove, muttering, "Philistines."

I started after him to escort him to the front door, but a group swarmed in on the refreshment table and I lost track of where everyone went.

By the time I finished serving the crowd and checked the store, Quistgaard had disappeared. However, several others were milling around the store, and I herded them back to the craft alcove, all the while trying to figure out what had happened.

Did book-club speakers generally storm away from a meeting like that? I certainly hadn't expected to have to deal with a third ticked-off male this evening. The two in my private life had been more than enough for one day, thank you very much.

Shrugging, I put on my shopkeeper's face and made sure everyone was happy. At least none of the encounters had ended in bloodshed. To me, that was one for the win column.

Chapter 3

"Who scraped the salt off your pretzel?" Birdie demanded when I trudged into the living room and threw myself on the couch.

"Nobody." It was nine-thirty exactly, and I'd had to channel my inner drill sergeant in order to get the Stepping Out Book Club, or SOBs as I now called them, to leave the store. "It's just been a long and weird day. The guest author stormed out of the meeting."

"Sweet Jesus!" Gran was sitting in her favorite chair, watching a rerun of *Law & Order*. "What on God's green earth made him do that?"

"I'm not sure." I eyed Banshee, Birdie's ancient Siamese, who was scrutinizing me from the protected position of Gran's lap.

While I loved animals, Banshee was less a cuddly kitty and more a bloodcurdling beast. Hostilities between the cat and me had commenced the day he ate my pet gerbil, and there'd been no sign of a cease-fire in the ensuing twelve years. He relentlessly attacked me from the tops of bookshelves and around corners, and I retaliated any way I could.

"I knew that group would be nothing but

trouble," Birdie *tsk*ed, puckering her mouth so tight her face looked like an albino raisin.

"Really?" I got off the sofa and headed toward the kitchen. "Why?"

Gran followed, elbowing me aside as she grabbed a couple of pot holders from the drawer. "Those people have too much time on their hands if they can waste it yakking about some darn fool poems." The heavenly aroma of mozzarella and pepperoni drifted up to me as she opened the oven door and took out a round pan.

"At least I made a nice profit from the evening." I hadn't eaten since one o'clock, when I'd wolfed down a peanut butter and jelly sandwich while continuing to work the register, so my stomach was growling too loudly for me to be able to concentrate on coming up with a really good rebuttal.

"You worry too much about money." Birdie slid the homemade pizza onto the tabletop. "We've always managed to squeak by."

"With the property tax increase on both the store and this property, and having to pay for my own health insurance, I need to make sure you and I are okay financially." I quickly gathered dishes, silverware, and napkins, then poured a glass of iced tea for myself and popped the top of a can of Miller Lite for Gran.

I didn't add that I wanted to avoid having to sell off any more of our land. We lived on the ten remaining acres of the property my family had settled in the 1860s. My grandfather's death fifteen years ago and my father's incarceration twenty-four months later had forced Gran to begin selling off the parcels surrounding the old homestead in order to pay the taxes and support us. Foot by foot, my heritage had been traded for our survival, and I couldn't bear to lose another inch.

"I know you just want to be fiscally . . . uh . . ." Birdie hesitated, a slice of pizza poised near her mouth as she struggled to complete her thought.

"Responsible," I supplied. Her doctor had said it was best to provide the word she couldn't recall rather than let Gran become stressed trying to come up with it. What I couldn't understand, and the gerontologist hadn't been able to explain, was how she could remember a less common word like *fiscally* but not an everyday word like *responsible*.

"Right." She flipped her long gray braid over her shoulder and said, "But we'll be fine, and you should be out having fun on a Friday night, not working."

Uh, oh. What was this about? "This is a once-a-month meeting." I bit into my pizza, then paused to savor the hit of oregano and crushed red pepper. "Besides, I usually spend my Friday nights here with you, and I don't see you going to happy hour at the bars."

"For me, at seventy-five, happy hour is any hour I spend aboveground," Birdie said. Then with a sly look in my direction, she added, "You spend too much time with me. You need to get out more. Go on a date."

"Oh?" What was she up to? Maybe I should have poured myself wine instead of iced tea. "What makes you say that all of a sudden?" She'd been fairly quiet about my love life, or lack of one, during the past month. "Does the fact that a certain deputy U.S. Marshal is back in town have anything to do with your sudden interest in my social calendar?"

"So, did Jake come by to see you today?" Gran beamed. "When he stopped here"—she sipped her beer—"I told him Noah Underwood had called to see if you were due home after work, and even though I told him I had no idea, I figured that rascal was probably planning on asking you out, so Jake had better hustle his buns over to the dime store right away."

"They both dropped in for a few minutes," I admitted, then muttered to myself, "So, that's how Jake and Noah just happened to be there at the same time."

"Are you going out with Jake tomorrow? Remember I'm taking an overnight casino bus trip with Frieda, so you don't have to worry about me being alone."

Jake was the grandnephew of Birdie's old high school flame, Tony Del Vecchio, and she and Tony were bound and determined to see me married to Jake. I was pretty sure they were trying to live their own interrupted romance through us. Despite my questions, Birdie had never fully explained what had happened when Tony went MIA in Korea, and she'd abruptly married my grandfather. And because I didn't want to cause her any more pain, I hadn't pressed the matter.

To avoid getting her hopes up about Jake and me resuming a romantic relationship, I was tempted to deny that I was seeing him the next evening. But Shadow Bend was too small to keep it quiet. I doubted we'd go all the way into Kansas City, the nearest place we could be together without running into someone we knew, and I sure as heck wasn't inviting Jake into my empty house. We had way too much chemistry for that to be either a smart or a safe move. Which meant we'd most likely go someplace where we'd be seen by one of Gran's cronies, who would tell her we'd been together.

After chewing and swallowing, I said, "As a matter of fact, Jake and I are getting together tomorrow night. But . . ." I held up my hand. "I've decided that with him living in St. Louis, it's best if we don't continue dating. We can be friends, but that's it."

"Right." The smirk on Gran's face belonged on a teenager, not an octogenarian.

Sighing, I didn't argue with her. She'd find out soon enough that no matter how hot things were between Jake and me, any future we might have had if he'd stayed in Shadow Bend wouldn't stand up to the geographical distance that now separated us. With our busy lives and demanding careers, a four- to five-hour drive each way would make it impossible for us to forge and sustain a serious relationship. And I wasn't interested in being his sleepover buddy whenever he strolled into town.

"What are you wearing?" Birdie asked, breaking into my reverie. "How about that pretty pink dress you bought for that date he had to break last month?"

"It's too fancy for a Saturday night in Shadow Bend." I got up and started to clear away our dishes. Sadly, there were no leftovers to put away. While Birdie had eaten her usual two slices of pizza, I had polished off the remaining six. Stress eating was something I had to watch. I was okay with being curvier than magazines and movies implied I should be, but I didn't want to gain so much weight that I'd be forced to buy new clothes—mostly because I couldn't afford them.

"How about—"

"Actually," I cut her off, "I've already decided on dark jeans and a black tank under my blush pink cropped jacket. I have those Jimmy Choo nude pumps and my pink Miu Miu purse, which will pull the outfit together."

Although I had sold most of my designer

clothing, especially the suits, when I quit my city job, I had kept the shoes, since I was reasonably sure the market for used footwear was limited. Hanging on to the purses had been an act of pure indulgence. But if the time came when I absolutely needed the cash in order to keep Gran at home with me, I'd sell them in a heartbeat.

And, yes, I'd been thinking about what to wear when I saw both Jake and Noah. Even if I didn't view either occasion as technically a date, I still wanted to look good. So sue me.

As we finished cleaning the kitchen, Gran made a few more efforts to tweak my wardrobe. First, she suggested a skirt instead of jeans; then she recommended a bustier instead of a tank top. I vetoed both, having neither a bustier nor any plans to lure Jake into bed.

By the time the dishes were done, it was after eleven and Gran and I retired to the living room for the late-night news. We had just sat down and some sports jock was yammering about the Royals' starting lineup, when I heard music playing from my purse.

It was Boone St. Onge's ringtone, so I jumped up, hurried into the hallway, grabbed my cell from my bag, and said, "Hey, B. What's up?"

Boone was my other best friend. He, Poppy, and I grew up together, and except for the years when we were off pursuing higher education—college for all three of us, then grad school for me and law school for Boone—we had remained in Shadow Bend.

"Sorry to call so late." Boone took a breath. "But I need a favor."

"No problem," I assured him. "As long as you're not in jail again."

"Thank God, no!"

Last month the police had arrested Boone when one of his clients had been murdered. It had been a harrowing experience for him, and he still hadn't fully recovered from the ordeal. I hoped that by teasing him about it, the whole episode would lose its power to upset him.

"Well, that's a relief." I walked into my bedroom and closed the door so our conversation wouldn't disturb Gran. "What's up?"

"A friend of mine from California called a few minutes ago and invited me to go on a cruise with him." Boone's voice rose in excitement. "His girlfriend got a part in a movie and had to back out of the trip at the last minute, so he offered me her ticket."

"That's sounds great." I sat down on my bed and took off my shoes.

"Since I don't have anything pressing in the office this week and I really need a vacation after what happened with Elise, I said yes. It leaves Sunday, so I'm flying out tomorrow."

"Terrific." I hoped he'd come back his old lighthearted self. "What do you need from me?"

"Cat-sitting."

Along with his freedom from incarceration, Boone had also acquired a cat—Tsar, the murdered woman's Russian Blue.

"Can't you board him?"

"No." Boone's tone was adamant. "He's just now getting over the trauma of being homeless after Elise's death. Boarding him would be cruel."

"You know I'd love to take care of such a sweet kitty, but I'm afraid Banshee would eat Tsar as a midnight snack if I brought him into the house." I paused, trying to think of an alternative. "Could I stop by your house once a day to feed him and clean his litter box?"

"Uh-uh. Tsar's therapist says he needs to be around people and shouldn't be left alone for extended periods," Boone explained. "I even take him to my office so he doesn't feel abandoned."

"Really?" Since when were there kitty psychologists?

"Hey," Boone broke into my musing. "How about if you keep Tsar at your store? Lots of shops have pets, and you're there as much as you're home anyway."

After several minutes of protesting, during which Boone assured me that the feline loved people and would not try to run out of the constantly opening door, I finally agreed to babysit Tsar at the dime store. We arranged for Boone to deliver the cat the next afternoon on his way to the airport.

After clicking off my cell, I walked back into the living room to tell Gran about Boone's upcoming trip, but she had evidently gone to bed, because the television was dark and her chair was empty. I decided to hit the sack, too, and turned out the lights. As I was making sure the front door was locked, the house phone rang.

Glancing at my watch, I saw that it was almost midnight. Who in the world would be calling so late? Boone would have rung back on my cell. And small-town etiquette prohibited phoning after ten, so it couldn't be any of Birdie's friends.

Feeling my chest tighten, I hurried into the kitchen, intent on answering before the ringing woke Gran. Anxiety made me a little breathless as I snatched up the receiver and said hello. And when I heard the chief of police's voice on the other end, I felt dizzy.

Chief Kincaid's next words made me sick to my stomach. "Devereaux, we need you to come down to the dime store right away."

"What happened?"

"I'll explain when you get here," he said. "See you in fifteen minutes."

He hung up before I could ask any more questions, but as I put my shoes back on and drove into town, visions of fire and burglary danced through my head. Damn, I hoped I'd paid that last insurance premium.

Chapter 4

Normally, Shadow Bend's village square was my favorite part of town. It was the soul of the community and always reminded me of why I never wanted to leave the area. But tonight, as I turned right onto Main Street, the moonlit bandstand with its cast-iron columns and decorative arches didn't charm me the way it ordinarily did.

Instead, as I cruised the four blocks leading to my store, a sense of dread settled on my chest like a beached sumo wrestler. Passing the familiar landmarks increased my fears. Shadow Bend Savings and Guaranty Bank, in its Greek Revival building, reminded me of my mortgage. What if my store had burned to the ground? The newspaper's unadorned cinder-block structure had me picturing a headline that read DEVEREAUX'S DIME STORE AND GIFT BASKETS VANDALIZED! And as I zoomed past the movie theater, with its limestone facade and Art Deco entrance, the marquee advertising *The Hunger Games* made me wonder if something had happened to destroy my business, would Gran and I starve?

When Brewfully Yours or the dry cleaner didn't

inspire any further doomsday scenarios, I tried yoga breathing in a vain attempt to settle down. But as I turned left at the hardware store and had to stomp on the brakes to avoid bursting through the yellow crime-scene tape strung across the road, my blood pressure skyrocketed. What in the world had happened? Why had the police cordoned off the entire block in front of my store?

At twelve thirty in the morning, few people were gathered at the barricade—mostly only older teens or twentysomethings who had probably been heading to the theater's five-dollar midnight movie. No doubt they'd decided that real-life drama was more exciting than the cinematic version.

Realizing I would have to walk if I wanted to get any closer to the dime store, I backed up and parked my sapphire black Z4 in the nearest spot. The BMW was the only truly valuable asset I had kept after quitting my job with Stramp Investments. Although I rationalized that in this economy I'd never get what it was worth if I sold it, if the truth be told, I adored that car, and I knew there was more chance of me starring as the next James Bond girl than ever owning a vehicle like it again.

As I approached the barrier, I hoped that the chief had left word to allow me through the blockade. While I had at least a nodding acquaintance with most of the officers on the Shadow Bend police force, it wasn't as if they were my buddies, so their fear of their boss made it a safe bet that none of them would bend the rules for me.

Now, if my BFF, Poppy, was with me, it might be a different story, especially if there was a male cop on duty. Not only was Poppy the chief's daughter, but her incredible beauty also made men stupid. Something she was more than willing to cash in on.

It took me a few seconds to attract the attention of the cop on duty—he'd been flirting with a pretty girl carrying a crossbow and with a quiver full of arrows on her back. At first, I wondered if we had skipped straight from Easter to Halloween, but then I realized she was supposed to be Katniss Everdeen from *The Hunger Games*. A lot of people dressed in costume for the twelve o'clock show. The crowd was a sight to behold during a *Star Wars* marathon.

I was counting my blessings that it wasn't the *Rocky Horror Picture Show* weekend when the young cop finally pulled himself away from the object of his lust and sauntered over to me. He jerked his thumb behind him and said, "Whole street's blocked off."

"So I see."

"Something happened at the dime store," he offered, expanding his chest. "Only official police personnel allowed past this checkpoint."

"Yes, the chief called me to come in." I squinted at the guy's name tag, which read CURLY WATSON. Talk about false advertising. His thinning hair didn't hold even a hint of a wave, and he certainly didn't appear to have any great powers of deduction, since I was wearing a sweatshirt with the store logo on it. "I'm Devereaux Sinclair." I pointed to the writing on my chest. "The owner."

I didn't recognize Curly, which was odd. With a population of 4,028, Shadow Bend was your typical small town; everyone knew everyone, which made me wonder if the cop had just moved here. The population explosion had skidded to a near halt a few years ago when the real estate bubble burst, but we still had the occasional newcomer.

Instead of the standard uniform, Curly wore a light blue shirt with navy epaulets and black pants, indicating he was a member of the auxiliary police force, a group of volunteers who provided traffic control, helped on searches, and supplied manpower for our poorly funded, perennially understaffed police department. Unfortunately, the imitation cops were often not the smartest cats in the litter box.

"Do you have any identification?" Pomposity flowed off Curly like stink off an onion. "I got a shirt with *Peyton Manning* written on the back."

He sucked his teeth. "That don't make me no football star."

I so wanted to retort that the badge on his chest didn't make him a cop, either, but instead I forced a smile, dug through my purse, pulled out my wallet, and slid my driver's license from behind its plastic window. I kept my voice even as I said, "Here you go."

He examined the laminated rectangle as if it were written in Sanskrit and ran a fingertip over both sides. Did he think there was a secret message stamped in Braille on the plastic-coated card?

Finally, he keyed the radio strapped to his shoulder and said, "There's a woman down here claiming to be Devereaux Sinclair. Says the chief called her. Should I let her past the barricade?"

Through the static I heard, "You'd better not be the reason it's taking her so long to get here. The chief's ready to spit nails."

Curly's demeanor changed from dictatorial to cowering, and he shoved my license at me. While I was putting it into my purse, he grabbed my elbow, untied the tape from the lamppost, and yanked me through the opening. Now that my mind wasn't occupied in dealing with a moron, the anxiety about my business returned full tilt and I raced down the block toward the pulsating red lights.

As I neared the dime store, my pulse kicked into

overdrive, but as I examined the building, it appeared undamaged. There weren't any flames billowing out from the roof or windows, and I couldn't see any hook-and-ladder trucks parked nearby, so I felt safe in concluding that the shop wasn't on fire.

Blowing out a tiny puff of air, I let my shoulders sag in relief. Seeing my dream go up in smoke would have been a blow from which I might not have recovered. So many of my hopes had been dashed throughout my lifetime, and I didn't know how many more times I could pick myself up, dust myself off, and start over again.

A nanosecond later, a chilling realization struck me. In the rush to get home, I had left the day's receipts in the safe rather than take them over to the bank's night-deposit box. If there had been a break-in and the thief had managed to open the safe, I was in big trouble. I couldn't remember how much I had in there, but I was fairly certain my insurance wouldn't cover a cash loss, since I had opted for the cheapest policy.

Racking my brain, I tried to come up with a third alternative for the extensive police presence at my store. Certainly a simple act of vandalism wouldn't have necessitated closing off the street or the presence of so many officers. What else could be going on? Biohazard? Bomb threat? No. I didn't carry dangerous material, and who would want to bomb a dime store?

Out of breath, I skidded to a halt in front of my building. A squad car was parked on the sidewalk, blocking the entrance, and another cruiser was positioned diagonally across the mouth of the alley. As far as I could tell, the display windows were unbroken and the front door didn't appear to have been forced open.

Spotting Jessie Huang, one of two female officers on the force, I trotted over to her and asked, "What happened? Was there a burglary?"

"The chief's in the back." She looked somewhere over my shoulder, clearly avoiding my gaze. When I opened my mouth to repeat my questions, she interrupted, "You'd better hurry. He's waiting for you and he's not in a good mood."

"Fine." A chill ran down my spine. What was the big secret?

As I sprinted toward the alley, I heard her mutter, "Better you than me."

Emerging from the dark passage, I blinked, temporarily blinded by the 1,800 watts of illumination that were aimed at the rear of my building. Half a dozen lights mounted on tripods were arranged in a semicircle, and several people wearing white Tyvek coveralls, booties, and rubber gloves were swarming over the tiny parking lot. One was kneeling beside an unzipped wheeled duffel, and another had a professional-looking camera hanging around his neck.

Oh. My. God! No way could this be good. I had watched enough *CSI* and *Law & Order* episodes on television to know that this kind of crime-scene activity could mean only one thing—a dead body.

Before I could jump to any more conclusions, Chief Eldridge Kincaid materialized at my side like a snake springing out of a hole, scaring the bejeezus out of me. I stepped back, stumbled on an electrical cable, and ended up on my butt with gravel embedded in my palms.

Chief Kincaid sighed, extended a hand, and hauled me to my feet. When I was once again vertical, he asked, "Have you been drinking?"

"No!" I brushed the pebbles out of my wounds. "I just tripped on a cord." No way was I admitting to Poppy's father that he had frightened me. I had my reputation as a tough chick to maintain. "What's going on here?"

"Let's go sit in my car." The chief tilted his head toward the black Chevy Suburban parked behind us. "You can clean up your injuries while we talk."

He took off without checking to see if I was following him, and I hurried to keep up. Chief Kincaid's heavily starched khaki uniform looked as if he'd just put it on a few seconds ago, and his gray buzz cut was impeccably barbered. Eldridge Kincaid demanded perfection from both himself and all the people around him.

Although I was getting sick and tired of

everyone ignoring my questions, I held on to my patience. There was no rushing the chief, and I'd find out what was happening faster if I cooperated with him. A lesson Poppy had yet to learn, which was why they weren't speaking.

Once we were seated, he tossed me a first-aid kit and said, "What time did you lock up the store?" His steel blue eyes drilled into me.

"About nine fifteen—give or take." I tore open a foil pouch and took out a moist towelette. "I didn't look at my watch, so I'm not sure."

"Why so late?" He took a notepad and mechanical pencil from his shirt pocket. "The dime store closes at six on Fridays, doesn't it?"

"The Stepping Out Book Club held their meeting here tonight." After wiping my palm, I squeezed some antiseptic cream on the scrapes. "It ended at nine. The members helped me put the chairs and tables back in the storeroom; then we all went home."

"You're sure everyone was out of the building when you left?"

"Well, I didn't search the place." I frowned. Had I seen everyone leave?

"Were there any cars in the rear lot when you drove away?"

"Nope." I stuck a couple of bandages on my abrasions. "And none in front of the store, either." I had glanced back to make sure I'd remembered to turn off the lights. "But earlier I heard some people mention that they had walked over, since it was such a nice night."

"Are you still wearing the clothes you had on at the book-club meeting?"

"Yes." I pursed my lips. Was another man questioning my choice?

"How many sweatshirts like that do you have?" Eldridge's words were short and clipped.

"Seven. One for each workday and an extra in case of emergencies." I fingered the aqua material. "But they're all different colors."

The chief suddenly changed the subject. "How many people were at the book-club meeting? Do you have a list of the members?"

"Nineteen attendees and the author." I crumpled up the debris from my medical ministrations and looked around for a litterbag. Not seeing one, I tucked the trash in my purse. The inside of the Chevy was immaculate and I wasn't about to be the one to mess it up. "The list is probably still on my computer, or you could get it from Mrs. Ziegler. She's the club president."

"Anything unusual happen at the meeting?" Chief Kincaid jotted something down.

Where to begin? I paused to gather my thoughts, then told him everything—including the late arrival of the guest speaker, the disastrous Q-and-A session, and the poet's storming out.

When I stopped, the chief said incredulously, "All of that over poems?"

"Apparently."

"Do you recall who seemed the most offended by the content of the verses?"

"Let me think." While I tried to remember who had gone toe-to-toe with the author, I stared at the Tyvek-suited figures, most of whom were now working near the Dumpster by the back door.

How did a town as small as Shadow Bend have such an extensive crime-scene team? Not to mention the white pimped-out RV with SHADOW BEND POLICE CRIME-SCENE UNIT painted in navy blue along its side.

Oh, yeah, the infamous grants. Because Chief Kincaid and our esteemed mayor, Geoffrey Eggers, didn't get along, the city council had been voting down police-department budget increases for years. In frustration, the chief had begun applying for federal funds to remodel the station, train personnel, and purchase up-to-date gear.

Everyone had been surprised when the chief's applications began to bring in money. So far, he'd been able to complete all three of his projects. Evidently, he must have hit the mother lode if he'd been able to purchase his very own crime-scene unit and mobile lab, and train his people to use them.

I hid a smile. His Honor the mayor must be beyond livid that once again the chief had managed to get what he wanted without financing from the town's coffers. Geoffrey Eggers hated being bested at his own game.

Focusing back on the question, I said, "Addie Campbell was the most upset. The others were more annoyed than angry at the author's attitude."

"Who was this guy?"

"Lance Quistgaard." That name would be hard to forget. "Supposedly he's local, but I don't recall ever seeing him before."

"Can you describe him?" Eldridge tapped his notepad with his pencil.

After I told the chief what Quistgaard looked like, Eldridge nodded, then gazed out the windshield for what seemed like a long time.

Finally, he opened the Suburban's door and said, "Come with me."

This time as the chief led me toward the back door of my store, he made sure I was following him. He stopped as we passed a man leaning against a car and snapped, "Krefeld, if you won an award for laziness, you'd send someone else to pick it up."

The man scurried off, and we were a few steps from the building when Chief Kincaid ordered me to wait. Once he was satisfied that I was following his command, he approached a woman wearing a Tyvek coverall and hairnet, standing near a large cardboard box that had held a shelving unit that had arrived Friday morning. I couldn't hear what he said to the crime-scene tech, but she moved out of the way.

Motioning for me to join him, the chief used a black rubber glove to flip open the flaps of the carton. It took me a millisecond to grasp what I was seeing, and when I did, I gulped and leapt backward. Inside the coffinlike box, eyes wide-open and staring, lay Lance Quistgaard, both hands clutching a wooden stake, which had been driven through his heart.

Chapter 5

"Yes." I answered the chief's question, rubbing my arms. I was suddenly chilled despite my sweatshirt and the mild May temperature. "That's the speaker from tonight." I fought to keep down the pizza I'd eaten earlier as nausea rose in my throat and threatened to empty my stomach. "I mean, last night, since now it's today, so the meeting was yesterday."

Chief Kincaid ignored my babbling. Evidently, my green complexion didn't make an impression on him either, since he didn't offer me a barf bag. Instead, he demanded, "You're sure the stiff in the cardboard box is Lance Quistgaard, the author at the meeting?"

"Definitely." I cringed as I took another peek at the dead man. "Why are you asking me who he is? Doesn't he have any identification?"

"No." The chief nodded to the crime-scene tech that she could resume whatever she'd been doing, then took my elbow and steered me back toward his SUV. "There's no wallet or keys in his pockets."

"So you think this was a robbery gone bad?" I opened the door and climbed into the Chevy's passenger seat, grateful to sit down.

"It's too early in the investigation to form a viable theory." Chief Kincaid's eyebrows rose when he noticed my chattering teeth and uncontrollable shivering. Scowling, he cranked up the Suburban's heat, reached behind him, and tossed me a blanket. "When you closed the store last night, I assume you left by the rear exit, since that's where you were parked?" He waited for my nod, then continued. "Are you certain you locked it?"

"Yes." I thought back, then nodded emphatically. "I let everyone out the front, turned the knob on the dead bolt on that door, went into the storeroom, got my purse from the desk drawer there, and used my key to lock the back door once I was outside."

The chief stared at me. Then, as if making a decision, he said, "It was unlocked when the first officer arrived on the scene."

"Was—" I started to ask a question.

Chief Kincaid held up his hand. "Nothing appears to be disturbed inside the store, but I do need you to take a look and confirm that. As of now, we believe the murder took place between the building and the Dumpster. We don't have a time of death—obviously it's between when you left at nine fifteen and when the officer noticed the blood trail on his ten-o'clock rounds."

"Oh." Well, that explained how the body was discovered. "I didn't know the police had appointed rounds. Do you have the same slogan as mail carriers?"

"Of course, my officers do regular foot patrols of the business area. They pay special attention to the back-alley entrances of businesses. If the doorways aren't illuminated by the halogen flood-lights we recommend to discourage break-ins, the officer examines the area with his Maglite. All of my people are equipped with the ML125, which is among the brightest flashlights available." The chief rolled his eyes. "And, no, we do not have the same motto as the post office."

"Good to know." I'd forgotten how much Poppy's father liked to lecture. I took a breath and asked the question that I'd been avoiding. "I'm not a suspect, am I?" After my experience with a Kansas City detective who had been determined to pin the murder of my ex-boyfriend's fiancée on me, I wanted to be absolutely clear about my status in the investigation. "Right?"

"Not if you can produce your other sweatshirts for the officer who will accompany you to your house when you leave here." Eldridge's voice was firm as he added, "And as long as the people who were at the meeting last night say you were wearing the color sweatshirt you presently have on, then, no, you are not a current suspect."

"Why is my choice of clothing so important?" I asked, then answered myself, "Duh! Earlier, you mentioned a blood trail." I paused to think, then said, "Which means whoever killed Quistgaard would be covered in blood, either from the stabbing itself or when he or she was dragging the body and wrestling it into the box."

"Exactly."

"But how would they do it?" I tried to remember the anatomy course that I had taken my freshman year in college. "Wouldn't it take a lot of strength to drive a stake into someone's chest?"

"If the weapon was aimed directly over the sternum, yes, it would take a great deal of power to do so." The chief rolled his pencil between his palms.

"So the stake is off center?"

"We don't have that information yet." Eldridge reached for the door handle. "Are you ready to take a look inside your store?"

"Totally." I jumped out of the Chevy and headed toward the building. As sorry as I was for the murdered man, my business was vital for Birdie's well-being. It was what put food on the table and kept shelter over our heads. Without it, I'd have to take a job in the city and Gran might have to go into assisted living. To say that I was anxious to make sure everything was okay was like saying that Hurricane Sandy had been a light breeze.

Chief Kincaid escorted me to the front entrance, watched as I used my key to open the door, and followed me across the threshold. We walked the aisles in silence, and my anxiety lessened with every step. I didn't see any evidence of theft or vandalism. Next, we checked out the back room, and I let out an audible sigh of relief when I saw that the safe was undisturbed. Still, I opened it and verified that the contents hadn't been stolen.

Once I confirmed that nothing appeared to have been touched, the chief asked, "Who, besides you, has a key to the building?"

"No one." I hadn't felt the need to give one to any of my employees.

"How many sets do you have?" Eldridge paced the length of the storage area.

"Three." I counted off on my fingers. "The one in my purse. The one at home in my desk. And the one that I keep in the safe here."

"Have you lost one at any time or had your pocketbook stolen?"

I shook my head. "And I've never misplaced a set or been mugged."

"The key was in there just now?" Eldridge pointed toward the safe.

"Right here." I reached inside, grabbed the vintage Coca-Cola bottle cap key chain, and dangled it in front of the chief's face.

"I'll need you to allow the officer to see the key at your home when you show her your sweatshirts." Eldridge continued to pace.

"Okay," I agreed, willing to help the police in any way I could.

"You are absolutely, positively sure you locked the back door?" Eldridge stopped in front of me and stared at me until I squirmed.

"Yes." I did a quick mental rewind of the evening. "I'm sure."

"Then someone had to have hidden in the store and unlocked the door from the inside." Eldridge crossed his arms. "But from the trail of blood, the murder took place outside. We looked earlier and there was no sign of blood in here."

"Will you have to dust the store for prints?" I asked, cringing at the thought of the mess the fingerprint powder would leave behind.

"There's no point." Eldridge ground his teeth. "In a public place like this there are thousands of prints, and we'd expect to find evidence here of everyone who was at the meeting."

"True," I quickly agreed, happy that they were leaving my store alone.

"The question is, Was the person who hid inside and then unlocked the door Quistgaard?" Eldridge refocused the conversation. "Maybe when he walked out of the meeting, he didn't leave the store. Or could it have been someone else in attendance?"

"He's one possibility." I leaned against a file cabinet and closed my eyes to help remember everything that had happened that evening. "But Addie left the meeting early, too, and I didn't see him leave the store, either."

"Who do you recall leaving when the meeting was over?" Chief Kincaid continued to stare at me as if he could force my memory to improve.

"Uh." With the chief glaring at me, I suddenly wasn't sure who I'd seen and who I hadn't. "I just don't remember." I nibbled on my thumbnail. "I was in the storeroom most of the time, stacking the chairs and tables as the members brought them back there."

"You must at least remember the last person, since you said you locked the door after him or her." Eldridge's mouth was a white line of frustration. "Who was the final one? The lingerer?"

Had it been Mrs. Zeigler? No. In fact, she and I had both forgotten about the basket she'd said she wanted to order. I'd have to call her and get the information. How about Xylia? No, definitely not my clerk. I would have remembered her, because I'd wanted to ask her if she could work a couple of extra days this coming week, since I had a lot of basket orders to fill. So who had it been?

"The newspaper guy," I blurted out, having finally realized the identity of the man who had looked so familiar. "I can't think of his name."

"Grant Edwyn?" Eldridge asked. "The *Shadow Bend Banner*'s editor?"

"That's the one. I kept trying to figure out how I knew him, and it just popped into my head a couple of seconds ago." I stepped over to my desk and dug an old newspaper from the bottom drawer. Flipping to the second page, I pointed to a picture. "This is him."

"He was the last to go?"

"Yes. I can't recall the others, but he offered to walk me to my car." Slumping, I fought back a bubble of hysterical laughter. "I told him that this was Shadow Bend, not Kansas City, and I'd be fine alone. After all, we didn't have much street crime around here."

Chief Kincaid patted me awkwardly on the shoulder, then pretended to study his notes while I regained my equilibrium. Once I was sure that I wouldn't embarrass us both by either bursting into tears or demanding a hug, the chief asked if I was ready to leave.

The rear exit was off-limits until the crime-scene techs were finished gathering their evidence, so when I nodded, we made our way to the front of the store. As we passed the APRIL SHOWERS BRINGS MAY FLOWERS display facing the entrance, I glanced at it and frowned. Something was off. I turned to look at the scene full-on. All the merchandise was present—the table, chairs, flowers, even the borrowed grill. So what was wrong? I examined it one more time, then silently gasped.

It was the picket fence that I had arranged across the front of the display. I had installed it by sticking each post in a dozen or so clay pots filled with dirt. A stake at the very end was missing. Probably no one else would notice, but I had worked on that fence on and off for the better part of an entire day to make it perfect.

Suddenly I knew where the murder weapon had been obtained. The question was, Should I mention it to the chief? I couldn't afford to have him shut down my store. Saturday was my busiest and most profitable day, and with the unexpected expense of the new roof that I'd had to put on a couple of weeks ago, I didn't have any extra funds to make up for the loss of revenue. The police already knew someone had been in the building and the chief had said dusting for prints was useless, so what kind of evidence could they possibly find?

"Is there a problem?" Chief Kincaid asked as he paused halfway out the front door.

"Not at all." *Shoot!* Now he was suspicious. "I . . . uh . . . just thought of something I have to do tomorrow. I'm free to open the store, right?"

"Yeah." He twitched his shoulders. "We'll keep the back lot barricaded until the techs have a chance to look over the evidence they've gathered, but the dime store itself is fine."

"Great." I hurried over to him and once we were outside relocked the front door. "Do you need me for something else or can I go now?" I glanced at my watch. It was nearly two in the morning. "I have to be back here in less than seven hours, and I'd like to get a little sleep."

"You can leave as soon as I assign an officer to accompany you." The chief escorted me outside and said to Jessie Huang, "Follow Ms. Sinclair to her home. Escort her inside, have her show you her sweatshirts—there should be seven, including the one she has on—then make sure her spare key is accounted for and report back here."

"Yes, sir." Jessie touched the brim of her hat, not quite saluting, then said to me, "I'll take you to your car, and we can depart from that location."

"Thanks." As I got into her squad car, I assured myself that I'd tell the chief about the missing picket-fence post after I closed the store tomorrow. That way, if Chief Kincaid felt he needed to have the crime-scene unit process my shop, they would have from six p.m. Saturday until I reopened at noon on Monday. And I wouldn't lose any business.

As I drove home with the cruiser's lights in my rearview mirror, my conscience nagged at me a bit. I knew an upright citizen would report her suspicions about the stake to the police straight-away, but I had spent a long time in the field of investment counseling, and that job had demagnetized my moral compass so that I was no longer sure which direction was true north.

Was telling the chief immediately really the right thing to do if no one would be hurt by delaying the information, while fessing up right away might mean hardship for my grandmother? Her medication was expensive, and Medicare Part D didn't pay half the cost. Then there were those other little necessities, like food and shelter.

People who received regular paychecks had no idea of the fine financial line walked by those of us who owned our own business. Besides, I was only waiting sixteen hours, not even a whole day. What could go wrong?

Chapter 6

After Officer Huang pawed through the laundry hamper and messed up the stack of clean sweatshirts in my drawer, I showed her the third key to the store, wished her a good night, and locked the door behind her. Gran must have taken a sleeping pill, because despite the police presence in our home, she didn't wake up.

Banshee, on the other hand, had followed the cop around as if she were catnip-coated tuna, purring and rubbing against her ankles. The woman had fussed over and petted the traitorous Siamese, ignoring the fur he'd deposited on her uniform and declaring that he was a sweet boy. Until that moment, I had always considered Jessie a good judge of character. Obviously, I'd been mistaken.

Needless to say, it took me quite a while to relax and fall asleep, which meant that when the meteorologist's voice woke me at six, I was too groggy to hear the entire weather report. I did manage to catch the word *thunderstorm*.

Once I had pried myself out of bed, I lurched into the bathroom. When I emerged, I must have showered and dressed, since my hair was wet and I had on something other than my nightshirt, but I had no memory of the two events. Avoiding the mirror—I knew the reflection wouldn't be a pretty sight—I put on my shoes and socks. Then, following the enticing odor of bacon, I trudged into the kitchen.

Gran had her back to me as she worked her culinary magic at the stove, but she must have heard my footsteps, because she chirped, "Good morning."

"Prove it," I mumbled as I staggered toward my friend Mr. Coffee, who, unlike most of the men in my life, had always been there for me. His red light greeted me with a welcoming glow, and his little round pot was filled with caffeinated ambrosia.

Gran turned from the griddle and ran her gaze up and down me until I felt like a cut of meat that she wouldn't serve her cat. "Why do you look like crap?" she demanded. "Did you even comb your hair after you washed it this morning?"

Taking a gulp of liquid energy, and burning my tongue in the process, I explained what had happened after she went to bed. I concluded with, "So, I didn't get to sleep until after three."

"Humph." Gran turned her attention back to her cooking. "Why does the name Lance Quistgaard sound familiar?"

"You got me." I poured myself another cup of get-up-and-go, put away the half-and-half, and nudged the refrigerator door shut with my hip.

"Supposedly he's a local, but I don't remember ever seeing him around before. Does he attend St. Saggy's?"

St. Saggy's was also known as St. Sagar's Catholic Church. While attending catechism as a child, I had inquired about the church's name. The priest who was visiting our schoolroom had explained the identity of St. Sagar, but further interrogation had revealed that he had no idea why Shadow Bend's Catholic Church had been christened for a martyred bishop from Turkey. Especially since the Turkish population of our little town was somewhere near zero.

After my cross-examination of the priest, our teacher, Sister Thomasine of the order of The Not Amused, no longer allowed me to ask questions. Shortly afterward, I refused to go back to CCD classes.

"I don't remember ever meeting anyone by that name at church," Birdie said, placing two plates on the table. Both contained three strips of crisp bacon, a pair of sunny-side-up eggs, and hash browns. "But the name does ring a bell from somewhere."

"I can't quite picture him on a senior bus trip." I grabbed the bread as it popped from the toaster and tossed a slice on each of our dishes.

"Very funny." Birdie sat down and grabbed the salt shaker. "Speaking of which, Frieda is picking me up in an hour. We'll be back late tomorrow afternoon. Will you be home, or should I take my key?"

Oops! I deliberately hadn't mentioned that I was seeing Noah for brunch on Sunday. Gran had never forgiven him for deserting me when my father was sent to prison. Birdie had spent her whole life in a town that took family feuds extremely seriously, and although the betrayal had taken place nearly thirteen years ago, in her mind Noah's treachery was as recent as last week.

I had been trying to persuade her that Noah may not have been totally at fault, but so far, she wasn't convinced. Like a lot of folks, Gran assigned to people the role they were at their worst, and without an act of God or at least a memo from the pope, she refused to change her mind about them.

Although she knew that Noah and I were working on a fresh start, mentioning my high school boyfriend's name would send Gran into an explosion of swearing that would make a gangbanger blink, so I stuttered, "Uh. Well. I'm not sure." I ran through my options and chose what I considered the most believable lie. "Poppy mentioned doing something together, so you should probably bring your key." Then I tried to change the subject. "I don't think I told you that Boone is leaving today for a cruise."

"I'm glad to hear it." Birdie took a bite of egg. "That poor boy needs a break." She swallowed, then pointed her butter knife at me. "But you spending tomorrow afternoon with Poppy is hogwash. She's in Chicago."

Jeez! If Gran was the one with the memory problems, how come she could keep track of my friends' whereabouts better than I could? I'd completely forgotten Poppy was spending the weekend with her current boyfriend, Tryg Pryce, an Illinois attorney whom she'd met last month when he'd come to Shadow Bend to defend Boone against a murder charge.

"I think Poppy said she'd be back by noon." I played for time by shoving a slice of bacon into my mouth and mumbling around it, "We might get together then."

"Don't try to fool me." Birdie lasered me with her pale blue eyes. "You have a date with that scum-sucking doctor, don't you?"

How to answer that? True, Noah was a physician, but I was fairly sure he never slurped slime. Still, arguing with her over that point would be futile, so I tried another tactic— weaseling. "It's not a date. It's just going to brunch with a friend."

"Don't prevaricate." Birdie stabbed her fork at me, and I ducked as egg yolk flew toward me. "He's trying to win you back, and I don't trust him. I'm, uh . . ."

"Suspicious," I supplied.

"Right." She wiped the yellow spatters from the

tablecloth with her paper napkin. "I'm suspicious that Noah and his mother are up to something. Maybe Nadine has ordered him to try to snake his way into your affections so she can figure out how to stop your dad's release from prison."

It had come to light last month that my father was innocent—sort of. Yes, he had killed a woman while driving under the influence. And there had been a controlled substance in his vehicle at the time. But the man who had been trying to frame him for embezzling money from the bank they both worked at had roofied my father's drink. Then, once Dad was drugged, he'd fed him beer after beer before putting him in his car and planting pills in his glove box.

"Why would Nadine Underwood want to do that?" I was no fan of Noah's mother, but why would she care if my dad were freed from prison?

"Because she's never gotten over the fact that Kern picked your mother instead of her to marry," Birdie explained, then muttered, "Talk about jumping from the frying pan into the fire."

"Dad dated Nadine?" I yelped. "She's got to be ten years older than him."

"Your point?" Birdie got up and started to clear the table. "Back in the day, Nadine was a sophisticated thirtysomething femme fatale, and your dad was the most eligible bachelor in Shadow Bend. She set her cap for him, and it almost worked. But your mother moved to town, got a job as a teller at Kern's bank, and that was the end of any romantic feelings Kern had for Nadine." Gran put the dishes in the sink, then turned to me and winked. "Hell hath no fury like a woman who sees the fella she considers hers pick another gal."

It took me a moment to sort through all of Gran's clichés, but when I finally finished, I nodded to myself. Nadine's intense dislike for me over the years now made a lot more sense. She'd probably been horrified when Noah and I had started dating as teenagers, and been thrilled when she was able to force him to walk out on me, just as my father had walked out on her. I shivered.

Nadine bent on revenge was a scary thought. Definitely another minus in Noah's column. It was looking more and more as if he and I were destined to remain friends rather than become lovers. Too bad I was still so attracted to him.

Surfacing from my musings, I narrowed my eyes at Gran and demanded, "Why haven't you ever told me about Nadine and Dad before?"

"When you were young, did you really want to know about your parents' previous love life?" Gran asked. When I winced and shook my head, she continued. "Then when Kern went to prison, you never wanted to talk about him or your mother."

"True," I mumbled, ashamed. I'd felt too angry and abandoned to even think about my parents without crying or punching something during those years.

"But now that Kern's coming home and you're an adult, it's time for you to know everything so you can be ready for any fallout from his return." Gran took off her apron. "Some people will still blame him for that poor woman's death, even if he was drugged when his car hit her."

"I hadn't thought about that," I admitted, pushing away the twinge of guilt I felt about my own poor treatment of my father while he'd been in jail. I suspected that the claustrophobia I'd developed that kept me from visiting him might have been a convenient excuse.

"Nadine will be stirring up any anti-Kern feelings in town that she can," Gran pronounced. "Especially if you're dating her precious son."

Thankfully, Frieda's arrival distracted Gran, and I was able to shoo her out the door before I had to respond to her implied demand that I should call off brunch with Noah on Sunday. After a flurry of assurances that I'd clean up the kitchen before I left for work, and an exchange of hugs good-bye, I watched Frieda's Impala drive away. With one last backfire, the old Chevy disappeared from view.

Tempting though it was to leave the dishes until tonight, with my luck, Gran would come home early for some reason and see the dirty plates. With that in mind, I filled the sink with water, pushed up my sleeves, and started to wash. In less than a quarter hour, the kitchen was sparkling and I was free to finish dressing.

Having done my granddaughterly duty, I tamed my mostly dry curls into a ponytail and hit the road. I wanted to get to the store early and make sure the cops and all their paraphernalia were gone—or at least confined to the rear of the building, as Chief Kincaid had promised.

Ten minutes later, when I arrived, I was excited to see that the alley was no longer blocked by a squad car, and was ecstatic that my rear parking lot no longer resembled the opening credits of an *NCIS* episode. Nevertheless, after I pulled my Z4 into its usual spot, I hesitated. Would there still be blood by the exit? And if there was, whom did one hire to mop it up? Was there a biohazard department of the Merry Maids?

Holding my breath, I walked the few feet across the asphalt from my car to the exit, stopping short of the door. I studied the ground, then exhaled noisily. The only mark I could detect was a section of the blacktop that was shinier than the rest. God bless Chief Kincaid's tidy little soul. I followed the clean path to the Dumpster and was relieved to see that the file carton and its gruesome contents were gone.

Not that I had expected the cops to leave the

dead body for the trash collectors, but, hey, it was always good to check out stuff like that. Smiling, I entered the storeroom, stowed my purse in the bottom drawer of the desk, and looked at my watch. I had an hour before the shop opened, and a lot of basket orders to finish.

I was placing the Trojan Vibrations Twister—an object that the package described as an intimate massager that provided unique and intense pleasure—in the Girl's Night Out Basket when a disturbing question popped into my head. No, not whether the batteries were included, but whether a murder committed a few steps from my store might keep people away.

By now, word of the crime would have spread like a burst water balloon. Would the good folks of Shadow Bend shun my business and me? News of my father's innocence and pending release from prison had stirred up a lot of sympathy for our family; I could only hope that those positive feelings would extend to this situation.

Still, as nine a.m. rolled around, I worried I might not have the usual Saturday-morning crowd. When I unlocked the front door, I was pleasantly surprised to find people lined up on the sidewalk. The group spilled across the threshold and I hurriedly got out of their way.

Xylia was at the front of the pack, but we didn't have time to exchange more than a quick greeting before getting down to work. The customers were already three deep at the candy counter, and as I rushed over to help them, my clerk manned the register.

The first woman in line placed her order for a pound of cherries jubilee fudge, then said, "Were you the one that found the body?"

Until she asked that question, it hadn't occurred to me that the news-flash factor might motivate people to drop by my store, although I certainly should have anticipated that possibility. After all, rumors flew around Shadow Bend like New Year's Eve confetti, and scandal was a taste everyone savored. The community didn't stand for gossip; it sat down and got comfy with it. A grisly murder would bring out both the connoisseurs of calumny and the occasional back-fence conversationalists.

And because I was unprepared, I wasn't sure how to handle the situation. What information had the police released? *Crap!* I should have listened to the news this morning instead of slapping off my clock radio after the weather forecast. Or at least I should have had it on in the car. Chief Kincaid would not be happy with me if I gave away a detail he was holding back to help catch the killer.

"No. I didn't find the body." A firm denial surely couldn't get me into trouble. "Would you like anything else?" I handed the tiny white box to her. "If not, you can pay at the register."

Before she could ask another question, the next person in line pushed forward. The morning continued in the same vein, with me evading the inquiries as best as I could. From what I gathered, the local anchorman had announced that the body of Lance Quistgaard had been found late last night behind Devereaux's Dime Store, and the police suspected that foul play was involved.

I had to snicker when I heard that last bit. Really? They *suspected* foul play? I would have guessed that a stake through the heart confirmed a criminal act.

The mob finally thinned out around two, and while I was overjoyed at the sales we'd made in the past five hours, I was exhausted. Lack of sleep, serving the larger-than-usual throng, and being careful about what I said concerning the murder had zapped my energy, and I felt my control slipping.

By the time Boone and Tsar arrived, I was happy the only customers left were a trio of teenagers camped out at the soda fountain, munching on chips, sipping vanilla Cokes, and taking advantage of the free Wi-Fi. After telling Xylia that I was taking a break, I helped my BFF carry all his stuff into the backroom.

Boone was an urbanely handsome man who wore designer suits, Italian leather shoes, and Serge Lutens Borneo 1834 cologne. His swath of tawny-gold hair fell in a flawless wave on his forehead, and his straight white teeth were striking against his tanned face.

All this made the picture of him wheeling a red cat carrier behind him all the more surreal. As he parked the kitty transporter, pushed down the telescoping handle, and unzipped the mesh flap, I sank wearily into the desk chair. The elegant Russian Blue poked out his nose, took a couple of sniffs, then extended one sleek gray paw. Apparently finding the floor to be acceptable, he exited the carrier and began to check out the perimeter of the room.

Meanwhile, gesturing to the cat's luggage, which I'd set on the floor, Boone said, "Here's Tsar's bowls, food, toys, treats, and bed." Pointing to a shallow plastic pan filled with a sandlike material, he instructed, "This is Tsar's litter box. Keep it immaculate, or you'll be sorry."

"Why?" I made it a point not to go anywhere near Banshee's litter box, so I had no idea what a cat's bathroom requirements entailed. Pun intended.

"If you don't clean it after each use, Tsar will find another place to relieve himself and it will most likely be in something you treasure." Boone smiled evilly. "He's partial to designer shoes."

"Point taken." I made a mental note to check the box every time I walked past it. "Anything else I should know about His Fussiness?"

"He'll only drink bottled water, will cry if his

dry food bowl isn't full, and he gets one can of Fancy Feast a day." Boone paused, then smacked his head. "Oh, and make sure he has his special treats, or you'll be mopping up hairballs."

"What I have gotten myself into?" I groaned. Tsar sounded like more work than taking care of a baby. "Are you sure you can't board him?"

"You'll be fine." Boone glanced at his watch, then said, "I've got to leave in fifteen minutes. Tell me all about the murder."

"Fine, but I'm saying this to you as my attorney." I'd decided to ask him his professional opinion about the stake situation. "That means what I say is completely confidential, right?"

"Give me a dollar." He held out his hand.

"Okay." I dug through my jean pockets and slapped four quarters into his palm.

"Are you somehow involved in the case?" A slight crease marred his usually smooth brow.

"Not exactly." I reached down and stroked Tsar's velvet fur, glad the cat had decided to rub against my ankles. I needed the comfort. "But I do have some information that I haven't shared with the cops." I explained my discovery of what I suspected was the murder weapon, then asked, "So, am I obligated to tell the police what I think?"

"Well." Boone's hazel eyes showed concern. "Since my law practice is more divorce and estate than criminal, I'd have to do some research to be sure, but it may fall under withholding evidence."

"So it's probably best that I do pass on my thoughts." I had guessed as much. "And when I do, I had probably better present the idea as having just occurred to me minutes before I telephone the cops." I waited for Boone to nod, then added, "And maybe I need to do that ASAP, rather than wait for the store to close."

"That would be best." Boone glanced at his watch again. "Now quick, tell me the whole story. Start from when Chief Kincaid called you."

"Okay. But this is still confidential, since I'm not sure what the cops are making public."

After I finished, Boone shook his head and was silent for a few seconds, then said, "Wow. That is just too bizarre to be real. Who knew a Shadow Bend book-club meeting would turn into the Dead Poet Society?"

Chapter 7

When I phoned Chief Kincaid, he was extremely interested in the possibility that the picket-fence stake was the murder weapon. He immediately ordered me to close the store, and less than fifteen minutes later, he and his forensic team were swarming over my shop. I was instructed to hand over my key, gather my belongings, and vacate the premises.

Unfortunately, I was informed that Tsar couldn't stay in the building, either. As I put the cat's possessions back in his luggage, Xylia came into the back room to tell me she was leaving. Until that point, the Russian Blue had been curled in his carrier, purring, but when my clerk opened the flap and tried to pet him, he hissed and darted into the store.

"I'm so sorry. I didn't know he'd run away." Xylia cowered almost as if she expected me to slap her. "I'll go catch him."

"No." I must have spoken too sharply, because Xylia hung her head, her posture subservient. I gentled my tone and said, "Let me. You can go ahead home."

"I could pack the cat's gear while you find

him." She bent over and her cotton skirt rode up, giving me a peek at her underwear.

"Thanks. When you're finished you can leave." I hurried after Tsar, silently chuckling that my buttoned-up clerk wore a black lace garter belt and matching thong beneath her demure clothing. I would have never guessed Xylia had it in her.

As I rounded up the cat, I worried about him having to face the wrath of Banshee. But my concern for the sweet Russian Blue's safety around the evil Siamese was pushed aside as Chief Kincaid followed me to my car and told me exactly what he thought of my behavior.

He was convinced that I had noticed the missing fence post the previous night when we'd walked through the store together, and he reamed me out for not telling him about it at that time. Although I maintained plausible deniability, I don't think he believed me.

In my defense, I reminded the chief of his prior statement that in a public place like my shop, there were thousands of prints, and that traces from everyone who had been at the meeting would be present just because they attended the book club, not because they were the murderer. When that argument failed to placate him, I asked what evidence he expected to find in my store now.

He didn't answer me; just growled, turned on his heel, and marched away. As I got into my car,

I worried that I had ruined my amicable relationship with the chief. Although he and Poppy were currently on the outs, he and I had always had a certain rapport. I'd helped him on his last murder case, for which he'd publically acknowledged and thanked me.

During my drive home, I reminded myself that Chief Kincaid knew that I often kept his daughter out of trouble—or at least the more serious kinds of trouble—and he had said that the crime-scene techs would be finished by Monday morning, so I could reopen on schedule. If he'd been really mad at me, surely he wouldn't have been so accommodating regarding my business.

With that positive thought, I pulled into the lane that led to Gran's house. As I maneuvered my Z4 through the shadow of the white fir and blue spruce lining either side of the road, I felt myself relax. Dorothy was right; there really was no place like home. At least not for me.

Glancing at the duck pond that I liked to picnic alongside when the weather was nice, I wondered if the next time I spread a blanket there, my father might join me in savoring Gran's fried chicken. According to his attorney, Dad would be released from prison any day now. Although in exchange for a lighter sentence the true embezzler had admitted to having framed my father, it had taken a long time to get all the paperwork completed.

I had so many conflicted emotions regarding his return that I'd been purposely not thinking about it. I felt guilty about doubting his innocence. I was nervous about how his presence would change both Gran's and my life. I had no idea if he'd be able to get a job. And if he couldn't, I was worried about whether I could financially support a third person.

His skills would be out-of-date, but, worse, he'd have a criminal record because in the end, Dad's lawyer had persuaded him to settle for parole instead of taking a chance on a retrial. He *had* been the one behind the wheel of the car that had killed an innocent girl. Even though he'd been drugged at the time, there was no guarantee a jury would find him innocent. That argument, plus our not having the money it would take to finance a whole new trial, had convinced my father to agree to the less risky option.

As the attorney had also pointed out, if Dad was paroled it was highly unlikely that there'd be any new media attention. His wasn't a high-profile case, and there was no one who might protest his release and stir up the interest of the press. A new trial, on the other hand, would probably result in an onslaught of newspaper and television reporters camping out in Shadow Bend.

Since there wasn't anything I could do about my father issues right now, I turned my attention to sneaking Tsar into the house without incurring Banshee's fury. Parking my car in front of the house, I left the Russian Blue in the BMW while I went inside to scope out the situation. As usual, the Siamese was in the living room, sunning himself on the cat tree in front of the picture window.

As I entered, he opened one eye, saw that it was me, and went back to sleep. Only Gran's presence could induce Banshee to move—well, her and the sound of a can of tuna being popped open. For the spoiled Siamese, it was always food o'clock somewhere.

Deciding to bring Tsar in through the back, I unlocked and propped open that door, then went to fetch the Russian Blue and his paraphernalia. The elaborate pet transporter could be transformed from a rolling carrier to a car seat to a backpack, so I strapped the Russian Blue on my body, balanced his litter box in one hand and grabbed his luggage in the other, and eased into the utility room.

After a quick peek to make sure the coast was clear, I tiptoed through the kitchen, then crept down the hallway to my room. My plan was to keep Tsar there behind closed doors until Monday, when I went to work. Banshee would never know his kingdom had been invaded by another animal.

In my bedroom, I set the pet carrier and suitcase on the floor. Looking around the twelve-by-twelve space, I opted to put the litter box in the attached bathroom. After I made sure that the litter was perfectly smooth for the finicky feline, and feeling smug at having outsmarted Banshee, I strolled back into my bedroom and froze.

The Siamese was poised in front of Tsar's carrier and he had managed to hook a claw in the zipper tab. As I watched in horror, the malevolent monster pulled downward, licking his chops and looking exactly as if he were unrolling the top of a sardine tin.

I still couldn't believe it. Instead of snacking on Tsar, Banshee had sniffed him, given his ears a few licks, and then the two cats sauntered out of the bedroom as if they'd been friends for years. Once I recovered from my shock, I followed them, sure that the Siamese was luring the Russian Blue to his doom. But the kitty couple was curled up together on the sofa, fast asleep.

Thankful for small miracles, I left the dozing duo and went into the kitchen for a snack. I'd skipped lunch and I didn't want to be so famished by dinner that I inhaled my food. That was so not the picture of me I wanted in Jake's mind.

One negative of the store closing early was that I had way too much time to fuss with my clothes and hair. Jake wasn't picking me up until seven, which should have left me with thirty minutes to get ready, but having nearly two hours made me crazy.

I decided to shower, set my hair, put on makeup, and even give myself a manicure. Well, I would've given myself a manicure, but since I couldn't find any polish that hadn't solidified in the bottle, I had to settle for filing and buffing my nails.

Still, my hands looked better than they had in months. In fact, I looked pretty good, which wouldn't help me any when I told Jake that I couldn't see him anymore. But was that what I was going to tell him? To say that I was torn would be an understatement of epic proportions.

For years, I hadn't been truly interested in any man. Now two of them made me tingle. And the truth of the matter was that I didn't know if it was Jake or Noah that I really wanted. Which was beyond awkward. Complicating the situation was that neither guy was the type to accept a non-exclusive relationship—at least not for very long. My initial reaction had been to cut them both loose, but that wasn't what I truly wanted to do.

If I was completely honest with myself, what I wanted was a chance to see which man was right for me. I wanted a chance at love. I wanted a chance at the brass ring of happiness. Did that mean I had to choose one now and hope for the best, or could I convince both guys to give me a little time? I guess I'd find out in the next couple of days if I could have my man, and a second one, too.

Finally, about quarter to seven, I wiggled into

my dark jeans and slipped on a black camisole. I'd compromised with Gran. I sure wasn't wearing a bustier—hell, I didn't even own one— but since the cami was edged in lace and had a lower neckline, it was a little sexier than my original idea of a tank. As I adjusted the top, I checked my butt in the mirror. Had it gotten bigger? No. That was just nerves talking. If I'd really gained weight, my pants wouldn't fit.

After I put on the blush pink cropped jacket, I slid into my Jimmy Choos. I was squeezing out the last little bit of lip gloss from the old tube of Venom that I'd unearthed from the bottom of a purse when I heard a vehicle thundering down the lane. Scooping up my bag and taking a deep breath, I sprinted into the foyer and glanced out the side window.

Even if I hadn't been expecting him, I would have known it was Jake. The enormous Ford F250 reminded me of its owner—strong, tough, and determined, with just a whisper of sexiness and a dash of playfulness for good measure.

As always, the pickup's black paint gleamed as if it had just left the dealership. Since I knew that unlike a lot of men who drove gigantic vehicles, Jake actually used his on a working ranch, I wondered how he kept it so clean. Did he wash it every time he came to see me? While that was a nice idea, I kind of doubted he'd make that sort of gesture. Noah, yes; Jake, not so much.

To avoid any awkwardness at the front door, I hurried outside. If I invited him in, we might never leave the house. I was determined to have a serious talk with him and not be swept away by our physical attraction. Of course, if he weren't so damned sexy and gorgeous, concentrating on something other than getting busy with him would be a hell of a lot easier.

As soon as I stepped off the porch, the truck's passenger door popped open and Jake leaned out, grinning. "Where's the fire?"

"Uh." My pulse doubled. This would be tougher than I'd thought. In the weeks since he'd been away, I'd managed to convince myself that the chemistry between us couldn't be as strong as I'd remembered. "Huh? Oh, you mean me coming out of the house so fast? Gran's resting, and I didn't want the doorbell to disturb her."

"Really?" He raised a dark brow. "Uncle Tony said that your grandmother is away on a senior bus trip. Did he get the dates mixed up?"

"Did I say Gran? I meant Gran's cat." I hated it when I got caught in a lie. "Banshee hasn't been feeling well, and the vet doesn't want him agitated." There, he'd made me tell another whopper.

"Seriously?"

I nodded, studying the man before me. Jake seemed to get better-looking every time I saw him. His thick ebony hair curled over the collar of his white Western shirt, making me want to run my fingers through the silky strands. And his full lips tempted me to climb into the pickup and onto his lap. What could one little kiss, or ten, hurt?

"Come on. Invite me inside." His voice held a satin-edged persuasion. "With Birdie gone, we could have the place to ourselves."

"Um." I searched for an excuse. "But what about dinner? I'm starving."

"So am I." His expression made it clear that he wasn't talking about food.

"Terrific." I chose to ignore his hint. "Then let's get going." I placed my foot on the step and used the handle inside the doorframe to hoist myself up into the pickup. *Jeez!* I'd forgotten that it was like climbing a sequoia just to get inside the cab.

"Are you okay?" Jake's sapphire eyes twinkled with laughter. "I can't believe how hard you make it seem to get into this truck."

"Hey, big boy, I'm only five-six, with the upper-body strength of a toddler. Maybe if I were six-four, like you, I wouldn't have a problem. I bet Meg doesn't have any trouble at all." Meg being his ex-wife. I'd never met her, but the image of her in my head was a cross between Wonder Woman and Miranda Priestly in *The Devil Wears Prada*.

"Meg's never been in my truck." The bronze skin tightened over his cheekbones and he muttered, "And she damn well never will be."

As much as I wanted to explore that statement, I contented myself with settling into the brown, saddle-leather passenger seat, then said, "I guess I should start lifting weights or working out or something."

"No." He chuckled good-naturedly. "I like you soft and curvy."

"Then don't tease me about my ascent into the lofty regions of your pickup." I clicked my seat belt buckle into its slot and asked, "Where are we going to eat?"

"How does Chinese sound?" He put the Ford in gear and made a three-point turn. "I hear the new place in town is good. Have you been there yet?"

Oops! I'd been there with Noah last month, but I wasn't ready for that conversation, so I hedged, "I had lunch there with my friends a few weeks ago. The food was fabulous."

"Great." He turned onto the main road. "How are Poppy and Boone?"

"Fine." Was it my fault he assumed that by friends I meant my BFFs? Of course, I could have corrected his misimpression, but why ask for trouble? "Poppy's spending the weekend in Chicago with her new boyfriend, and Boone's taking a cruise. He caught a flight out this afternoon." It was a relief to talk about something other than our love life, and I gave Jake all the details of what Poppy and Boone were up to as he drove toward town.

I briefly considered mentioning the murder to Jake, but I was sick of thinking about it, since it had been constantly on my mind since Chief Kincaid showed me the body. I'd tell Jake sometime before he took me home, but for right now I wanted a break and a few hours of fun.

During the ride, I was happy that Jake had to His striking blue eyes were fringed with dense black lashes and wisps of dark hair curled against the V of his open shirt. He had an air of authority, as if he were used to receiving instant compliance to any order he issued. And although he'd never get obedience from me, it was a comfort to be with someone to whom others acquiesced. Someone who wouldn't take any shit from anyone and didn't care what people thought of him.

"So Boone is okay now that the murder charge is behind him?" Jake pulled the pickup into the Golden Dragon's parking lot.

"He's getting there." I unfastened my seat belt and prepared to exit the truck, wishing I had a parachute for the descent. "Spending time in jail took its toll on him." I blew out a breath. "I suppose it will have changed my father, too."

"Tony told me your dad's been cleared but is taking parole so he can get out of prison sooner." Jake came around to my side of the pickup and helped me to the ground. "Are you good with that?"

"Yeah. Although I'd rather he didn't have to go through life with a criminal record." When we'd met, I had told Jake about how my father's conviction had affected my adolescence. "But I feel guilty for not believing in him and for resenting him all these years, so I don't feel I can say anything to him about it." I sighed. "Gran never doubted him for a minute. Hell, even the chief of police thought he was innocent. But his own daughter didn't have faith in him."

"It's tough to trust someone you think has let you down." Jake took my hand. "You can't blame yourself for having resented him."

"Maybe." It was hard to think with Jake's thumb drawing circles on the sensitive skin of my wrist. "I'll just have to try to make it up to Dad when he gets home."

"Don't go overboard." Jake opened the restaurant door for me.

"As if," I sniffed. "You never talk about your folks. Why is that?"

"We're not close." Jake's voice was even, but a crease had formed between his eyebrows. "I generally see them about once a year, and that's usually too much."

"For them or you?" I was curious about Jake's ability to have a relationship.

He was saved from answering, as the hostess, a stunning Asian woman in her early twenties, glided toward us and asked, "How many, please?"

"Two," Jake answered, then added, "And we'd like a quiet booth."

She glanced at me, a puzzled look in her eyes, then smiled and said in a melodic soprano, "Ah, now I remember. You were here with Dr. Underwood. Would you like his table? He's not expected tonight."

Shit! Caught in another lie. I just couldn't get a break. Maybe it was time to be a little more truthful. Nah. That would be too easy.

"Sounds good." Jake shot me a look that promised we'd talk about this later.

Once we were seated and the hostess left, in a rush to distract him, I said, "Tell me about the case you've been on this past month. Did you catch the guy before he killed the witness?" Jake had been undercover trying to locate a cartel boss who had skipped bail.

"We got him a few days ago." Jake studied the menu. "He was about fifty yards from the Mexican border."

"He sounded like a real bad guy."

"Yeah, but in terms of pure evil, he doesn't even rank in the top ten." Jake's expression darkened.

"Oh?" I was curious about Jake's life as a marshal. "Who heads that list?"

"The psychos are the worst." Jake's jaw tightened. "And the serial killers, like the Doll Maker." I opened my mouth to ask for details, and Jake cut me off. "Believe me, you don't want to know more."

"Okay." I sort of did, but I'd wait for another time. Instead, I asked, "What happened to the cartel boss?"

"I escorted him back to jail, then came straight here." He put the leatherette menu down and looked at me. "I'm sorry I've been out of touch for so long."

"I understand." I took a sip of water, wanting to ask how many days he'd be in Shadow Bend, but unsure how to broach the subject. "It's your job. It's not as if you have time to make calls and drop in for a visit when you're out catching the bad guys."

He didn't respond, and it was a relief when the waitress appeared to take our drink order. Jake asked for a Tsingtao, and I went for a lychee martini. After she walked away, the silence was starting to grow uncomfortable when I spotted a familiar figure hurtling toward me.

I was about to warn Jake that we had company—he had his back to our approaching visitor—when the whirlwind trilled, "Dev, you're just the person I wanted to see."

Winnie Todd's frizzy gray curls bounced as she charged up to our table. She and her daughter, Zizi, were members of the Blood, Sweat, and Shears sewing group that met at my store on Wednesday nights. Winnie was the original flower child, and she still dressed the part. Tonight she had on bell-bottoms, a fringed suede vest, and a flowered scarf tied around her forehead. Winnie was one of a kind, and I loved that she never allowed the Shadow Bend Peer-Pressure Posse to make her conform and blend in.

"Tell me about the murder at the dime store," Winnie demanded, breathless from her mad dash across the restaurant. "Zizi said the dead guy acted like a real dickweed at the book club."

Zizi had been so quiet during the meeting that I had almost forgotten she had been there. Come to think about it, it was strange that she hadn't been more vocal. Zizi was a social work graduate student and usually extremely outspoken if women were being dissed.

"There's not really—" I started to deny any knowledge of the murder.

But Winnie caught sight of Jake and cut me off. "Ah, I see the hot U.S. Marshal is back in town. How delicious. Is he edging out our gallant doctor in the competition for your affections?"

There was no way to answer that question, so I ignored it and said, "Jake, this is Winnie Todd, a friend of mine from the sewing group."

They exchanged greetings, and then Jake asked, "What murder?"

"Last night, a man named Lance Quistgaard was found dead *behind* my store, not inside it." I emphasized the word while staring at Winnie.

"Did you know him?" Jake's law-enforcement antenna had clearly been engaged.

"Earlier that evening, he'd been the guest speaker at the local book club that met there." I summarized the event for Jake, with Winnie avidly taking in every syllable I uttered. I ended with, "So, no, I didn't *know him* know him, but I had met him."

"I heard that he was a poet," Winnie commented. "Poets are very passionate men, and passionate men make enemies. I knew a lot of them when I lived in Haight-Ashbury." She had left Shadow Bend to live in San Francisco during the midsixties, and had returned, sans husband, in the late eighties to have Zizi, her only child.

"Well, I'm sure the police will sort it out," I assured Winnie.

"But with the murder being *behind* your store, don't you think you should help them?" Winnie fiddled with the silver peace symbol hanging from a leather thong around her neck.

"No." Actually, I sort of did, but it really wasn't any of my business.

"You figured out who killed Dr. Underwood's fiancée, and you cleared Boone's name when he was arrested."

I saw a gleam in Winnie's eye and could almost hear a click. *Oh-oh.* A figurative lightbulb must have just gone on over Winnie's head. "That was pure luck." All I needed was Winnie with an idea.

"You seem to have a knack for detective work." Winnie ignored my attempt to dismiss my previous investigative success. "Zizi and I could help."

"Thanks, but I think I'll leave this one to Chief Kincaid." I looked over her shoulder. A group of sixty-something women was beckoning her. "I think your friends are trying to tell you that your food's arrived." I pointed to a lady waving a large red hat with a purple plume.

"Yikes! I hate cold moo goo gai pan." Winnie leaned in and hugged me. "Got to go. But call me if you need a Watson for your Sherlock." Before she let go of my neck, she whispered in my ear, "By the way, keep both guys. I always did."

After Winnie walked away, the waitress served our drinks and took our appetizer order for hot and sour soup and pot stickers.

Once we were alone again, Jake said, "Tell me more about the murder."

"Why?" I took a sip of my martini. "It doesn't have anything to do with me."

"Because I know you're holding something back." He quirked an eyebrow. "Humor me."

Figuring Jake was one of the few people in Shadow Bend who could keep his mouth shut, I told him everything I knew about the case.

When I finished, he said, "So, you withheld information from the police?"

"Not withheld so much as deferred revealing it

until a more convenient time." Hey, I'd told the chief—eventually. And shouldn't the cops have figured it out without my help? After all, they were the so-called experts. "Anyway, what kind of evidence can they really expect to get from my store? Anything they find could have gotten there during legitimate business hours. There's no way to sort that stuff out, is there?"

"There isn't a way to time-stamp fingerprints or trace, so it's highly unlikely the crime-scene techs will come up with anything," Jake admitted, then frowned. "But back to someone hiding in your store. How did they manage that?"

"As I said, both Quistgaard and Addie Campbell stormed out of the meeting." I chewed my thumbnail. "Although I didn't like the idea of them wandering around my store unsupervised, I was mobbed and couldn't follow them right away." I shrugged. "I figured all they had to do was turn the knob on the dead bolt to let themselves out, and at least one of them did that, because the door was unlocked when I was finally able to break away and check."

"What I don't like is that someone was in your store and you weren't aware that they were there." Jake stared into my eyes. "You do realize that once everyone left, you were alone with a killer."

Chapter 8

As when I'd previously eaten at the Golden Dragon, the food was wonderful and so was the company. I had a good time talking to Jake. I loved his wicked sense of humor, and his stories about being undercover were riveting. For my part of the conversation, I brought him up to speed about what had been happening in my life since I'd last seen him, and how I'd helped figure out who had really killed the woman that Boone had been accused of murdering.

We lingered over dessert, but finally our server brought us the check with two fortune cookies on top of the ticket. Jake tossed me one of the cellophane-wrapped clairvoyant confections before reaching for his wallet. I momentarily considered offering to pay half, but decided against it. Jake wasn't the kind of guy who'd be okay with going Dutch treat on what he considered a date.

As he laid money for the bill on the little plastic tray, I opened my cookie and read aloud, " 'The current year will bring you much happiness.' " I tucked the little slip of paper in my purse. "I hope that means my father's homecoming will go smoothly." I wondered how Dad would get along with Jake and Noah. Would he like them or feel threatened by the men in my life?

"Just take it slow," Jake advised, then handed the cash to the server, who had returned to pick up the check, and told her to keep the change.

Once she thanked him and left us alone, Jake cracked open his cookie. His face was expressionless as he read, " 'You will take a chance in the near future, and, if you have faith, win.' "

"What's that supposed to mean?" I slid out of the booth and when Jake joined me, I asked him, "Are you planning a trip to the casino boats?"

"Nope." Jake's palm on my lower back guided me to the exit. "The only gambling I do is part of my job."

"You mean because you put your life on the line every time you go after a bad guy." I preferred not to think of that aspect of his profession. Another reason I was hesitant about getting too serious about him.

His answer was a twitch of his shoulders. When we got to his pickup, he opened the passenger door and said, "Here, let me help you up."

"Thanks." His hands on my waist sent a shiver of awareness sizzling though me.

Apparently, Jake felt it, too, because instead of lifting me into the truck's cab, he pulled me toward him and, his voice thick, rasped, "It's been so long since I had my arms around you."

"Yes." Something about his expression made

my mouth go dry. I had to clear my throat in order to continue. "It has."

He cradled my cheek in his palm and murmured, "You know, all those nights lying in some cheap hotel room, waiting for morning, I kept thinking about how soft your skin was and trying to convince myself that it couldn't be as silky as I remembered."

I tried to inhale, but his mouth was so near, I could barely draw enough breath to ask, "And is it the way you remembered?"

He gathered me closer, pressing me against his hard length, making me hotter than chocolate fondue. The callused feel of his fingers as he slid them down the neckline of my cami made me gasp. And when he moved his hand to my breast, a delicious shudder ran down my spine.

What was it about this man that made my body commandeer the decision-making process from my head? How did he sweep away all my good intentions? We needed to talk about Noah, but I couldn't seem to find the strength to stop him as he placed his lips on mine.

The hunger of his kiss shattered what little self-control I had retained. I was overwhelmed with sensation as erotic images flashed through my mind—images of Jake and me on a king-size bed. I tried to remind myself that he'd be returning to St. Louis and that I was only a convenient stopover while he visited his uncle.

But the primitive part of my brain urged me on.

While I was rallying all the reasons I should stop him, I slid my hands over his rock-solid pecs, then around his neck, and finally tunneled them through his hair. He grunted his approval and deepened the kiss, licking into my mouth as he pressed me against the side of the truck. His heat created an ache inside my soul and I pulled him even closer. I worked his shirttail loose from his pants, burrowed under the crisp cotton until I reached his broad shoulders, then scraped my nails down his back. I loved the feel of his firm muscles under my fingertips.

I knew this evening probably wouldn't end well, especially when I told him that I intended to keep seeing both him and Noah until I was sure which man I loved. But Jake drew me like those dark chocolate curls that decorate a French silk pie. I always told myself not to gobble them down, but I never listened to my own good advice.

My rational side was losing the battle against my craving, and his hands were fumbling with the button on my jeans, when a chorus of voices heading in our direction grabbed my attention. It took us both a long moment to put the brakes on our lust, but it finally penetrated our sexual haze that we were seconds from becoming the *show* part of *dinner and a show*.

With a groan, Jake pulled up my cami, adjusted my jacket, and tucked in his shirt. An instant later, a group of ladies rounded the aisle, heading toward a silver Lincoln MKX.

Before I could scramble into Jake's truck and hide, a familiar voice purred, "Devereaux, my dear, what a surprise to see you here. Noah told me he had tickets for you and him to attend a concert tonight."

Shit! Shit! Shit! Nadine Underwood, aka a cross between a cockroach and Satan, walked over to me with a smirk on her face. I hadn't noticed Noah's mother in the restaurant, and evidently she hadn't spotted me there, either. If only Jake and I hadn't gotten distracted, I could have made a clean getaway. Now I had to pretend to be pleasant or at least civil.

Pasting a social smile on my lips, I tried to sound nonchalant. "Hi, Nadine. You must have misunderstood. Noah and I are having brunch tomorrow." Knowing how much she disliked me and how upset she was that I'd been seeing her son, I added, "But thanks for your concern."

"I see." Nadine may have been a beauty at one time, but years of tanning and vitriol had taken their toll, and the wrinkles around her mouth became even more pronounced when she gloated, "He must be taking someone else tonight."

"That must be it." I kept my tone unperturbed but felt a flicker of jealousy, which was totally unfair since I had just been in heavy-duty lip-lock with Jake. "Well, we were just leaving, so . . ." I trailed off, hoping she'd get the hint and skitter away like the insect she resembled.

"Is something wrong?" she asked. "Is that why you're in a hurry to go?" Nadine's expression brightened; she was clearly cheered at the thought. "You seem out of breath."

"Everything's fine," I lied. Nothing like running into the mother of the other man in your life to douse your desire. "Jake has an early morning. He's helping out on his uncle's ranch," I improvised.

"I don't think we've met." Jake turned on the charm. "I'm Jake Del Vecchio, Tony's grand-nephew. And you must be Dr. Underwood's mother."

"Yes, I am." Nadine extended her hand. "Do you know my son?"

"We've met."

When Jake didn't elaborate, she drew her Magic Marker–drawn eyebrows together. She was used to people fawning over her and her son, and, apparently, Jake's indifference upset her. Pursing her mouth, she turned her attention back to me. "Devereaux, I hear that you've managed to get involved in yet another murder. What is it with you and crime?"

"I don't know what you mean." I put a steel edge in my voice.

"The body found at your store." Her tone oozed condescension. "Surely you can't be so distracted by this pretty boy you're with that you've forgotten the poor man who was killed inches from your door last night. Even you can't be that self-centered and coldhearted."

"Pretty boy?" Jake chuckled faintly and tapped my arm. "Seriously?"

I shot him an amused glance, then said to Nadine, "Of course I haven't forgotten about the victim, but I hardly consider myself involved. The investigation is in the police's capable hands."

"I don't know about that." Nadine's eyes gleamed with malice. "They'll certainly have their hands full with all the suspects."

"What do you mean?" I had no idea what she was talking about, unless somehow she had heard about the ruckus during the book-club meeting and was referring to the club members who'd argued with the victim.

"Didn't you know?" Nadine's expression reminded me of Banshee after a particularly successful attack on my ankles. "Lance Quistgaard was the man who wrote 'The Bend's Buzz.' He'd ticked off half the town."

"The Bend's Buzz" was the gossip column in our local newspaper. The writer's identity was a huge secret, so how had Nadine found out that it was Lance? Or had everyone known except me?

"You're sure?" I asked. "How do you know Quistgaard wrote the column?"

"Grant Edwyn is a good friend of mine."

Nadine bared her teeth in what I assumed was her attempt at a smile. "When his paper started featuring that awful column, I demanded to know who was behind it and threatened to sue if I was ever mentioned."

"Of course you did," I muttered. "Well, don't let us keep you, Nadine. I'm sure your friends would like to leave."

"Certainly." Nadine smiled serenely. "There's no excuse for being inconsiderate of one's friends, is there?" She turned to go, then added over her shoulder, "I'll tell Noah you *both* said hello. He'll be so glad to know you weren't spending Saturday night alone and missing him."

After releasing her stream of venom, Nadine slithered away. When she rejoined her cronies, I couldn't hear what she said, but they all tittered like a flock of magpies before piling inside the Lincoln.

Jake and I exchanged a mutual sigh of relief; then he helped me up into the truck and we got the hell out of Dodge before someone else wanted to comment on our being together. This was why I hated going out in a small town—no privacy, and everyone felt they had the right to share their opinion about your date, whether it was asked for or not.

I was silent, my thoughts whirring too fast for me to focus on just one. I wasn't ready to think about what Nadine had interrupted, and I didn't want to consider how she'd twist the situation when she reported it to her son.

Apparently, Jake had decided to ignore our make-out session, too, because we were halfway to my house before he said, "I almost feel sorry for Underwood. Having a mother like that can't be fun."

"He's been better at standing up to her lately." I thought about the conversation Noah and I had had when we'd started seeing each other again. Noah had assured me that he'd issued an ultimatum to Nadine. If she did anything to upset me or tried to take any action against my family, my friends, or me, he would sever all ties with her. Although she'd promised to be good, I suspected she hadn't actually surrendered and had instead taken the battle underground.

"Really?" Jake's tone was skeptical. "That's a big change for such a mama's boy."

"Maybe." I had doubts myself. "I know it can't be easy for him."

In the past, I had never quite understood why Nadine disliked my family and me so much, but now that I knew about her history with my father, it made more sense. It also made it less likely that Noah would be able to keep her need for revenge under control.

"Which should be a point in my favor." Jake's tone was casual. "My uncle loves you and would be happy to see us together."

"True," I agreed, turning in my seat so I could gauge his expression. I realized this was the opening I had been waiting for. "Now that you mention it, I'd like to discuss the situation with you."

"Oh." Jake tensed, then pulled the pickup over to the side of the road, cut the motor, and looked at me. "What situation is that?"

"All of them." I closed my eyes, trying to decide which to bring up first.

"Let's start with you and me." He unfastened his seat belt, flipped up the center console, and scooted over so that his thigh pressed against mine. "I think we have a pretty good thing going."

"When you're here." I stared straight ahead, not allowing myself to be captivated by the enthralling scent of what I was coming to think of as Eau de Jake—a mixture of lime, saddle soap, and sexy man. "Now that you're back working as a marshal, you're gone for weeks at a time. That doesn't seem like such a good thing."

"You know, Tony's been talking to me about managing the ranch for him." Jake's casual tone was contradicted by the rigid way he held his body. "If I did that, I'd be around all the time."

"Are you going to take him up on his offer?" I felt an ember of hope start to ignite in my heart.

"How about you and Frat Boy?" Jake asked, ignoring my question.

"He and I have a lot of history," I said carefully.

"And I admit there's still a spark between us." I met Jake's stare and immediately was sorry that I had. The intensity in his dark blue eyes made me swallow, and for a millisecond, my mind went totally blank.

"From what you've told me, that history isn't good." Jake moved closer.

"Some of it is; some of it isn't." I studied Jake's face. The only sign that he was upset was the tensing of his jaw. But a sadness hung over him, and my conscience ached for having put it there. "Noah explained his reason for breaking up with me when we were in high school, and I've forgiven him. We've made a fresh start."

"As friends?" Jake's hands were fisted. "That's what you told me a few weeks ago." His massive chest rose and fell rapidly, as if he'd been running up hill. "Has something changed?"

"No. Yes. I don't know." I wanted to be honest with Jake, but I hadn't figured this whole thing out myself. "Noah and I are still just friends, but maybe there could be more if I let it."

"Don't let it." Jake stroked my chin with his thumb. "He's too analytical, too inflexible, too insular. He's not right for you."

"Probably not," I admitted, thinking that Jake had pretty much described me as well as Noah. Maybe the two of us being so much alike would become a problem. "But I'll never know if I don't give him a chance."

"Underwood had his chance thirteen years ago and he blew it." Jake twined his fingers in my curls. "How about you give me mine?"

"I want to." I closed my eyes. The sensation of Jake's hands stroking my hair washed over me like a waterfall. "I really do want to."

"Let yourself go." Jake leaned toward me, his breath, sweet from our dessert, fanning my face, and his voice low and gravelly. "Go ahead. Take a leap of faith."

Without realizing I was going to ask, I heard myself say, "But if I jump, will you be around to catch me? Are you going to stay in Shadow Bend and manage your uncle's ranch, or are you going back to St. Louis and the Marshals Service?" When he didn't answer, I could see the indecision in his eyes. "Which is it?"

"I . . . I . . ." He stopped, then sighed and said, "The best I can do right now is maybe."

"Maybe?" I pulled away from him. "You want me to take a chance on maybe?"

"There are no guarantees in life." Frustration colored his voice. "I'm trying to figure some things out right now. Give me a break."

"I will if you will." Staring at him, I said, "I'd like to keep seeing you, but I'm going to keep going out with Noah, too." I crossed my arms. "If we're lucky, maybe we'll both figure out what we want at the same time. Can you live with me dating you both?"

Jake let out a loud, audible breath. "Do I have a choice?"

"Yes." I watched as he slid across the seat, fastened his seat belt, and started the engine. "You can walk away."

"No." Jake's lips flattened into a hard white line. "That's one thing I can't do."

Chapter 9

Jake ground his teeth in frustration. In the few minutes that it took him to drive to his uncle's ranch, adjacent to the Sinclair property, he thought about how badly his date with Devereaux had ended. How had the situation deteriorated so quickly?

The evening had started out well, even if she'd met him in the driveway. It had been hilarious to see her making excuses for why she didn't want him to go inside her place. She was such a strange mix of tough businesswoman and vulnerable female. She never did what he expected her to do, and normally he hated being caught by surprise, but she always managed to charm him.

Jake ground his teeth again as he pulled his truck up to his uncle's front door. Devereaux also always managed to light his fuse, then turn him away before he could complete the mission. Now, at a few minutes past midnight, Jake was raring to go, with no one to go with.

He stared at the dark house. Thank God Tony had gone to bed! The last thing Jake needed was his uncle asking about the stick of dynamite in his pants threatening to blast his fly wide open.

Sighing, Jake climbed out of the pickup's cab and winced. The docs had told him that his leg was healed and that he was fit for duty as a marshal, but they had also warned him that he'd always have some pain. And after his latest stint undercover, his knee seemed to be bothering him more often. He probably shouldn't have attempted that flying tackle when the cartel boss made a run for the Mexican border.

Ignoring the twinge, Jake went inside and headed to the liquor cabinet in the living room. He needed a drink if he had a hope in hell of falling asleep anytime soon. He poured himself two fingers of Bourbon and flopped down on the couch.

As he sipped the booze, his thoughts skittered to Devereaux's announcement. Did she really expect him to sit back and accept her going out with Dr. Dweeb? Jake's stomach churned. He'd never been good at sharing. When she'd declared that she would date them both, a wave of fury had nearly choked him, and it had been all he could do not to smash his fist through his truck's windshield.

Jake toed off his Durangos, set his stocking feet on the coffee table, and balanced his whiskey glass on his stomach. After he'd swallowed his anger at the thought of Devereaux with another man, he'd felt something else, something he wasn't used to feeling. He'd felt fear. What if he lost her? What if she was the one for him, but she decided that he wasn't the one for her? Could he live with that? He wasn't brave enough to answer that question.

But was it fair to expect her to give up someone who would always be there for her? At best, Jake would be in Shadow Bend one week a month, and if he was on a difficult case, it could be a lot less often than that. Underwood offered her dependability and status in the community, things she'd had ripped away from her when her father had gone to prison and her mother had dumped her on Birdie. Maybe he should bow out.

Hell, no! Jake abruptly sat up, barely catching the glass before it went flying. There was no guarantee that Frat Boy would stand up to his mother. He'd betrayed Devereaux once, and if push came to shove, he might do it again.

Jake paced the length of the living room. No woman before Devereaux had ever tempted him to quit the Marshals Service and settle down, but he'd been thinking about it a lot lately. In many ways, it would be the ideal solution to his problems. He'd be able to take over the ranch for his uncle, who needed him. Although ranching wouldn't be as easy on his leg as some desk job, he wouldn't have to worry that it would give out in a crucial moment, when it could endanger his or other's lives. It was also a lot less likely that while working on the ranch he'd become so severely reinjured that he couldn't walk. *And* he could concentrate on winning Devereaux.

She'd haunted him this past month. She was always in the back of his mind. Just before going to sleep at night, he'd fantasize that she was beside him. It had been sheer torture pretending that his ex-wife was his girlfriend. Every time he'd had to touch her or kiss her, he'd compared her to Devereaux and asked himself why he'd ever married Meg. How had he thought he loved her?

After chugging the last of his Bourbon, he walked into the kitchen and put the empty glass in the sink, then pulled out a chair and sat at the table. Something else was bothering him. The murder. The idea of Devereaux being alone with a killer ate at his gut.

What if the murderer wasn't just some run-of-the-mill violent asshole with a grudge? What if he was a totally deranged nut job who didn't care who he offed? Devereaux could have been the victim instead of that poet.

Jake had a week before he had to report back to work, and since he was in the area, maybe he should take a gander at the case. After all, the local cops didn't handle many homicides, especially ones where the vic ended up with a stake through his heart.

As Jake headed to bed, he smiled. Nothing like a juicy case to take his mind off his troubles.

Chapter 10

With Gran on her casino trip with Frieda and my store off-limits due to the police search, I seized the rare opportunity to sleep late. It was quarter to ten when I got out of bed Sunday morning, and the cats were waiting at my bedroom door when I emerged from my room. Both meowed loudly at me as I passed them, and Banshee lashed out at my bare ankles. I did a quick hop to avoid his claws and landed on a hard plastic mouse that one of the foxy felines had deposited strategically in my path. I swear the Siamese sniggered when I yelped in pain.

Clearly, the cats were ticked off by their delayed breakfast, so it was a good thing I had moved Tsar's litter box from my bathroom to the utility room the night before. Otherwise, I was fairly certain he would have displayed his displeasure at not being able to get to his potty in an unacceptable manner. No doubt by depositing a little gift for me in the Jimmy Choos that I'd kicked off and left in the hallway.

Once the cats' needs were taken care of, I put on the coffee and went to take a shower. Noah was picking me up in an hour and I needed to hustle if I was going to be ready in time. While I got dressed, I sipped a cup of liquid renewal and considered what Nadine had said. No, not that Noah had taken someone else out the night before—well, I spared only a fleeting thought about that—but what she had revealed about Lance Quistgaard.

Did Chief Kincaid know that Quistgaard had written "The Bend's Buzz"? Now that I was aware of that fact, his behavior at the book-club meeting made a lot more sense, especially since the news-paper's editor had turned out to be the man that had forced the poet to stop arguing and leave. Had Edwyn been afraid Lance would reveal himself as the gossip columnist if he continued to express his acerbic opinions about Shadow Bend?

Was it the editor's idea to keep the identity of the gossip columnist a secret? Or had it been Quistgaard's choice? Either way, in the face of his employer's displeasure, Quistgaard must have decided that he'd better back down, or risk being fired.

Now that I knew that Lance was the voice of the "Buzz," what he'd said that night about small towns and hypocrisy added up. And with his writing for the *Banner* being credited to Anonymous, his comment about his published poetry finally giving him something that he was proud to put his name on fit, too.

Time had slipped away while I pieced together the traces of Lance's secret life; and when I checked the clock, I had exactly five minutes to put on my clothes or I would have to answer the door in my robe. Noah would arrive exactly on time, so I couldn't count on any wiggle room, and I didn't want to give him the wrong impression by greeting him less than fully dressed and ready to hit the road.

Noah had mentioned that he wanted to try a restaurant in Kansas City called bluestem, and I'd Binged it to figure out what to wear. I noticed from its Web site that the name began with a lowercase b, which led me to expect an avant-garde atmosphere. Based on that and the prices on its Web site, I'd chosen a short black-and-white dress that I paired with black tights and Kate Spade patent-leather ballet flats.

I had sold all my good jewelry, but I still had some nice costume pieces. Rummaging around in my drawer, I located a long snowflake-obsidian necklace and dangling ebony earrings that were perfect for the modern yet elegant look I was going for.

As expected, Noah arrived precisely at eleven, and because I knew I could trust him not to try to charm his way inside, I didn't feel the need to meet him at the curb. When I opened the door, my pulse did a little Macarena of excitement. He was so handsome—and everything you'd expect of a wealthy, socially prominent young doctor.

His gray eyes twinkled as he greeted me. "Dev, you look amazing."

"Thank you." I twinkled back. "So do you. I love your jacket."

He wore a dark gray Dolce & Gabbana cotton blazer, a Pembury plaid shirt, and black twill pants. At six-foot-two, with his lean build and classic features, he might have stepped straight out of the pages of *GQ*.

"Thanks, but I can't take the credit." Noah shrugged. "My Nordstrom guy delivered it yesterday. He sends me new stuff every season. I keep what I like and ship the rest back. I don't have time to shop, so that works best."

"I used to have a personal stylist at Nordstrom," I said with a nostalgic sigh. I'd almost forgotten what it was like to have money to burn. Wait. Now that I thought about it, I really didn't miss that lifestyle. At least not as much as I'd expected to.

"It is convenient." Noah shoved his hands in his pockets. "Especially if you work sixty hours a week."

"True, but keeping current with fashion isn't quite as vital to me now that I wear a sweatshirt to work every day." I glanced at my watch. "We should probably get going if our reservation is for twelve thirty." Even without commuter traffic, it took a good hour to get into the city from Shadow Bend. And that didn't include finding a parking place, which was often a pain in the city.

Like Jake's F250, Noah's Jaguar reflected his personality. The taiga green Jag was sleek and powerful, and as he assisted me in, I couldn't help but let a contented groan slip out. The ivory leather seat was like a warm embrace, and the scent of Amouage Dia Pour Homme, Noah's after-shave, filling the car's interior completed that feeling. I was surprised at how comfortable I felt with Noah. After the initial awkwardness a few weeks ago when we'd first started seeing each other again, we'd picked up where we'd left off so long ago. It was almost as if it had been thirteen days rather than years since we'd been together.

Noah concentrated on driving. It was sort of funny that the roads in Shadow Bend were busier than the freeway. What with people on their way to and from church, folks going to the grocery store to pick up the Sunday paper, and others stopping at the diner for a late breakfast or early lunch, our little town was hopping.

When Noah finally merged onto the nearly empty highway that would take us into the city, he put the Jag on cruise control and asked, "Any news about that murder? Have the police found any evidence?"

"Well . . ." I hesitated. Noah had heard on the radio about the body behind my store and called me at work Saturday morning to see if I was all right. I'd assured him that I was fine, but I hadn't mentioned my suspicion regarding the fence post or that I'd decided not to inform the chief about it until later that afternoon. Now I had to fill him in without admitting my omission. "After I talked to you yesterday, I noticed something that might be connected to the murder weapon, so now the cops are processing the inside of the dime store."

"What did you notice?" Noah put on his turn signal, accelerated, and passed a slow-moving Buick.

I explained about the stake, ending with, "I don't think the chief is releasing exactly how the guy was killed. At least I haven't heard it on the news, so please don't share that tidbit with anyone."

"I won't," Noah promised. He changed lanes to allow a semi to merge, then asked, "Do you want me to meet you at the shop tomorrow morning and help clean up? If those crime shows on television are any indication, the police will leave the place a mess."

"That would be terrific." I was touched that Noah would offer his help, and noted that Jake hadn't done the same. "Don't you have to work?"

"I'm not scheduled at the clinic until the afternoon." Noah grinned. "I finally found a doctor who's willing to take some hours. I'm hoping she'll like it here and will consider coming on board full-time."

Noah had attended the combined BA and MD program at the University of Missouri's School of Medicine, which had allowed him to graduate in six years. Afterward, he'd done a three-year residency in family medicine, then returned to Shadow Bend and opened the Underwood Clinic. It was the only medical facility in a forty-mile radius and perpetually crowded, but until now, due to the long hours and low pay, he'd been unable to lure another physician into joining his practice.

"That's terrific. I'll keep my fingers crossed for you," I said. Wanting to forget that the police were ransacking my business as we spoke, I decided to change the subject and asked, "So, how was the concert last night?"

As soon as the words left my mouth, I tried to suck them back in. When I couldn't, I gave myself a mental slap upside the head. How could I be such an idiot? I didn't want to discuss my own Saturday night until later, which meant that bringing up Noah's evening was just plain stupid.

Damn! Now I'd have to admit to seeing his mother, a little factoid I had intended to neglect to mention. Not that I didn't think he'd find out about our little tête-à-tête; I just didn't want to be the one to tell him.

"Uh." He glanced at me with a puzzled frown. "Okay. How did you know I went to a concert? I don't remember our discussing it."

"Your mother." For a split second, I'd considered claiming that Noah had told me. But I only lied if I was pretty damn sure I could get away with a fib, and Nadine would probably relay our parking-lot encounter to him in exquisite detail. "I ran into her at the Golden Dragon last night. She seemed surprised to see me there, rather than with you at the symphony."

"Ah." Noah's lips twisted into a cynical smile. "Mom knew I was escorting my cousin. In fact, my mother was the one who volunteered my services as a chauffeur when Patti's husband was called out of town on business at the last minute. My cousin doesn't like to drive in the city, and originally offered my mother the tickets."

I made a face. "What a surprise, Nadine trying to stir up trouble."

"I bet she was thrilled to see you with Del Vecchio." Noah grimaced.

"She called him a pretty boy." I snickered. "But I wouldn't actually say she was pleased. She can be fairly hard to figure out."

"Tell me about it." Noah's gaze met mine, and we both chuckled.

Before Noah could pursue the topic of Jake, I steered the conversation back to the concert he'd attended, and we talked about music the rest of the way to the restaurant. The Underwoods were big supporters of the Kansas City Symphony, and although Noah was knowledgeable about classical music, it wasn't his favorite type of music, so our discussion drifted to performers we both admired.

The entrance to bluestem looked a little like the one to my dime store. Although theirs was covered by a navy canopy and my awning was green, both front doors were flanked by two large windows. An interior wall of red brick and a ceiling of exposed heating ducts made for unadorned elegance, or at least that's what their Web site claimed. We were seated at a table for two in a quiet corner, handed the menus, and told our server would be with us shortly.

As I studied the selections, I decided to keep the conversation light while we ate, then debate the whole relationship mess on the way home while Noah was distracted by driving. With any luck, we'd finish our talk just as we arrived at my house. Birdie would be back from her trip by then, so there would be no possibility of inviting Noah inside.

When our server approached, Noah asked me, "Do you still like champagne?"

My pulse jumped at his roguish little grin, and I nodded, remembering the first time I'd tasted it. Noah had stolen a bottle of his mother's Cristal and we'd gotten tipsy drinking it out of red plastic cups. Neither one of us had had any idea that we'd guzzled two hundred bucks' worth of bubbly until Nadine found out and impressed upon us just how much each swig had cost.

After sending the waitress off to get a bottle of Piper-Heidsieck, Noah took my hands and said, "I hope this isn't a farewell meal."

"Of course not." I really didn't want to discuss that topic yet.

"Good." Noah's brow instantly smoothed and he squeezed my fingers.

I was trying to think of a way to postpone the relationship conversation when I heard someone say, "Well, isn't this a small world."

"Hi, Vaughn." Noah and I greeted the owner of the voice simultaneously.

Vaughn Yager strolled over, grabbed a chair from an adjacent table, and, without being invited, joined us. He had been a classmate of ours, but he was an entirely different person today. Because he'd been an unattractive, studious boy from a less than prestigious family, he'd been bullied. But as nerds often do, he'd grown up to become a successful man and an eligible bachelor.

After using his considerable mathematical skills and his genius for tactics and strategy to make a fortune playing professional poker in Las Vegas and Atlantic City, he'd bulked up, had his nose straightened, and gotten a chin implant. His appearance transformed, he'd come back to town, bought a factory that was approaching bankruptcy, and turned it into a thriving operation. Now the teenagers who had snubbed him in high school were the adults who pursued him for his connections, money, and status.

I beamed at the brash man who had replaced the shy adolescent and said, "Someone must have forgotten to blockade the Shadow Bend exit." He and I had both been teased and ostracized by our classmates, which was a bond that could never be entirely forgotten.

"I think all the cops are busy at your store." Vaughn's recently straightened and whitened teeth gleamed against his tanned skin. "I passed it on my way here and it was swarming with our gallant men and women in blue. Did they find another body?"

"No." This was beginning to feel like a repeat of last night, with Vaughn taking Winnie's role as nosy friend. At least I didn't have to explain it all to Noah, as I had with Jake. "They're just being thorough, since the store's back door was found open." I pasted on a "dumb me" expression and lied, "I'm pretty sure I must have forgotten to lock it, but you know Chief Kincaid. He likes to dot all his *i*'s and cross his *t*'s."

"That's the chief, all right," Vaughn agreed.

I noticed that my old classmate's smile turned on and off like a broken neon sign, and wondered what he was really thinking. He'd been a brainiac in school, and it occurred to me that he might no longer be the honest, straightforward person that he once was. It made me question whether transforming himself into a charming man about town had cost him a piece of his soul.

The three of us were silent until Vaughn glanced at his diamond-studded Rolex and rose. "I'd better not keep my date waiting any longer, or she'll order the four-hundred-dollar bottle of Krug just to spite me. And considering she wouldn't know a good wine from a bottle of Boone's Farm, that would be a crying shame." He touched his finger to his forehead and said, "Be good, you two." He winked. "Or at least don't get caught."

After Vaughn left, our waitress served our champagne and took our food orders. Noah and I both started with smoked salmon, but while he selected chicken livers and grits for his main course, I stuck to the traditional eggs Benedict. For the kind of money the restaurant was charging, I wasn't eating poultry organs and ground corn. Gran would be happy to cook either of those items for me anytime.

The food was amazing, and as we savored our after-brunch coffee, I told Noah about Nadine's revelation that Lance had written "The Bend's Buzz." I concluded, "So, did everyone in town know but me?"

"I don't think so." Noah set his cup down. "I certainly didn't know, and a lot of my patients have been really curious about who's been writing that stuff. They and my staff talk about who the Bend's Buzzard is all the time."

"The Bend's Buzzard?" I chuckled. "How appropriate."

"I think so." Noah nodded sagely, a smile playing along his lips.

"So, if someone found out that Lance was the one dishing the dirt on everyone, they might have a good motive for killing him." I toyed with my spoon while I thought about that, then asked, "Have you heard of anyone who was really angry about being gossiped about in the paper?"

"My physician's assistant, Yale Gordon, wasn't happy to have the details of his recent divorce trotted out for everyone to read." Noah wiped his mouth on his napkin and sat back. "Yale was livid and said if he knew who the Buzzard was, he'd wring his neck."

"Really?" I had to start reading the paper more. That is, if they found someone else to write the column. "Yale was at the book-club meeting. I wonder if he found out about Lance that night."

"Or if Yale didn't, maybe someone else did," Noah suggested.

"Hmm." I contemplated Quistgaard's secret identity while Noah took care of the bill, and we walked back to where we'd parked. I didn't even consider offering to chip in this time. No way could I afford bluestem's prices.

Noah helped me into the Jag, then headed the car back to Shadow Bend. After several miles of silence, he commented, "You're awfully quiet. Is something wrong?"

"No. Yes. I mean, the more I think about the murder, the angrier I get." I scowled. "That someone used my fence post to kill that obnoxious poet, and evidently hid out in my store after hours, just frosts my cookies." I narrowed my eyes. "Do you think the murderer was trying to set me up to take the fall? Maybe because of my past involvement with the police and the judicial system?"

Between my ex-boss having been arrested for fraud shortly after I resigned from Stramp Investments and my being a prime suspect in a murder investigation in February, I'd had more than my share of suspicion cast on me. It could be that whoever had killed Quistgaard might have intended to take advantage of my past misfortunes and try to pin the crime on me.

"I suppose it's possible you were a target." Noah twitched his shoulders. "But the whole crime appears to be impulsive rather than planned. The killer used a weapon of convenience rather than bringing one with him or her. And he or she put the body in a box rather than throwing it in a river or burying it where no one would ever find it."

"True." I crossed my arms. "It still makes me mad. I'm being dragged into a mess that I didn't make. I hate not being in control."

"It seems to me the killer didn't come prepared. He or she had some sort of issue with Quistgaard, hid in the store to confront him, and grabbed what was handy to kill him." Noah glanced at me. "Which goes back to your original theory that someone found out that night that the poet was also the gossip columnist."

"I guess I should tell the chief about that." I slouched in my seat. Chief Kincaid would so not be happy to hear yet another tidbit of information that I hadn't immediately shared. What if he thought I was involved in the murder? "But I really don't want to get on the cops' radar any more than I already am."

"You could talk to some of the book-club members and see if any of them knew about Quistgaard's other job," Noah suggested. "And I could ask around to see whether his identity had recently been disclosed. If it had, you'd have something more solid to go to the police with, and maybe the chief would take your tip more seriously."

"Good idea." I was impressed with Noah's willingness to help me.

"Thanks."

We whizzed past a mile marker. We were about halfway home, so it was now or never to bring up Jake. "About you and me," I started. "We . . ." I trailed off, unsure how to finish that sentence.

"Yes?" Noah's knuckles were white where they gripped the wheel.

"I'm really happy that we're friends again and it's been terrific being with you." *Yikes!* That sounded lame even to my ears.

"But?" A muscle ticked in Noah's jaw. "What are you trying to say?"

"I'd like to keep seeing you." I twisted around to look at him.

"But?" Noah asked again, then abruptly crossed from the left lane all the way to the right and took an approaching exit. Once we were off the highway, he pulled the Jag into a gas station and parked in back of the building.

Great! I had hoped to avoid having his full attention. I took a deep breath and said, "But I also want to keep seeing Jake." The announcement fell off my tongue in a rush of words.

"Oh?" He stared straight ahead through the windshield, and his voice became dangerously quiet. "So you want to date us both? We are talking about more than friendship, right?"

"Right." I squirmed, not at all comfortable with having to verbalize my feelings. "I know there's still something between you and me, but there's also something between Jake and me."

"He's not right for you." Noah unbuckled his seat belt, leaned over, and cupped my cheek. "I am."

"Funny. That's what he said about you," I

squeaked, taking a shuddery breath. The heart-rending tenderness of his expression speeded my pulse rate. "He suggested that you and I didn't have so much a mutual attraction as a common trajectory."

"Then he's a liar." Noah leaned closer and whispered into my hair. "Because we've been meant for each other since we were born."

"I . . ." Heat ripped through me. This felt so right. Noah and I had always been good together.

"Not I—us." Noah's sexy mouth was a hairsbreadth from mine.

I gave a ragged groan and closed the distance between our lips. His kiss was hard and searching, yet still as sweet as the first bite of a red velvet cupcake. It sent the pit of my stomach plunging, as if I were on a roller coaster. Then at the strong pull of his hot, wet tongue, the amusement-park ride derailed and I felt as if the floor had dropped out from under me. As we free-fell, fireworks lit up my world.

I don't know how long we made out, but thank goodness the console kept us from going much further than kissing and groping. The gearshift digging into my thigh finally brought me to my senses, and I pulled away from Noah's caressing hands and moved out of his reach.

Straightening my clothes, I cleared my throat, then cleared it again. Finally, I got my breathing under control and felt as if I could trust my voice enough to ask, "So, is that a yes or a no?"

"What was the question?" Noah's gray eyes were like clouds of smoke.

"Is my seeing both you and Jake an arrangement you can live with?"

"Do I have a choice?" Noah's words echoed what Jake had said.

"Not if you truly want to find out if what we have between us is real."

"And I do." Noah steered the car back toward the highway. "So I guess that's a yes."

Chapter 11

By six thirty Monday morning, Noah was out of bed, dressed in sweats, and walking Lucky, the Chihuahua he'd inherited from his deceased fiancée. He'd slept poorly, his emotions ping-ponging between jubilation that Dev had finally admitted that there was more than just friendship between them and frustration that she also thought she felt something for that jerkwad Del Vecchio.

After several weeks of Dev insisting she and Noah were pals and denying the spark that ignited anytime they were together, she had acknowledged the attraction. Now he just had to figure out how to win her away from Deputy Dork and keep Nadine out of Dev's path. The last thing he needed was his mother screwing up his love life.

As Noah led Lucky down the sidewalk, the Chihuahua pirouetted in excitement. Noah lived in an upscale neighborhood that boasted a beautifully maintained, fenced area where the local pets could run free and socialize. Because Lucky was so small, Noah took him to the dog park only when he was sure the Chihuahua could have fun and be safe from the larger breeds. He'd found that if they arrived before seven a.m., they usually had the park to themselves.

Humming Cheap Trick's "I Want You to Want Me," Noah made his way through the double-gated entry and scouted the space for any potential doggie danger. When he was assured that the area was secure, he unhooked Lucky from his leash. The Chihuahua took off like a mutt on a mission, and Noah sat on a nearby bench, admiring the sun as it slowly climbed above the horizon.

He and Lucky were the only ones in the park, so Noah stretched, put his hands behind his head, and stared at the blue sky as he relived the day before. Having Dev in his arms, even for the short time they'd kissed in his car, had been indescribable. In the long years they'd spent apart, he'd nearly forgotten her softness, her intoxicating scent, and her sweet mouth. The few embraces they'd shared since then had only whetted his appetite for her.

While Lucky raced back and forth over the park's meticulously groomed lawn, Noah daydreamed about Dev, but his grin faded when his thoughts turned to the reality of their situation. In actuality, he'd barely had an opportunity to hold her, let alone get her somewhere alone. He sighed, then smiled again. Maybe now that she'd admitted their mutual attraction, she'd let herself go and they could explore the chemistry between them.

Of course, she'd said she would be doing a similar exploration with Del Vecchio. At that thought, Noah felt as if a Great Dane had landed on his chest. What if she decided she loved that jerk and not him? Flinching, Noah realized there was a very real possibility that he could lose Dev again. And this time it might be forever.

The sound of the gate opening jolted Noah from his gloomy revere, and he turned to see Riyad Oberkircher and his Saluki, Persia, entering the park. Persia and Lucky were friends, and once Riyad had released his dog, he joined Noah on the bench.

"Good mornin', Doc." Riyad was one of only three attorneys in Shadow Bend. "You all got the a.m. shift again at your clinic?"

"No. Just couldn't sleep." Noah smiled. His neighbor was a curious mixture. His mother was from Saudi Arabia, and his father was German. How the two had ended up together, let alone living in southern Missouri, was a mystery. But the combination of cultures resulted in Oberkircher's exotic appearance and his slight drawl. "Do you have an early client?"

"Yep." Riyad crossed his legs, straightening the crease on his gray suit pants. "They claim to need to see me before they go in to work, so I agreed to a seven-thirty meeting. I've got to keep a leg up on the competition."

"Do you get many requests for emergency consults?" Noah asked. "I thought you mainly practiced family law."

"I do, but on account of the homegrown angle, every once in a while someone wants to consult a local lawyer instead of getting a hotshot criminal attorney from the city." Riyad shoved his fingers through his coal black hair. "I usually end up referring them, 'cause felony cases are reachin' out there for me, but, boy howdy, was this client insistent."

"Did the person give you any idea what the problem is?" Noah glanced at his watch, then whistled for Lucky. He needed to get going. He was meeting Dev at her store to help clean up at eight.

"Nah." The tall, spare man shrugged. "And I couldn't say if I did, but if you think about the big news this weekend, you might have a pretty fair guess."

"The murder?" Noah deduced.

Riyad shot a finger at Noah. "Bingo."

Once he'd attached Lucky's leash, Noah said good-bye to his neighbor and left the park. Riyad's mention of the murder brought his thoughts back to Dev. If she chose Del Vecchio over him, Noah wasn't sure he could take it. He needed to make sure she knew how he felt about her, stop acting like the detached town doctor, and make her see his passion. The only way to win Dev's heart was to show her his soul. Was he capable of doing that? He damn well better be!

After dropping Dev off at her place yesterday afternoon, Noah had gone over every word she'd spoken and examined his own responses. He thought he was in pretty good shape and he was glad that he'd get to spend several hours with her this morning. He bet Marshal Dillon wouldn't be around to help clean up.

Back home, Noah fed Lucky, started the Keurig, and hopped into the shower. Later, while he shaved, he drank his French roast and listened to the local radio station. He frowned when he realized that the newscaster was the station owner's nephew rather than the usual morning anchor, who was a responsible broadcaster. The small, family-owned station had only three or four regular employees, and if one of them got sick or had an emergency, whoever was around took the microphone. Even a cocky college kid with no journalistic ethics.

Noah was putting on his jeans when the DJ said, "As we reported earlier, there's been no progress reported on Friday night's murder. The police aren't releasing any details, but an anonymous tip reminded us that the victim was found behind the store of a woman who is no stranger to police investigations."

"Damn!" Noah pulled on his polo shirt, took one last gulp of coffee, and slammed his mug down on his dresser. Dev was right. Even though the chief may have said she wasn't a suspect, someone still thought of her that way, or at least wanted to put the possibility of her involvement in the crime into everyone else's mind.

Noah rushed out of the bedroom, grabbed his keys, and hopped into his car. He'd decided to make a stop before going to the dime store. If he wanted to hear the town's reaction to that BS about Dev's possible connection to the killing, he knew just the place to go.

Chapter 12

"Oh. My. God!" I swung open the front door of my store and stood gaping at the chaos the crime-scene techs had left behind. It looked as if a volcano had erupted, littering its path of destruction with bits and pieces of people's lives and sprinkling the remains with ash. Thank goodness Banshee had taken a liking to Tsar. There was no way the Russian Blue could have come to work with me today.

I stood frozen, unable to make myself move farther into the room until Poppy finally pushed me aside. She barreled into the shop, then stopped dead in her tracks, sputtering. She'd called me last night when she'd gotten back from Chicago. We'd discussed her weekend—she'd had a great time with Tryg. Then I'd told her about mine. She heartily approved my decision to continue seeing both Noah and Jake, and was shocked by the rest of my news.

After hearing about the police search of my store, she'd insisted on coming this morning to help with the cleanup. Though I was glad for the assistance, I had tried to dissuade her. I was afraid that having Poppy witness the condition in which the cops would doubtlessly leave my shop would worsen the relationship between her and her father, since there was no way on earth she wouldn't blame him.

Before I could stop myself, I muttered, "How in the world did they make such a mess in less than thirty-six hours?"

"I'll kill him." Poppy twirled around, taking in the disassembled displays, ravaged shelves, and items heaped into the middle of the floor, and then she ground out between clenched teeth, "This time he's gone too far. I'm going back to my bar, get my gun, and shoot him."

She meant her dad, Chief Kincaid, and I hurriedly said, "I'm sure he was only doing his job." Tugging on Poppy's hand, I towed her into the backroom to stow our purses and gather cleaning supplies. "You know he had no choice. He had to process the place."

The storage room hadn't been spared, and Poppy's gorgeous heart-shaped face turned as red as the sole of the Louboutin pumps in her closet. Her relationship with her dad had been precarious since Poppy had reached adolescence, but something had happened last Christmas to push both of them over the edge. I'd never found out exactly what had caused the final rift, but I assumed the reason was the obvious one. Poppy's reckless lifestyle must have clashed one too many times with the chief's rigid view of the world, and one of them finally did or said something the other couldn't forgive.

"So you had a good time with Tryg?" I asked, attempting to distract her before she had an aneurysm.

"Yeah." A reluctant smile played around her lips. "He can be a real dumb-ass sometimes, but a fool and his money are fun to go out with."

"That describes most of your dates." I thrust a hand vac at Poppy while she giggled her agreement; then I led her back to the front of the store and said, "I'll start putting things where they belong and you follow behind me, vacuuming up the fingerprint powder."

Flinging her arms wide, she said, "You realize my father did this just to spite me." She narrowed her amethyst eyes. "There's no way they *had* to make this much of a mess. It was deliberate."

"You need to find a way to get along with your dad." I put my hands on my hips. "It's time to get over your issues."

"No way." Poppy put her own hands on her hips, mirroring my stance. "I stopped fighting my inner demons a long time ago. Now we're on the same side and we both think my father's an uptight, controlling, vengeful jerk."

"Oh, for crying out loud. If the chief intended to get back at anyone, it was me." I began to sort through the items strewn across the floor. "He was pretty ticked when he guessed that I figured out about the murder weapon over twelve hours before I shared that bit of intel with the police. Not that I admitted that to him."

"That would piss him off, all right." Poppy's waterfall of platinum curls floated around her shoulders as she bent to run the Dirt Devil over a stack of books lying beside the metal spinner rack.

"Yep." Although Chief Kincaid had never come right out and ordered me to keep the information about the murder weapon confidential, I suspected that was his wish, since I hadn't heard any gossip about the bizarre way Quistgaard had been offed. But I'd had to tell Poppy about the fence post being used to kill the poet when I couldn't come up with any other good explanation for why the police had waited until the next day to search my store.

That made four people I'd told and sworn to secrecy, and Poppy was the only one I was really worried about blabbing. Not that she would purposely break her word to me, but she tended to blurt things out first and think about the consequences later—giving the chief another reason to be upset with both of us. Too bad letting the cat out of the bag was a whole lot easier than putting it back in.

Though I truly hoped I hadn't screwed up the police investigation by revealing how Lance had died, I was pretty darn sure it wasn't in my best interests to keep that information from any of the people I'd taken into my confidence—except for Poppy. And if there was one thing I'd learned from my previous run-ins with the law, it was to look out for my family, my friends, and myself first, because the cops certainly wouldn't do so.

Poppy and I worked in silence for a few minutes, and then she glanced at the clock and said, "I thought Noah was supposed to be helping us out. What time did you say he was planning to be here?"

"Eight." I checked my cell phone to see if I'd missed a text from him, but there were no messages in my in-box. "It's not like him to be late. Maybe he got an emergency call from the clinic."

"Shoot!" Poppy wiped her forehead with her arm, leaving a smudge. "This will take forever with just the two of us. Trust Boone to be off on a cruise when there's any physical work to be done."

"He does hate to get dirty." I chuckled at the image of a less than immaculate Boone. The man disliked having his hair mussed, much less getting his hands filthy, or ruining the crease of his pants.

"We should have gotten someone else to help us," Poppy complained.

"I did." As I started to rebuild the May flowers display, I noticed that the entire length of fencing was missing and guessed it was in police custody. Making a mental note to stop at the hardware store on the way home to replace it, I said, "I asked Xylia if she had class this morning and she doesn't, so I hired her to help us out. She'll be here at nine." I looked around. "I just hope she doesn't freak out. She's another one who doesn't like it when things are out of order."

Before Poppy could comment, I heard a thud and saw through the glass door that Noah had arrived, bearing gifts. In one hand he held a tray with four coffee cups, and in the other was a pale pink box tied with white string. The thumping sound must have been him kicking the bottom of the door to get our attention.

Poppy elbowed me in the ribs. "Clearly, Noah thinks the way to your heart is through your stomach."

"Which is true," I informed her loftily, then leered at his tight-fitting jeans. "Although there are alternate routes."

Poppy elbowed me again, then shoved me in Noah's direction.

As soon as I unlocked the door and held it open for him, he stepped inside, kissed me on the cheek, and said, "Sorry I'm late. I stopped at the bakery to pick up some donuts and gossip."

"Since when do you indulge in that local sport?" Poppy asked, grinning.

"Since someone was murdered behind Dev's store." Noah set the carton on the soda-fountain counter, shrugged off his hooded sweatshirt, and looked around. "Wow. The mess here is even worse than I thought it would be."

"Yep." I nodded toward Poppy, whose expression had darkened again, and gave a tiny shake of my head, then said, "But I'm sure the police were only doing their jobs."

Understanding dawned in Noah's eyes, and he changed the subject. "Did you two hear the local news this morning?"

"I didn't." I looked at Poppy and she shook her head. "What about it?"

"An 'anonymous tipster' reminded the reporter that Dev was involved in a couple of other police investigations." Noah looked into my eyes and added gently, "The insinuation was that you might have something to do with this one, so I wanted to check out the town's reaction, and I figured the bakery was my best bet."

"Fu—" I cut myself off. I had vowed to stop dropping the F bomb. "I was afraid of that." I sat down on a stool and asked Noah, "Do you think I'm in trouble? What did the rumor mill have to say?"

"About thirty-seventy in your favor. The majority didn't put much stock in the idea that you're involved," Noah assured me. "In fact, they were promoting the theory that the cops were being deliberately led astray by someone. I wonder who phoned in the tip."

"It has to be my dad," Poppy growled. "Who else would dare?"

I put my hand on her arm. "This is not your father's doing." I hoped that my faith in the chief was justified. "He plays by the rules and would never make an anonymous statement like that."

"Humph," Poppy grunted. "You might be right. He's not much for covert action. He'd much rather look you in the eye when he stabs you in the back."

"Huh?" I raised my eyebrows at her mixed metaphor. Or whatever that was she'd said. "How can you look at someone if you're behind them?"

"Fine," she huffed. "Knifes you in the chest." She smiled cruelly. "And if it isn't him, he's going to be blowing his stack that someone is revving up the press's interest in the case."

"Let's hope he finds out who it is and does something about it before my reputation is smeared." I felt another one of those remorseful twinges that I'd been having since finding out my father was innocent. When he'd been sent to prison, I'd worried so much about what the people of Shadow Bend thought of me, I hadn't even considered that Dad might have been set up. Now that he'd been exonerated, I'd been thinking that I could quit being so concerned, but if I was implicated in another murder, I could kiss that hope good-bye.

"Even if my father says you're in the clear," Poppy said, interrupting my guilt trip, "we can't count on him to staunch the gossip. We need to do something about it ourselves." Crossing her arms, she turned to Noah and demanded, "Did you hear anything else about the murder? Any clue?"

"Uh . . ." Noah hesitated, taking a sip of coffee and then opening the donut box and staring at the contents for several seconds.

"Yes?" I prompted. I could tell that something was making him uncomfortable and whatever it was might be important, so I prodded, "What?"

"I ran into Riyad Oberkircher at the dog park this morning." Noah handed me a vanilla cream–filled Long John—my favorite.

"The lawyer?" Poppy waited for Noah's nod, then snatched a cruller from the carton. "What about him? Did he have something to say about the murder? Spill it, Doc."

"Maybe." Noah selected a Bismarck. "He mentioned that he was going into his office at seven thirty today because a client had phoned him, begging for an emergency meeting." Noah took a bite, chewed, and swallowed. "He wouldn't say who the client was or what he or she wanted, but—"

"But it sure could be about the murder," Poppy deduced.

"Yes." Noah nodded. "That would certainly be my guess, and I think Riyad thought so, too. Not that that bit of info will do us any good."

"I don't suppose you thought about hanging out in front of his law office and seeing who went inside?" I asked, knowing the answer was no. Noah was too good a person to do that to a friend who had confided in him.

"Of course not." Noah raised a brow. "That wouldn't have been right."

Poppy and I exchanged a look, indicating that Noah's personal moral code wouldn't have stopped us; then I asked, "Anything else interesting? Maybe something that we can actually use?" I knew I sounded testy, but I was sick and tired of people talking about me.

"I considered making a few phone calls this morning to see if anyone would admit knowing that Quistgaard wrote 'The Bend's Buzz.' " He twisted his lips. "But you really need to tell the chief about that before we start asking people. It's sure to get back to him, and he'll be furious if he's the last to know."

"The murdered guy was the gossip columnist?" Poppy squealed.

After we filled her in on that development, Noah looked around at the mess and said, "Now, don't you think we'd better get to work?"

"Definitely." I handed him a rag and the spray bottle of detergent solution that I had prepared according to the directions I'd found on a Web site devoted to cleaning up fingerprint dust. It's amazing what you can find online these days.

"Use this on any items the vacuuming hasn't completely cleaned." He nodded, and I added, "Make sure they're waterproof before you spritz them, and you might have to do it two or three times to remove all the powder."

When Xylia arrived half an hour later, she was wearing her usual sweater set and had even added a silk scarf. Why she was so dressed up to clean was beyond me, but I didn't want to make her uncomfortable, so I didn't comment. We left Poppy and Noah wiping down the front displays, soda fountain, and cash-register counter areas, and went to tackle the craft alcove.

As we worked, Xylia said, "According to the radio, the murder took place behind the building, so why did the police search the store?"

"The back exit wasn't locked," I explained, but didn't add my theory about the murder weapon. I'd already told my quota of people.

"How odd." Xylia continued to sort skeins of yarn, placing them in their proper sections. "Is there any chance you forgot to lock the door?"

"Maybe." I decide to stick with the story I'd told Vaughn. "It was a little frenzied around here that night with people getting mad and storming out of the meeting and all." I started in on the scrapbooking supplies. "I lost track of where everyone was. Did you notice anything? Someone who wasn't where they should have been?"

"I don't think so." Xylia scrunched up her face

in a visible attempt to dredge up that night's activity, then shook her head. "Sorry, no. Like you said, with all the comings and goings, it's hard to remember."

We worked in silence while I thought more about that evening. Earlier, after Noah had told me about the newscaster's innuendo, I'd checked my computer for the list of book-club attendees. I really needed to talk to everyone who had been at the meeting and get his or her impressions, recollections, and alibis. If someone was trying to implicate me as an accessory to the crime, I wanted to be proactive rather than reactive. The more info I could give the police about that evening, the faster they'd catch the killer.

Glancing at my clerk as she carefully straightened bins of embroidery floss, I decided to practice my questioning technique on her. "By the way, Xylia . . ." I waited until she looked my way so I could see her expression, then said, "I'm curious about what you thought of the book-club discussion. You mentioned previously that you felt you didn't fully understand the poems and was hoping Mr. Quistgaard would help you interpret them better."

"Uh." Xylia bit her lip. "I, uh, I'm still not certain." Her cheeks turned red and her body went rigid. "Mr. Quistgaard's reasoning wasn't really clear."

"He sure didn't like explaining himself, did he?" I forced a chuckle, hoping Xylia would relax. "Did you talk to any of the members who didn't voice their dislike of the poems during the discussion but were still offended?"

"Not directly." Xylia blinked several times. "I overheard Bryce Grantham and Zizi Todd talking about the book while we were putting away the chairs."

"What did they have to say?" I'd met Bryce last month when he helped me search for Tsar. The single father had found the cat and brought him to me. It turned out that Bryce was involved in a custody battle that was exacerbated by his sexual orientation; he was gay. I liked both him and Zizi, and I would have thought that they'd share similar opinions about the poems.

"Bryce agreed with Mr. Quistgaard about the negatives of small-town life." Xylia finished arranging the floss and moved on to the bolts of fabric that had been pulled from their shelves and tossed in a heap on the floor.

"Zizi didn't?" I moved to help Xylia with the cloth. The stiffness in her shoulders made it clear that the mess was upsetting her. "Or were their differing views about another issue?"

"Zizi said something about the obvious misogyny of Mr. Quistgaard's poetry making any other social commentary in them questionable."

"That sounds reasonable." I returned a bolt of

calico to its rightful place. "What did Bryce say to that? Did he disagree?"

"No."

"Anything else you might have overheard?" I had been hoping for more. Xylia was quiet, which gave her the potential to be a keen observer. I had figured people might almost forget she was around and talk more in front of her.

"The police asked me all this when they interviewed me on Saturday," Xylia said, her expression a mixture of apprehension and something else. "I sort of forgot about it until now, but I followed Grant Edwyn when he walked out of the meeting early. He didn't leave the store, so I was keeping an eye on him." She looked at me, and I nodded my encouragement. "Then as Mr. Quistgaard was leaving, I heard Mr. Edwyn say to him, 'If you don't learn to keep your mouth shut, you're going to blow your cover as "The Bend's Buzz" columnist.' "

"Wow." I pretended amazement, all the while thinking that if Xylia had overheard Grant, someone else at the meeting might have, too. "I had no idea he wrote the 'Buzz.' Do you think other people knew?"

"I sure didn't." Xylia wrinkled her brow. "I really don't want to talk about that night anymore. Thinking about it makes me feel like I can hardly breathe."

"I understand." I awkwardly patted her

shoulder. Neither one of us were comfortable with touchy-feely stuff. "I just hate the thought of someone getting away with murder."

"Sure." Xylia glanced around the alcove. "Anything else we have to do here?"

"It looks good." I dusted off my hands. "Let's move onto the toy aisle."

It was hard work, but by eleven thirty, Noah, Poppy, Xylia, and I had put the shop to rights. The backroom was still a disaster area, but the store itself was ready for its usual noon opening. I made a fresh pot of coffee, and we were all taking a break as we finished up the last of the donuts when Noah's cell started to play "Mama Don't Allow."

"Yes, Mother?" Noah answered.

I laughed. The ringtone proved that Noah had a sense of humor.

"What?" Noah straightened and reached for his sweatshirt. "I'm calling nine-one-one. Take an aspirin, unlock the door, and sit in the foyer." As he ran for the store's exit, he called over his shoulder, "She thinks she's having a heart attack."

Chapter 13

After my helpers left, I used the employee restroom in the back to wash up, change into a fresh sweatshirt, put on nicer jeans, and redo my ponytail. Once I was fit to be seen, I retrieved the cash drawer from the safe, checked the soda fountain to make sure it was well stocked, and then, at exactly twelve, I flipped on the neon OPEN sign and unlocked the front door.

Seconds later, Hannah Freeman, my high school helper, arrived. A senior, she worked for me four mornings and one afternoon a week as part of her vocational-education program. Because she was not one to be influenced by how her fellow teenagers were dressing, I was never quite sure what to expect of Hannah's outfit du jour, but I knew it would be wild. She tended toward Hello Kitty chic, but didn't limit herself to that style.

Today she sported a pleated neon plaid miniskirt that she'd paired with a robin's-egg blue and black graphic T-shirt and Zara ankle booties. Like Xylia, she refused to wear a Devereaux's Dime Store sweatshirt. Her excuse was that since she went directly from the store to school, it would be too embarrassing to be seen in the hallways in something as uncool as a semi-uniform.

When I pointed out that she'd told me she didn't care what the other kids thought about her, she'd retorted that she didn't mind being thought of as weird, but only in a limited-edition way. Having no idea what she meant by that, I gave up my struggle to enforce a store dress code.

Today, Hannah's first words as she zipped past me were, "So, tell me about the murder."

"There's nothing much to tell." I was sensing a theme here, and I was sick and tired of everyone greeting me the same way. "Some poor man was killed behind the building. The store's exit was found unlocked, so the police searched the place. End of story."

"How loathsome." Hannah's voice rose incredulously. "But—"

Before she could question me further, the place began to fill with the first customers of the day. Tuesday through Friday, the hours after lunch and before school let out were usually slow, which was why during the rest of the week Hannah worked mornings. Often, I didn't see a single shopper from one to three, but on Mondays, because the store had been closed for the past forty-four hours, there was always a crowd.

As the cheerful voices created a merry hubbub, I was once again glad I hadn't replaced the tin ceilings with acoustical tile or cork matting to mute the energetic hum. To me, the sound of people socializing with their neighbors as their heels clicked along the hardwood floor was what made the shop a gathering place rather than just somewhere to buy life's little necessities. Both sides of the community—the newcomers who had moved to Shadow Bend to escape the city's crime and high prices, and the natives who had been born here and never left—felt at home in my store.

When I'd bought the business, I'd also purchased the adjacent building and knocked out the communal wall to double the interior space. And although I'd updated the plumbing and electrical and added Wi-Fi, I'd made a concerted effort to keep the character of the original variety store intact.

Hannah and I dove into the day's business, helping customers find items, reorganizing shelves that people had disturbed while rummaging through our carefully arranged stacks of merchandise, and, my favorite, ringing up purchases on the old brass cash register. Its distinctive *ting-a-ling,* which signaled that the business was bringing in cash, always made me feel warm and fuzzy inside.

While I worked, I went over my mental to-do list: call the chief to inform him about Quistgaard's work as a gossip columnist, call Mrs. Zeigler about the basket she had forgotten to order, and get hold of all the past "The Bend's

Buzz" columns. I wasn't sure how to accomplish that last one. Would they be online? Did I know anyone who kept all the local papers? Would the newspaper office have them? Too bad the Shadow Bend Library had been closed due to lack of funds. Now the nearest library was in the county seat.

Around two, the dozen or so members of the Knittie Gritties arrived. The knitting club, along with the other craft groups that met at the dime store, was the backbone of my business. I provided them with the space, and they bought the materials for their projects from me, as well as refreshments and any other merchandise that caught their fancy.

The members knew the drill and automatically headed to the crafting alcove in back. For the scrapbookers, quilters, and sewers, I set up long worktables, but when the knitters, crocheters, and needlepointers held their meetings, I hauled out the comfy chairs and ottomans. Another reason why I'd wanted the extra space the adjoining building had provided was to store the various pieces of furniture I needed for the clubs.

I waved as the knitters passed by, intending to check on the group when I had a free moment. I didn't hang around during their meetings, but I did like to make sure they knew that I valued their presence. If there was one thing I was good at doing, it was making nice with the customers. A big part of my job as an investment consultant had been keeping the clients happy so they would continue to give our firm their money, and it was a skill that I continued to use as a retail-business owner.

Today, along with my usual kissing up, I also wanted to talk to Addie about his run-in with Lance Quistgaard at the book-club meeting, and find out if the police had questioned him about it. The radio shock jock's mention of me in connection with the murder had spooked me, so I needed to know what was happening in the investigation and if the cops were doing their job.

Customers kept me busy at the register until the after-school crowd poured in a few minutes past three, and then I was occupied with the onslaught of hungry teenagers at the soda fountain and candy case for another half hour. Just as Hannah and I finished serving the last kids, the Knittie Gritties took their fifteen-minute break.

For five dollars each, I provided coffee, tea, and a selection of cookies and pastries that I purchased wholesale from the bakery. Although it worried me a little to trust people, I didn't have time to stand around and collect the money, so payment for the refreshments was on the honor system. The group members deposited their money in an old cigar box. After Addie filled his plate with goodies and doctored his cup of coffee with cream and sugar, I hurriedly completed the purchase of a customer at the register; then I followed him back to the crafting alcove.

While the other Knittie Gritties ate their treats and chatted about their projects, their children or grandchildren, and the weather—always a fascinating topic in rural Missouri—I took the seat next to Addie and said, "Wow! That was quite a heated discussion at the book-club meeting. I thought the evening would be super intellectual. I had no idea that the get-togethers could be so explosive."

"That guy was a punk," Addie growled around a mouthful of snickerdoodle. "I told the cops it's no surprise that someone offed him."

"He was certainly pompous and rudely opinionated," I agreed.

"Yeah, even duct tape can't stop that kind of stupid, although I was ready to give it a try." Addie brushed the crumbs from his pink T-shirt, which read KNITTING KEEPS ME FROM UNRAVELING.

"You should have." I bit back a laugh. "It might at least have shut him up."

Addie snorted his coffee, then wiped his nose with the back of his hand.

"Had you met Quistgaard before? I understand he lived somewhere here in town."

"I'd seen him around. He hung out at Brewfully Yours a lot." Addie took another slurp from his cup. "And he was in my shop a couple of times, trying to sell stuff."

"Really?" I couldn't picture the elegant, supercilious man pawning his belongings. "Do you remember what he brought in?"

"The first time, he sold a ring and a locket that he said belonged to his dead mother." Addie shoved an entire cookie into his mouth, then spoke around it. "And a couple of months ago he pawned his laptop."

"Ouch!" I cringed. Parting with his computer had to hurt a writer.

"He vowed he'd get the laptop back before his contract with me expired."

"Contract?" I asked. Who knew that there was paperwork involved in giving stuff over to a pawnshop? "I thought you just got some sort of receipt if you hocked your belongings."

"The contract states the amount of money loaned against the pawned item, the finance charge, and the due date," Addie explained. "Anyway, Quistgaard called the other day to say he'd be by to get his computer as soon as some big check he was waiting for came in the mail." Addie crossed his beefy arms. "I told him he had until the end of the month. Then I was putting the laptop up for sale."

"Do you think that was why he was so hostile to you at the book club?"

"I doubt he even recognized me." Addie

chugged the rest of the coffee and put the cup on the floor beside him. "The guy was driving without his headlights on."

I tilted my head questioningly.

"He never looked me in the eye the whole time he was in my shop," Addie clarified. "Lots of people don't. They're too embarrassed. And he definitely wanted to be anywhere but there."

"Did you know much about Quistgaard?" I asked. "I mean, before the meeting."

"Nope." Addie opened the canvas bag at his feet and got out his knitting. "I never heard his name mentioned by anyone before he came into my shop."

"Hmm." Since Shadow Bend Pawn Shop and Jewelry was a fertile field for the local grapevine, Addie usually had the lowdown on everyone in town. "Did you see Quistgaard after the book club let out?"

"Nah." Addie's concentration was on his needles as they flew through the red yarn. "After I left, I headed out to Gossip Central for a drink. That asshat left a bad taste in my mouth and I wanted to wash it away with a beer. I ended up closing the bar down."

Poppy owned Gossip Central, but she would have already left for Chicago by that time. Still, her staff should be able to verify Addie's alibi. He was fairly hard to overlook, and if he'd been there the whole night, someone should remember seeing him. He wasn't a quiet sort of guy.

The Knittie Gritties trickled out between four thirty and five, and the teenagers headed home to supper soon afterward. With only a few customers remaining in the store, I left Hannah in charge and ducked into the backroom to call the chief. I half hoped he'd be gone for the day, but the dispatcher put me right through to him.

"Chief Kincaid, it's Dev Sinclair. Do you have a moment to speak to me?"

"If this is about how we processed your store, I have nothing to say."

"That's not why I called, but, yes, the place was a mess." I wondered at the chief's defensive tone, which was unusual for him.

"So, then," he said, impatience lacing his voice, "what can I do for you?"

"I heard something that I thought might help your investigation." I paused to figure out how much to tell him. "Are you aware that Lance Quistgaard wrote 'The Bend's Buzz'?" When Chief Kincaid didn't answer right away, I added, "The gossip column in the *Banner*, written by Anonymous."

"Interesting." The chief clipped off that single word, then was silent.

"Yes, it is," I agreed. "And during the book-club meeting, Grant Edwyn, the *Banner*'s editor, gave Quistgaard a disapproving look that made him stop arguing and leave."

"You're not suggesting Edwyn murdered Quistgaard because the man had a big mouth, are you?" Chief Kincaid asked. "Because I don't buy it."

"No." I sat on the edge of my desk. "I'm suggesting that someone who'd been skewered by Quistgaard in the 'Buzz' overheard Edwyn and Quistgaard talking that night, confronted the poet about being Anonymous, and ended up killing him." I described the conversation Xylia had repeated to me.

"Hmm." The chief seemed to process that information then asked, "So, your clerk told you Quistgaard was behind 'The Bend's Buzz'?"

"Yes, but I first heard it from Nadine Underwood." I had briefly considered not revealing my source, but could find no reason to protect someone who would never return the favor. "Apparently she demanded Edwyn tell her the Buzzard's identity right after the first column came out."

"Which means that the identity of the columnist was never completely anonymous," Chief Kincaid mused, then sighed unhappily. "I'd better talk to Nadine and see who else she shared that little secret with."

"Questioning her might be a bit tough." I swung my sneaker-clad foot. "Just before noon, Nadine thought she was having a heart attack and called Noah. She's probably in the hospital by now."

"Son of a buck!" Chief Kincaid took a deep breath. "Anything else you'd like to disclose? Maybe something else you forgot or didn't think was important or didn't find convenient to share with me?"

"No." I didn't like his snarky tone. "And, speaking of inconvenient, did you find anything when you tore my store apart?"

There was such a long silence, I thought the chief might have hung up on me, but finally he muttered, "There were no prints on the stake in the vic's heart, but it definitely came from the fencing in your display."

"Oh?" I wasn't surprised. I'd been pretty damn positive it was a match before I told him about it. "So, the post did go through Quistgaard's heart and that's what killed him?" I asked.

"Yes," Chief Kincaid confirmed. "The killer didn't break through the sternum, but the stake ruptured the pulmonary artery, which was why there was so much blood."

"Anything else?"

"What we expected—a hell of a lot of finger-prints and enough trace to keep the lab busy for a year." The chief sighed again, then ordered, "From now on, if you hear anything, see any-thing, or have any hunches, I want to be the first to know."

"Yes, sir!" I saluted the phone, then pressed the OFF button. That had gone about as well as I'd anticipated. Actually, a tad better, because I hadn't expected Chief Kincaid to tell me what, if anything, they'd found when they searched my store. I tapped my lip with my cell; maybe the chief actually wanted my help.

Still contemplating Chief Kincaid's motives, I grabbed the phone book from my desk drawer. Mrs. Zeigler wasn't listed, and I didn't think anyone would be answering the telephones at the high school this late, so I wasn't sure how to reach her.

I was doing a quick Internet search for Mrs. Z's private contact info when Hannah called out, "Dev, a customer needs to see you."

As I came out of the back room, I heard a cultured contralto scold, "It isn't polite to shout, Ms. Freeman. A lady doesn't raise her voice."

I wouldn't have to call the principal after all. She was standing at the register, giving my clerk lessons in deportment.

I hurried forward and said, "Mrs. Zeigler, I was just trying to phone you. I'm so sorry I forgot to get your order Friday night."

"That's perfectly understandable." She smoothed the side of her chignon. "I'm afraid that awful man flustered all of us."

"The evening was a lot more confrontational than I thought a book club would be." I raised my brows. "Do the discussions often get that heated?"

As we chatted, I took a good look at Mrs. Z. She was a sturdy woman with toned arms and calves. Last summer at the lakeside recreation club just outside of town, I'd seen her doing laps, and she definitely had the muscles to drive a fence post into a man's heart. Could she have murdered the poet for disrupting her group?

I swallowed a chuckle. No matter how hard I tried, I couldn't imagine her staking the guy. Maybe rapping his knuckles with a ruler, but not killing him. Hell, if she couldn't handle an antagonistic individual, she'd have quit working in public education a long time ago. The PTO meetings alone probably had more hostile negotiations than the senate and congress combined.

"That was a first for our group. As was his later homicide . . ." Mrs. Zeigler frowned at the memory, and then she shook her head, glanced around the store at the remaining customers, and said, "May we speak privately?"

"Sure." My pulsed raced. Did she want to tell me something about the murder? Of course not. She just didn't want to be overheard ordering an erotic basket. I grabbed a binder with pictures of my past creations, an order pad, and pen. "Right this way."

Normally, we could step into the back room, but it was still a mess from the police search, so I steered her toward a locked door that opened to a short flight of stairs. I used my key, then led her up the steps to a small suite of offices that had been part of the adjacent building. I hadn't been able to figure out a good retail use of the space but I'd kept the rooms intact, hoping I could rent them out to an insurance agent or Realtor. So far, there hadn't been any takers.

Once we were settled on the ancient wooden chairs, leftovers from the previous occupant, I handed her the binder and said, "Here are some examples of my erotic line. Can you give me an idea what you have in mind?"

After she pointed out some baskets that she liked and indicated which items she found most interesting, I said, "Each of the baskets includes my trademark—the perfect book for both the occasion and the person receiving the gift. Do you have any suggestions?"

"The book aspect of your baskets is my favorite, so I've given it a great deal of thought." Her dark eyes sparkled. "I believe that new novel everyone is talking about by L. L. Charles would be ideal."

"*Ten Colors of Blonde*?" I squeaked, then cleared my throat. Considering the contents of the basket she'd ordered, I didn't know why I was so flabbergasted that she was requesting a book that was being touted as S and M–lite and mommy porn, but still . . . ew! "Uh, have you read it?"

"No." Mrs. Zeigler tipped her head. "I thought that was something my spouse and I could do together on our anniversary getaway."

I nodded, keeping my face down so she couldn't see how red my cheeks were. I was normally not one to blush, but, then again, I'd never had this sort of talk with a woman who had been my high school principal before, either. And no matter how many years ago I'd graduated, imagining Mrs. Z as a sexual being was still disconcerting.

After we finished up, I said, "Ever since the murder, I've been thinking a lot about Mr. Quistgaard. Did you know him before he requested to speak at the book club?"

"No." Mrs. Zeigler picked up her purse. "He must not have been a native to Shadow Bend, since I didn't recognize his name as someone who went to school here."

"Did any of the club members comment that they knew him or didn't want him to be one of your speakers?"

"A few people protested having to read poetry, but I don't recall any mentioning that they were acquainted with him." Mrs. Zeigler got to her feet and smoothed her skirt. "However, when the notice of this month's selection went out, Kiara Howard objected to us hosting Mr. Quistgaard. I was a little surprised when she attended the meeting."

"Did Kiara say what she objected to?" I stood up.

"Not specifically, no. She stated only that he wasn't the kind of writer that she wanted to encourage or support." Mrs. Zeigler took a deep breath and admitted, "She didn't explain what she meant, and I'm afraid I didn't ask, since by that time it was too late to rescind our invitation." Mrs. Zeigler shrugged. "Maybe I should have."

I held the office door open for Mrs. Zeigler, and as I watched her walk away, I wondered if Lance Quistgaard would still be alive today if Mrs. Z had heeded Kiara's warning and canceled the poet's appearance at the book club before someone else could cancel his life.

Chapter 14

Before returning to the store, I sat down at the old desk and sketched out my ideas for Mrs. Ziegler's basket. I liked to get my thoughts on paper while they were still fresh from the client interview. I was making a note to order a copy of *Ten Colors of Blonde* when I heard the steps creak.

Thinking that Hannah might be looking for me, I called out, "I'll be down in a second." I jotted one more note and added, "I'm coming."

I grabbed the binder and order pad and hurried out the door toward the stairs. Suddenly the hairs on the back of my neck rose, but before I could turn to see if someone was behind me, I felt what might have been a shove between my shoulder blades and stumbled. Unable to regain my balance, I pitched forward and fell, thumping down each step until I lay breathless at the bottom of the staircase. *What in the hell just happened?*

It took me a moment or two, and whatever was left of my pride, before I could get to my feet and ascertain that nothing was broken. By then Hannah had run from the cash register to where

I'd fallen. I spent the next thirty or so minutes trying to convince her I was fine.

While Hannah was watching me, I made myself walk around as if I were pain-free and frequently descended the stairs on my ass. But after I waved good-bye to her, I admitted to myself that I was in agony and grabbed the bottle of Advil from behind the counter. Dry swallowing a couple of tablets, I collapsed on a soda fountain stool. I was too sore to lock up or even flip on the CLOSED sign.

While my body rested and the ibuprofen started to work, I called the police. Chief Kincaid seemed to think my imagination was working overtime. He said that I had probably tripped rather than been pushed, but if I wanted, he could send an officer over to look around.

I hesitated. Just before Hannah left, I'd checked out the second floor and hadn't seen evidence of anyone's presence there. It was a shame that since the door to the upstairs area had been locked, the police had assumed that whoever had hidden in the store hadn't been able to gain access to it. If they'd processed that space, there'd be fingerprint power to smear. And because my cleaning lady kept the place spic and span, there wasn't even a layer of dust that might have had footprints to prove someone had been behind me.

Concluding that a search would probably be

futile, and realizing that the last thing I wanted was for the police to create another mess or cause any more rumors about me to float around town, I declined the chief's offer. Maybe he was right. Maybe my nerves had gotten the better of me. Maybe I had just tripped over my own big feet.

Sighing, I checked my messages. Still nothing from Noah about his mother's health. Earlier, I'd sent a text asking him to give me an update when he had a chance. He couldn't use his cell in the hospital, but I'd thought he'd be home by now, and I was getting worried.

Although Nadine was far from my favorite person, I hoped her symptoms had been a false alarm and she was all right. I wanted her to be okay, if for no other reason than because a sick Nadine would drive Noah crazy with her constant demands for his attention.

Setting aside my concern for Noah and his mother, I thought about all the stuff I needed to check up on regarding the murder. Number one was getting copies of the past gossip columns. A close second was confirming Addie's alibi. And third was finding out why Kiara had objected to Quistgaard speaking to the book club.

I reached for the single chocolate-chip cookie left over from the Knittie Grittie meeting and bit into it. Something else was niggling at the back of my mind. Someone else that I should consider a suspect. Someone who was angry with the Bend's Buzzard. But who? Nope, the glimmer of a memory refused to surface.

Realizing that I couldn't force myself to remember, I decided to concentrate on the things I had to do. With Gran expecting me for dinner in twenty minutes, did I have time to accomplish any of them before heading home? Confirming Addie's presence at Gossip Central would probably be the quickest item on my list.

I shoved the rest of the cookie into my mouth and was reaching for my cell when the sleigh bells above the front door jingled. *Shoot!* I *so* didn't want to deal with a customer, but I'd forgotten to switch on the CLOSED sign and lock the door. I'd have to suck it up and smile.

Twisting to ask whoever had entered if they could come back the next day, I found myself instead beaming at the incredibly gorgeous man entering my store. I was reminded of my first meeting with Jake. The circumstances were similar, although in our initial encounter it was a double dark-chocolate milk shake that I had just chugged. At least this time I had only a few cookie crumbs to brush off my chest, not a whipped-cream mustache for him to laugh at.

"Hi." I patted the stool next to me, an electrical charge running through my nerve endings as a burst of heat swept through my body. Jake's striking good looks completely seized my attention, and the pain from my tumble down the stairs seemed to melt away. "What's up?"

"Tony invited your grandmother over for chili and the *Bonanza* marathon on TV tonight." Jake's smile was both devastating and contagious. "When Birdie walked into the house a few minutes ago, I asked what you were doing for supper, and she said you'd have to settle for yesterday's tuna casserole." A dimple at the corner of his lips appeared. "From your grandma's expression, I'm guessing that's not your favorite dish, so I thought maybe we could get a bite to eat. I'll save you from leftovers, and you can save me from four hours of Ben Cartwright."

"Well . . ." This really did feel like déjà vu. The last time Jake had popped into my life with a message from my gran and his uncle, I was in a similar disheveled state of dress—sans makeup, with my hair scraped back into a ponytail, and wearing an oversize sweatshirt and baggy jeans.

"Come on," he coaxed. "You know you don't want to eat tuna casserole."

"True, but I should probably go home, take a shower, and change first." I sniffed discreetly. Yep. Whatever deodorant and perfume I'd put on at six a.m. were long gone. I smelled like a long day at work—not exactly hot guy–ready. "Once I'm a little more presentable, I could meet you somewhere in, say, an hour."

"You're fine." His chiseled face relaxed into a sexy smile and his gaze was so hot it was like a branding iron on my skin. "I like the natural you." He smoothed the faded Levi's that lovingly molded the muscles of his thighs. "I'm not dressed up, either."

"I *am* hungry." I realized that I'd missed lunch and I hadn't had anything to eat since breakfast. Except a whole lot of empty calories in the form of a donut that morning and the cookie I'd just scarfed. "Where did you have in mind?"

"Tony mentioned that a new barbeque place over by Sparkville is having a grand opening tonight." Jake pushed up my sweatshirt sleeve and stroked my inner arm. "You know no one there'll be dressed fancy." He beckoned with his fingers. "Tony said the brisket's supposed to be real tasty and the beer's guaranteed to be ice-cold."

The neighboring town of Sparkville had elected a German shepherd to office after their last mayor was caught trying to sell a city council seat to the highest bidder. The shepherd was a cute animal, and I wondered if he would be at the restaurant. The mayor in my own town wouldn't miss an opportunity for free food, but Sparkville's doggy head honcho might be more ethical.

"You've talked me into it." My mouth watered and I put my hand into his outstretched palm. "Just let me turn out the lights, stick the day's receipts in the safe, and make sure the back exit is locked. Then we can go."

"I'll get the lights." Jake stood, pulling me to my feet. "Birdie said you wouldn't be able to resist the lure of pulled pork, coleslaw, and corn bread." He winked. "But what I really hope is that you can't resist me."

I gave him a noncommittal look, then disappeared into the back room, clutching the cash drawer. Once we were in his truck driving the short distance between Shadow Bend and Sparkville, I brought Jake up to speed on all that had happened since I'd last talked to him. When I got to the part about the anonymous tipster trying to implicate me, he wrinkled his brow and grunted.

Finishing up my summary, I said, "So, I think it would be a good idea if I helped Chief Kincaid find the murderer. The longer it takes for the case to be solved, the more likely people will start looking at me funny."

"He may not be happy with your meddling," Jake suggested. "Local LEOs usually aren't real open to any outside interference."

"Leos?" I scrunched up my face. "Is that the chief's zodiac sign?"

"Law enforcement officer," Jake translated. "Federal agents call them that."

"Oh." I nodded. "I've heard that expression on various *CSI* shows but never knew what it meant.

I thought maybe they were referring to lions, since the cops on those programs seem to roar a lot."

Jake chuckled, then said, "So, do you think Chief Kincaid will be open to some external help? I was thinking of stopping by the station and seeing if there is anything I can do."

"The chief may not admit it, but as long as I approach him in the right way, I'm pretty sure he won't be adverse to receiving tips from me." I crossed my arms. "You might be more of a threat to his manhood. Sort of like saying he's not up to the job."

"In that case . . ." Jake paused as he swung the pickup into the barbeque joint's parking lot, found an empty spot, and pulled in. "Maybe we should look into some of the suspects on your list together and then you can bring the information to the chief."

"We?" I liked the sound of that. "Will you be around for a while?"

"I've got a week off and might be able to take a few more days if nothing comes up." Jake shoved his Stetson back. "I don't like the idea of your reputation being smeared, but what really worries me is that the killer might start thinking you know more than you do. What if you saw something that night that you don't remember seeing or that didn't seem important? The murderer could decide he needs to get rid of you."

"Well." I sagged back against the truck seat. I

hadn't mentioned my fall—the chief had half convinced me I'd imagined the push and the footsteps—but Jake's words made me rethink that conclusion. I hated to admit my clumsiness, but maybe I should get his take on what might have happened. "Do you really think I'm in danger?"

"It's hard to say." Jake shrugged. "But even the slightest possibility makes me nervous. And I . . ." He cupped my cheek, and for a millisecond, I could almost see the sexual awareness zinging between us. Then a shutter seemed to come down over his eyes, and whatever he'd been going to say was lost.

"Yes?" I wanted to know what Jake had decided not to tell me.

"Nothing." He moved away from me, got out of the pickup, and walked around to my side to help me down. "I just think it's better to be safe than sorry."

"Then I guess I should tell you what happened to me this afternoon." As we headed across the asphalt, I explained about hearing the footsteps, feeling someone put their hand on my back, and being pushed down the stairs. I finished with, "I called Chief Kincaid, and he seemed to think I had tripped over my own feet."

"But you didn't?" Jake's voice deepened with concern. "Why didn't you tell me this right away? Are you okay?"

"I'm a little sore. Otherwise I'm fine." I didn't

meet his eyes. "I didn't mention it because the chief sort of convinced me that I had stumbled and I was embarrassed about being so klutzy."

"Has something changed your mind?" Jake opened the restaurant door.

"You did." I bit my lip. "In the back of my mind, I wondered if being shoved was connected with Quistgaard's death. But I didn't want to admit to myself that his killer might be targeting me." I thought of the murderer coming after me and shuddered. If Jake was right, this wasn't just about me being the subject of gossip again. This time, my life might be in danger. "What could I possibly have seen?"

"Who knows?" Jake took my hands. "I hope you did just trip, but if someone is after you, we need to be careful."

"You're right." I took a breath. "If the murderer thinks I know something, then I'd better start figuring out what that is."

"Right." Jake squeezed my fingers, then looked around. He pointed to a corner booth and said, "Let's nab that table."

Once we were seated and had ordered the special and a couple of beers, I asked, "So, what do you think we should do first?"

" 'The Bend's Buzz' seems like a good lead." Jake took a notepad from his shirt pocket. "We need to get back copies of the *Banner*. Do you think the library has them?"

"It shut down last month. Most of the other little towns around here closed their libraries quite a while ago." I frowned. "I've heard there's a committee trying to raise money to reopen it, but right now the nearest library is over in the county seat."

"Then I guess the newspaper office is our best option." Jake jotted a note on his pad. "I'll stop by there tomorrow afternoon, then meet you at the dime store at six to go over the columns."

"Great." I paused while the waitress served our drinks and put a basket of steaming corn-bread muffins on the table. "I think we should concentrate on anyone who was both mentioned in the column and present at the book-club meeting Friday night. We can compare the list I have on my computer against people mentioned in the 'Buzz.'"

"Good idea." Jake took a swig of his Budweiser. "Your clerk mentioned two members who were arguing about Quistgaard's poetry. We should look for their names or anyone close to them. Remember, the motive for Quistgaard's murder might not be something that was printed about them personally."

"True." As I paused to spread butter on the warm muffin, I finally remembered what had been nagging me. It was something Noah had said about his physician's assistant. "There's one guy who I know was at the meeting and was ticked off at being mentioned in the column." I explained about Yale Gordon's beef with the Bend's Buzzard.

"He sounds like a good suspect." Jake jotted a note on his pad.

"Then there's Kiara Howard." I swallowed a bite of the corn bread, savoring the buttery goodness. "She objected to Quistgaard being invited to speak to the book club."

"Why?" Jake leaned forward and wiped a crumb from the corner of my mouth.

The touch of his rough finger on my lips made my heart stutter, but I ignored the zap of electricity between us and explained what Mrs. Zeigler had told me, ending with, "So, I don't know why."

By the time the food arrived, we'd added checking Addie's alibi to our list, but then run out of ideas. As we ate, I tried to put thoughts of the murder out of my head, but that left me wondering if there was any chance Jake would stick around. Or would the siren call of the Marshals Service and his ex-wife lure him back to St. Louis, and leave me with a broken heart?

Chapter 15

With a full stomach and a slight buzz from the beer I'd consumed, I was in a digestive stupor during the ride from Sparkville back to my car. When Jake pulled his pickup into the spot next to my Z4, I stretched and yawned, then squinted at the BMW's windshield.

"What's that?" I pointed to something white tucked beneath my wiper.

"Probably a flyer for the local pizza joint or a coupon for a car wash." Jake got out of the truck, grabbed the offending item, and handed it to me. "Here. It looks as if someone wanted to save on postage."

"Thanks." It was a business-size envelope with my name typed across the front. I slit it open with my keys and pulled out the single piece of cheap paper, then gasped. Printed in the exact center of the page was:

KEEP YOUR MOUTH SHUT AND STOP SNOOPING OR THE NEXT TIME IT WON'T BE JUST A FALL DOWN A FEW STEPS.

Jake took the note from my unresisting fingers. He snarled as he read it, then opened the Ford's center console, grabbed a plastic bag, and shoved the letter and the envelope inside, knotting the top.

Wordlessly, he put the truck in reverse and squealed out of the parking lot. I knew where he was heading, and it definitely wasn't how I'd pictured the evening ending. Instead of a prolonged make-out session, I was in for a lengthy interrogation. This was *so* not how I wanted to spend my time with Jake.

The Shadow Bend Police Station was located on the main drag between the hardware store and the dry cleaner. The lot behind the building was for police vehicles and employees only, which meant daytime parking was often a problem. But since it was now long past normal business hours, all five spaces out front were free. Jake swung smoothly into the slot nearest the entrance, cut the motor, whipped off his seat belt, and came around to help me out of the pickup.

Even the normally thrill-inducing feel of Jake's hands on my waist couldn't alleviate the anxiety I felt about going inside. The station's square cinder-block building, recently installed front window bars, and overall oppressive atmosphere reminded me of the prison where my dad had spent the past twelve years.

Which was a problem for me, because during my one and only visit to the penitentiary where my father currently resided, I had developed a sort of claustrophobia that kicked in whenever I stepped into anything that resembled a jail. I tended to lose the ability to breathe if I thought too long about being locked up. And swooning at Jake's feet did not project the image of the cool, independent woman I wanted to convey. In my experience, passing out rarely left a good impression on a man, unless, of course, alcohol was involved.

Seeing no other choice, I took a deep breath and allowed Jake to escort me toward the building. My chest tightened as he pushed open the door and waved me through, but I concentrated on inhaling and exhaling and remaining vertical.

The lobby was silent and empty, and we immediately ascended the short flight of concrete stairs that led to the main part of the station. As we headed toward the counter, the young woman manning the desk behind bulletproof glass was laughing into the telephone, but the minute she caught sight of Jake, she licked her lips, muttered a quick good-bye, and tossed the receiver onto the cradle.

She slid the window open—apparently hot guys didn't have to talk through the small speaker built into the glass—and leaned forward until she was close enough for her breasts to press against the counter. She fluttered her false eyelashes and sucked on her finger.

Once Jake had had enough time to appreciate the assets that were threatening to pop the buttons of her blouse, she said, "Can I help you with something, handsome?" Her sultry tone made it clear that her offer of assistance included getting naked and doing the horizontal mambo with him, if that was what he had in mind.

"Hi there, darlin'. I'm Deputy U.S. Marshal Jake Del Vecchio, and I need to speak to the officer on duty." Jake rested a hip against the desk and smiled seductively, then drawled, "Although I'd really rather deal with the chief, if that's at all possible."

"You're in luck, sugar." The dispatcher's gaze swept every delectable inch of Jake's six-foot-four frame, and she fluffed her intricate bottle blond updo. "He's in his office, working on another grant, and he told me not to disturb him, but for you, I'll risk it."

"I'd be grateful." Jake flashed a smile, his straight white teeth gleaming.

It appeared that I had somehow become invisible, because the dispatcher ignored me completely and winked at Jake. She shook a long pink fingernail at him, and said, "Don't you move now, gorgeous."

"Wild horses couldn't drag me away," Jake assured her.

"I'll be right back." She flipped open the counter and disappeared down the hall, her hips moving to some conga beat only she could hear.

Once she was gone, Jake grinned at my revolted

expression and said, "I thought I noticed the chief's car when we passed the back lot. I figured that it being so late, he wasn't officially here, but I hoped I could persuade the dispatcher to let us talk to him. I think it's best if we deal with him directly about this threat."

"Hmm." It had been interesting seeing Jake turn on the charm in order to get what he wanted. That image might be one I needed to keep in mind in the future when I questioned whether he was being sincere or just using me. "You're probably right," I said. "At least we shouldn't have to repeat ourselves as many times if we start with the head guy."

A couple of minutes ticked by before Miss Perky Boobs returned and triumphantly reported, "Chief Kincaid says you can go on back."

As we passed her, I saw her press a piece of paper into Jake's palm and heard her whisper, "Dump the chubster and give me a call."

It took considerable self-control not to throttle her. Instead, I slipped my hand into Jake's and stared into Nympho Barbie's overly made-up eyes. "Dream on. Inflatable dolls aren't his type."

Jake's broad shoulders were shaking with laughter, and I was trying to think of a comment that would squelch his mirth when we entered the chief's office. Eldridge Kincaid was as starched and pressed as if he'd just started his shift, rather than having been on duty for twelve or fifteen hours. Did he have multiple uniforms that he changed into when the one he had on got wrinkled?

Once we were settled in chairs facing his desk, the chief said, "So, Del Vecchio, what's so important that you had to seduce my dispatcher way past her usual level of stupid to see me?"

I couldn't remember when Jake and the chief had met. The chief hadn't been involved when I'd been accused of murdering Noah's fiancée; I dealt with the Kansas City police department then. And when Boone had been arrested, Jake hadn't been in Shadow Bend. Maybe they'd met socially, or casually around town. Jake mostly stuck to the ranch when he was staying with his uncle, but there was always the grocery store or the pharmacy.

"Take a look at this." Jake tossed the bag he'd been holding on to the chief's desk. "We found this on Devereaux's car windshield."

"Tonight?" Chief Kincaid asked, smoothing out the plastic and reading the note. When Jake nodded, the chief flipped the bag over and examined the envelope through the other side. He scowled, pulled the phone toward him, and dialed. After a brief conversation with someone I assumed was one of his crime-scene trained officers, since the poor guy had been ordered to get his butt to the station ASAP, the chief carefully placed the handset back in the base.

The chief stared at the letter, turning it over and over as if he could change what was written on the page. Finally, he looked at me with a strange expression and said, "I apologize. I should never have dismissed your fall when you called me earlier. That was negligent of me."

"Don't be sorry." I sat forward and put my hands on the desktop. Despite his quarrel with my best friend and his rigidity, I liked Eldridge Kincaid. I admired his determination to do the best possible job for the people of Shadow Bend. In a way, we were alike. He and I were both willing to risk being disliked if it meant doing what we considered necessary to protect those we loved—even from themselves.

The chief grunted and shook his head. "That's very kind of you, but—"

"Your assumption was logical," I interrupted him. "I had been under a lot of stress and I could easily have tripped and imagined that I was shoved."

"Thank you." Chief Kincaid dipped his head, then fingered his shiny brass nameplate and asked, "So, what kind of snooping have you been up to?"

"I've talked to a few people about that night." I shrugged. "Nothing more than what everyone else in town is doing."

"Who did you talk to?" Using his handkerchief, the chief rubbed off the mark his thumb had made on his nameplate.

"Poppy, Noah, my clerks, Addie Campbell, and Mrs. Zeigler." I closed my eyes. Had I mentioned the murder to anyone else? "Oh, and about a thousand customers asked me about the murder on Saturday."

Chief Kincaid adjusted the leather blotter so that it lined up more perfectly with the edge of his desk, then said, "Addie isn't the killer. He was at Gossip Central between nine fifteen and ten. The bartender and several of his drinking buddies swear he never left his stool."

"Great." Well, checking Addie's alibi was one thing I could cross off my to-do list.

"And Mrs. Zeigler was home by nine thirty," Chief Kincaid continued. "A teacher called her on her landline at that time to discuss a problem, and said they were on the phone for half an hour. Mrs. Zeigler lives way the heck in the country, so it isn't possible for her to have staked the vic in the heart, dragged his body into the box, and driven to her house in fifteen minutes."

"The murderer could have overheard Devereaux talking to someone about the crime," Jake said, then turned to me, and asked, "Who was around during your conversations?"

"The store was full when I was chatting with Addie, but I was alone when I spoke to everyone else." I tried to remember who had been present while the pawnbroker and I had talked that afternoon. "The entire Knittie Grittie group, a bunch of teenagers, and a handful of customers were there. It really could be anyone."

The chief posed a few more questions, said he'd have the letter and envelope dusted for prints, and asked for the dime store key so the crime-scene techs could process the second floor. I could tell he didn't hold out much hope of discovering any evidence, but he promised he'd let me know what they found.

As Jake and I left, I gave a warning glare to the sexpot at the dispatch desk, and she stuck out her tongue. I knew it wasn't reasonable to be jealous, considering that I was bent on seeing both Jake and Noah, but I assured myself that what I was doing was different from the flirting that the big-boobed, brassy-haired witch was doing with Jake right under my nose.

I was relieved when Jake stayed cool and didn't go all macho U.S. Marshal on me on the drive back to my store. I'm not sure what my reaction would have been if he'd tried to tell me to stop looking into the murder or attempted to convince me that the police could handle it without my help. But I know my response wouldn't have been pretty. I'd been taking care of myself for a long time, and it boded well for any future relationship that we might have that he seemed to understand that about me.

Instead, Jake and I discussed our plans for tomorrow. He reiterated his intention to get hold of the past issues of "The Bend's Buzz" and meet me at the store when it closed at six. After he'd filled me in on the contents of the gossip column, we'd go have a chat with Yale and Kiara. If we had time, we'd track down Bryce and Zizi, too, but I figured they would probably have to wait until the next day.

When Jake dropped me off at my car, he informed me that he would follow me home to make sure no ax-wielding psychopath was waiting for me at my place. Okay, he didn't say that last part, but it was implied. His tone indicated that he expected me to argue, but I was grateful for his concern. What red-blooded American girl wouldn't be a little thrilled to have someone as hot as Jake worried about her well-being? And while I was independent, I wasn't stupid. A killer had just threatened me, so I was happy to have a gun-toting lawman see me safely to my house.

On the short drive, I went over and over in my mind the events of Friday night. Nothing new occurred to me, and I kept wondering what I was missing. If the killer was intimidated enough to warn me off, there must be something I knew that could convict him or her.

Chapter 16

Jake had wanted to do a quick recon of Devereaux's house before she went inside, but she'd narrowed those pretty blue-green eyes of hers and said no. When he'd persisted, she'd put her hands on her lush hips, stuck out her cute little chin, and repeated the word *no* until he finally gave up.

After she'd proven her point—whatever the hell it had been—she'd agreed to allow him to wait in the driveway until she checked out the place. He'd spent an anxious ten minutes with his gun at the ready and the truck's door cracked open, until she gave him an all-clear signal from the living room picture window.

Once he knew Devereaux was safe, he made a U-turn and headed his F250 up the lane toward the main road, all the time wishing she were sitting beside him in the passenger seat. The smell of her spicy yet sweet perfume lingered in the truck's cab like a hint of what their future together could be if he quit the Marshals Service and stayed in Shadow Bend.

Jake had planned a very different end to their evening. With her grandmother occupied at his

196

uncle's place, he'd intended to suggest that after dinner they take advantage of her empty house. Instead, they'd spent those hours at the police station.

He'd given up fighting his attraction to the feisty cinnamon-haired woman, and even though he was back working as a U.S. Marshal and couldn't quite figure out how to manage their relationship, he still wanted her in his bed. Or him in her bed. Or on the couch. Or, for that matter, on the tabletop or the floor, or any other horizontal surface that could hold them.

Too bad she was so damn stubborn. This business of her insisting on continuing to date Underwood was bad enough, but now that she'd been threatened, probably by Quistgaard's murderer, Jake was afraid that her pigheadedness would get her killed. It had taken every ounce of self-control that he possessed not to order her to stop snooping. His common sense told him that even if he'd been able to wrangle an agreement out of her, she'd just keep poking around behind his back.

Which was why Jake had kept his mouth shut. At least this way she wouldn't be hiding her investigation from him. He'd be in the loop and at her side while she questioned suspects. If things went south, he'd have a chance to protect her. While he was confident she'd eventually pick him over Frat Boy, he needed to keep her safe—

even if that meant biting his tongue and not interfering with her plans to catch a killer.

Jake whacked his head against the back of the seat and stared out the windshield at the empty asphalt as he drove the few miles to his uncle's ranch. Why was his life always so damn complicated? How had he gone from deciding to tell Devereaux they should cool it, since he was back living in St. Louis, to suggesting that he might stick around for good? What had happened to letting her down easy? Why did logic fly out the window and his carefully planned life go to hell the minute he got near her?

Friday afternoon when Jake had stopped by the store to talk to Devereaux, he'd had every intention of giving her the "let's be friends" speech. But as soon as he saw Underwood sitting at the soda fountain, as if he belonged there, Jake had allowed his emotions to take over. And instead of saying sayonara to Devereaux, he'd insisted that she go out with him the next night.

Then, on their way home from the restaurant, when she'd accused him of asking her to take a leap of faith without planning to be around to catch her, he'd said he would be there—or at least he'd try to be. Why had he even brought up his uncle's offer to manage the ranch? Until that moment, he'd never contemplated quitting the Marshals Service and settling down in Shadow

Bend. Was that even something he'd be willing to consider?

A year ago, Jake would have said no effing way. Hell, six months ago, his fondest desire was to heal enough to get back to chasing the bad guys. Then he went and kissed Devereaux, and now he couldn't get her out of his thoughts. Jake whacked his head against the back of the seat again. No woman had ever affected him this way. Was it crazy to think that he might be happier as a rancher than as a marshal if it meant having her beside him?

Jake pulled his pickup into his uncle's garage and cut the motor. He pounded the steering wheel and reminded himself that he'd wanted to be a U.S. Marshal ever since he saw a documentary about them on TV when he was twelve years old. Then there were all the scum who would still be out there if he hadn't tracked them down and put them behind bars, where they belonged. Serial killers like the Doll Maker, drug bosses like the guy he'd just put back in jail, and pedophiles like the Candy Man might have gotten away if it weren't for him and his team.

Still, he'd always loved working on the ranch with his uncle, too, and Tony wasn't getting any younger. During Jake's recent stay with the old man, it had become increasingly clear that his uncle was slowing down. Tony had even been talking about signing on a foreman to help out.

Once he did that, it wouldn't be fair for Jake to decide he wanted the job anytime in the near future and ask his uncle to fire someone he'd just hired.

Which meant that Jake had to figure things out before Tony hired someone. He also needed to do it before Devereaux decided that Underwood was a better choice for her. Jake's breath hitched and his heart gave an agonizing squeeze at the image of her in another man's arms. He closed his eyes, trying to consider the pros and cons of marshal versus rancher, but the memory of Devereaux's soft warmth pressed against him crowded his thoughts.

He frowned at his own weakness and scrubbed his face with his fists. He couldn't allow his emotions to override his common sense. Undercover, that could get you killed, and, in this situation, the results might be almost as bad.

Jake took a deep breath and opened the pickup door. Sitting here stewing wasn't getting him anywhere. He'd go inside, get a good night's sleep, and do some police work tomorrow. Then, once he and Devereaux figured out who had murdered the poet, he'd make his decision.

Chapter 17

Tuesday morning, I woke to two pairs of feline eyes staring intently at me. Banshee was sitting on my head, doing his version of the Snoopy vulture pose, no doubt imagining me as roadkill. Tsar lay sprawled on my stomach, purring and kneading my chest, which explained the hot dream I'd been having about Jake, me, and a hotel room.

Groaning, I glanced to my right and discovered that my bedroom door was ajar. I must not have shut it tightly enough the night before, and the devious duo had managed to get it open.

I cautiously moved Tsar off me, then patted the comforter and crooned, "Here, kitty, kitty," trying to persuade Banshee to join him.

The Siamese made a sound halfway between a trill and a click and didn't budge. I lay perfectly still, trying to think of a way out of this situation that didn't involve me becoming scratched and bloody.

Finally, when "Sue Me" blared from my nightstand, I bit the bullet. Reaching up, I grabbed Banshee around the middle and lifted him off my skull at the same time as I sat up. He hissed, dug in his claws, then leapt to the mattress.

"Hey, Boone." I fingered the bleeding grooves in my scalp as I answered the phone. "Where are you? Are you having fun on the cruise?"

"I'm having a fabulous time," Boone answered, his words a little slurred. "I'm in San Francisco. We got here yesterday afternoon and the ship stayed in port overnight. Right now I'm on our balcony, since I can't get a cell signal inside the suite."

"Great." I was happy to hear the sparkle back in Boone's voice. This trip was just what he needed. "What's your next stop?"

"Santa Barbara. How are things at home?"

"Okay." I did a little quick mental math, not easy at six in the morning, and realized that it was four a.m. in California. "What are you doing up so early?"

"I haven't gone to bed yet." Boone giggled. Yes. He actually giggled. "My buddy and I have gotten friendly with the entertainers on board and we've been partying with them all night."

"Why am I not surprised?" I remembered the after-the-play bashes we'd had in high school. Boone had always been the last to leave.

"How's Tsar doing?" Boone asked, then crooned, "Does my little kitty miss me?"

"I'm sure he does, but he's fine." I turned my head and saw the Russian Blue curled up with Gran's cat. "Would you believe he and Banshee are getting along? They are actually grooming each other."

"That's terrific. I always said Banshee wasn't as bad as you made out." Boone paused, and I could hear him take a drink of a beverage that I seriously doubted was coffee or orange juice. "Does that mean Tsar's staying at your house instead of the store?"

"Yes. And it's a good thing." I paused, considering just how much to tell him about what had happened since his departure. Knowing Boone would be upset if I kept anything from him, I spilled it all—the police search of the dime store, Nadine's revelation about Quistgaard and her possible heart attack, my nose-dive down the stairs, and the letter on my windshield. When I finished my tale of woe, I took a breath and added, "So, Jake and I are investigating everyone who was trashed in 'The Bend's Buzz.' "

"Are you nuts?" Boone's tone implied his question had been rhetorical. "Why don't you just butt out, like the note said?"

"I can't." I stopped to ask myself exactly why I was willing to risk my life. Oh, yeah. I was ticked off and tired of being pushed around. "Someone used *my* display, *my* store, and *my* trash. The killer made it too personal for me to ignore." I stroked Tsar's soft gray fur. "Then to shove me down the stairs and threaten me—that's just not something I can tolerate."

"I know." Boone's voice sounded a lot more sober than it had in the beginning of our conversation. "Whoever did it doesn't know you very well. There isn't a less effective way to make you back off than to provoke you and tell you to mind your own business."

I agreed with Boone's assessment of my character. We exchanged a bit more chitchat; then I heard someone calling for Honey Boo Boo to return to the party, and we said good-bye.

Snickering at Boone's new nickname, I attempted to get out of bed. *Ouch!* Every muscle in my body shuddered with exhaustion and abuse. Maybe I should just go back to sleep. Except that I couldn't. No workee; no payee.

After a long moment, I heaved myself to my feet. As Gran always said, in order to succeed in this world, no matter how bad you feel, you need to get up, dress up, and show up. Limping into the bathroom, I turned on the shower.

Once the water had warmed past its initial glacial temperature, I stepped into the bathtub and pulled the curtain closed. While I let the spray stream over me, I thought about last night. Despite the death threat that had ended our date, I'd had a good time with Jake. A really good time.

I loved his dark sense of humor, and I was amazed by how much his concern for my safety meant to me. No one had been my protector since my dad went to prison and Noah walked out of my life. I smiled at the thought of Jake as my knight in faded denim and a cowboy hat.

What I really liked about Jake was that he knew when to let me fight my own battles. He seemed to recognize when I needed him and when I didn't. Or if he didn't figure it out on his own, he got the hint fairly quickly.

As I squeezed citrus and white ginger bath gel on my loofah, I admitted that what I truly liked about Jake was nearly everything. He was ruggedly handsome, fun to be around, and too damn sexy for his or my own good. He was almost the perfect man—except that he lived five hours away, regularly risked his life, and worked with his ex-wife. But, hey, all those things could be fixed.

Yeah. Right. Who was I kidding? The only one who could remedy those things was Jake himself. Short of moving to St. Louis, hiring a bodyguard for him, and shooting his ex, there certainly wasn't anything I could do about them. And none of the above options seemed like a good choice.

Sighing, I finished washing, dried off, and got dressed. Determined not to be caught looking like crap again, I tamed my curls with a flatiron, applied some bronzer, a little concealer, and a sweep of mascara, then grabbed a silk sweater to change into after work.

I hadn't had a chance to talk to Gran much in a couple of days. When she'd gotten back from her casino trip Sunday night, she'd been pooped and had gone straight to bed. Then yesterday morning, I left for the store before she was up, and she hadn't come home from the *Bonanza*-and-chili marathon at Tony's last night until after I was asleep. I planned to spend a little extra time with her this morning.

Lately, Gran seemed to be doing a lot better. Her memory appeared to be sharpening. I thought about calling her doctor to discuss her improvement with him, but ultimately decided against it. As my grandpa used to say, don't mess with something that ain't bothering you none.

I figured that with me being around more, Gran's renewed friendship with Tony, and the good news about my father, maybe she was just happier and more focused than she'd been in a long, long time. It was a count-your-blessings moment, and I was determined to enjoy the sensation.

While Gran and I chatted over our bowls of oatmeal, I filled her in on the past few days. I omitted my fall down the stairs and the threat to my life, since those tidbits would just worry her. What was the use of upsetting her about situations she couldn't control?

Once I finished bringing her up-to-date, Gran told me about her evening. For someone with memory problems, she amazed me by telling me the plot, setting, and outcome of every *Bonanza* episode she'd watched the night before.

When I thought I'd go crazy if I heard the

sentence *Little Joe got on his horse* one more time, I interrupted her and asked, "You read 'The Bend's Buzz,' right?"

"Every week." Birdie nodded. "I wouldn't know what they were talking about at bingo if I didn't. I can't figure out how the writer finds out all that stuff about everybody's dirty laundry."

I told Gran that the dead guy behind my store was the author, then asked, "Do you recall reading anything really juicy in the column recently?"

"Hmmm." Birdie cleared the table. "There was something a month or so ago about that girl you're friendly with, the one who runs the B and B . . ."

"Veronica Ksiazak," I supplied. Names were still a problem for Gran, but, then, they were often an issue for a lot of people.

"Right." Birdie put the dishes in the sink then opened the junk drawer. "I remember wanting to tell you about that. I tore that piece out to show you, but you know I can't abide a mess on my counters, so I put it away and forgot it." She pawed through the drawer's contents, then slammed it shut. "Nope. It's not there. Where could I have put it?"

"Don't worry about it." I patted her shoulder. "Jake is getting hold of all the columns today, so I'll look for the one about Ronnie when he brings them over after work." *Oops!* I hadn't meant to mention Jake to her. She was already too encouraged by our date the night before. Our evening together had been the first thing she'd asked me about this morning.

I scrambled to change the subject, but before I could come up with anything, Gran said, "And before I forget, I got a call late yesterday afternoon." She beamed. "Good news! Your dad will be released this coming Monday. He'll be home by the time you get back from work in the evening. The three of us can have supper together."

"Oh, my God! That's wonderful. I had no idea it would be this soon." I grabbed her by the waist and danced her around the kitchen. "Don't we need to go pick him up?"

"No. Kern's lawyer will go fetch him." Birdie shook her head. "I know you've been raring to go see him since you found out he's innocent, and that he's said no, he doesn't want you to come to the prison, since it upsets you so much."

"I should have gone anyway." The twinge of guilt I'd felt in my stomach ever since learning that I'd misjudged my father flared into a flaming ball of self-reproach. "I should never have doubted him. You didn't."

"Kern understood that you felt abandoned. You two were so close when you were growing up." She patted my cheek. "But, sweetie, it's best you just let him do this his way."

"Sure, Gran." I nodded, but how could I have not trusted my own father? "You're probably right about letting him ease back into things."

An unwelcome thought flickered through my mind. Would my father's presence change my life? How would it be with Gran, Dad, and me all living together? Would there be personality clashes? My father didn't really know me as an adult. I pushed my misgivings aside and said brightly, "We'll have to plan something special for his homecoming. Do you need any help getting his room ready?"

"Nope." Gran plunged her hands into the hot soapy water. "I'm going to tackle that today. I thought he'd like some privacy, so I'm cleaning out the apartment over the garage for him."

"Oh. I forgot about that space." Before my grandfather died, back when the Sinclairs were prosperous landowners, the hired hand had lived in the garage apartment. "What kind of shape is it in?"

"We'll soon find out." Gran rinsed a dish and put it in the drainer.

"Call me if you need anything." I glanced at the wall clock. It was eight forty-five. "I'd better get going. I probably won't be home until late. I need to talk to some people after work."

Grabbing my purse, my spare key to the store—Chief Kincaid had my regular one—and a change of clothes, I hopped into the car and broke a few speed limits getting to the store on time. It was one minute to nine when I unlocked the back door and stepped inside.

A note had been left on my desk by the crime tech who had processed the upstairs. It informed me that no evidence regarding my attacker had been found and my key would be dropped off sometime that morning. Even though I hadn't expected any big discoveries, I was disappointed. On the upside, the fingerprint-powder mess was confined to the second floor this time, and I could wait for my cleaning lady to tidy it up, rather than have to do it myself.

As I was heading to the front entrance, my cell dinged, indicating that I had a text. It was Noah, so I stopped and read the message: Mom OK, but cardiologist kept her in hospital overnight. she insisted I stay w her. Just dropped her off @home and am on my way 2 clinic. I'll call u when I've got a break btw patients.

I quickly texted back, Glad she's OK. Hope you're not 2 zonked. tlk2U l8r.

I thought about it, then added, Can u fnd out where Yale will be after 6pm? I hated to bother Noah, but I didn't know any other way to find out the physician's assistant's after-hours location.

Slipping my cell in my jean's pocket, I opened up the store and concentrated on my business. On Tuesdays, I hosted both the Quilting Queens and the Scrapbooking Scalawags. Regrettably, neither group's members nor any of my other customers yielded any good gossip about the murdered man. Still, none of the craft-group participants got into a screaming match, no guest speakers were killed, and no one threatened my life, so I deemed the day a success.

Chapter 18

It was late afternoon on Tuesday before Jake was free to go into town. As he drove, he noticed the green buds dotting the trees that lined the road. Spring was bursting out all over, and it was a particularly busy time on the ranch. Pasture season was in full swing, and Jake's morning had started at five a.m., when he'd helped the ranch hands take the cows and their calves to the native grass meadows. The livestock would graze there until the beginning of October, when the young would be weaned.

There'd been a hurt week-old bull calf that he'd had to see to. The calf's mother had accidently stepped on him and broken his leg. It had been gut-wrenching, seeing the baby struggling to follow its mama, but a fracture usually healed fairly easily. Too bad it had taken so damn long to catch the animal, get it to the vet, and have a cast put on his leg.

It had been noon before Jake got the calf back to its mother. Having been practically raised on a ranch, he knew that the cattle always came first. Their health and well-being were the rancher's priority. But dealing with the animal's injury meant that it was several hours later than he anticipated before he could head into the newspaper office. He just hoped it wasn't closed.

Jake drove the speed limit, giving himself a chance to collect his thoughts and figure out a strategy for approaching the editor. He'd never met Grant Edwyn and wasn't sure how receptive the guy would be to sharing information with a law-man. Journalists and cops weren't always on the same side. Most of the time reporters thought the First Amendment was more important than putting away the bad guys and keeping people safe, while law enforcement felt exactly the opposite.

Even going a sedate fifty-five, his F250 ate up the miles into Shadow Bend, and he arrived at four fifteen. As Jake crossed the sidewalk and entered the building, he noted that the *Banner*'s office was typical for a small-town paper. A long counter ran the length of the back wall, with stacks of newspapers piled on the wooden surface.

The front two-thirds of the space contained racks holding various preprinted signs, reams of paper, ink cartridges, and printing supplies. A teenager bobbing to whatever he heard through his ear-buds was sweeping the floor by the cash register.

Jake tapped the boy on the shoulder, and the teen jumped as if he'd been Tasered, then shouted, "What the hell, dude! You almost gave me a heart attack."

"Sorry, man." Jake bit back a lecture about

being more aware of one's surroundings. "I didn't realize you hadn't seen me."

Glaring, the boy said, "We're closed."

"The door was open," Jake pointed out. "Do you have a morgue with the past issues of the *Banner*? Or, better yet, is it digitized?"

"Yeah, it's all on the computer." The teenager leaned on his broom. "But it's only available to the public from eight to four. As I said, we're closed."

"I see." Jake knew that arguing with the hired help wouldn't do any good. He needed to talk to the guy in charge. "Is Mr. Edwyn around?"

The teenager peered at him for a long moment, then said, "Who's asking?"

"Jake Del Vecchio." He held out his palm. "And you?"

The teenager tentatively shook Jake's hand and muttered, "I'm Bobby."

"Good to meet you, Bobby." Jake smiled. "I'm visiting my uncle on the Del Vecchio ranch."

"So?" Bobby couldn't have been more than thirteen, but he had the adolescent attitude down pat. "Is that supposed to mean something?"

The boy wore a gray hoodie with a pair of Hawaiian-print board shorts, and neon green flip-flops, and his dirty blond hair was spiked with gel. Since it was still a cool fifty degrees out, Jake thought he was rushing the season a little, but evidently fashion was more important than practicality to this kid.

"Can't think of an answer, dude?" Bobby faked a yawn. "Tick. Tock." He pointed to his watch. "I'm getting bored."

The little bugger's lame attempt at being a badass was getting annoying, and Jake thought about flashing his tin. Instead, he said, "Son, just get your boss."

Bobby opened his mouth, then after staring at Jake's unsmiling face, he seemed to reconsider and said, "Fine." He shuffled off, yelling, "Uncle Grant, some big dude wants to see you."

While he waited, Jake rested a hip against the counter. He really hoped Edwyn would cooperate. Devereaux would be disappointed in him if he had to come back to look at the papers tomorrow. Jake groaned. Since when did he care about disappointing a girlfriend? He shook his head. Man, he had it bad.

A few minutes later, a middle-aged man with a receding hairline and a basketball-size paunch marched out from the back. His muddy brown eyes were full of curiosity when he said, "You're Tony's nephew, right? The one that's a deputy U.S. Marshal."

"I am." Jake shook the guy's hand and asked, "Do you have a couple of minutes? I'd like to speak to you about 'The Bend's Buzz.' "

Hitting his palm with the pencil he was carrying, the editor examined him as if taking his measure, then said, "Follow me."

Jake trailed him to a small desk stuck in a rear corner, where each of them took a seat and Jake explained his request to see back columns of "The Bend's Buzz."

"Are you working on a case, Marshal?" It was hard to read Edwyn's expression.

"Not officially," Jake answered. "Just checking out a hunch."

"Chief Kincaid has already talked to me about Quistgaard's tenure as our gossip columnist." Edwyn crossed his arms. "But he wouldn't tell me who informed him that Quistgaard was working for me."

Jake twirled his Stetson in his lap. "If it was such a secret, the question would be, Who knew, and who would be likely to blab?"

"Only one person was aware of Anonymous's identity." Edwyn's gravelly voice made it sound as if he were growling. "I regretted it the second she bullied me into telling her, but she had never revealed his name before and I can't see her running to the police now."

"Then maybe someone else recently found out." Jake tilted his chair onto its back legs. "Say, someone was eavesdropping when you talked to him at the book club . . ."

"How did you know I spoke to Quistgaard about the column that night?" Edwyn demanded, jabbing a finger at Jake's face. "There wasn't anyone around when I warned him to keep his mouth shut."

"Wrong." Jake's voice was cool. "And probably more than one person overheard you."

"Shit!" Edwyn slumped. "The minute I saw that Quistgaard was going to be at the book club, I knew he'd cause trouble. That man speaking to a local group was like a boy swilling spiked punch at the high school dance. You know he'll make a mess. You just don't know whose shoes he'll ruin. Quistgaard purely hated small towns."

"Which is why you hired him," Jake guessed. "Was it your brainchild for his byline to be Anonymous? So that people wouldn't clam up around him?"

"Actually, the whole shebang was his idea, although I thought it was smart and didn't want him to blow his cover at the book-club meeting. He'd never be able to gather the gossip he needed if everyone knew he wrote the 'Buzz.'" Edwyn's posture oozed contempt.

"I see." Jake wasn't sure if the editor's scorn was for the columnist or the townspeople. "Did Quistgaard agree?"

"To a certain extent, but the real reason he didn't want his name on the column was because he felt that that kind of writing was beneath him. He considered himself an artiste, not like the rest of us—and I quote—'Hacks writing drivel for the masses.'"

"So why did he take the job?" Jake asked immediately, not giving the editor a chance to think and possibly clam up. "It sounds like the last thing he'd want to do."

"As I said, Quistgaard proposed the column to me. He said he tended to work on his poetry at the bakery and at Brewfully Yours, and people were always disturbing him by gossiping with one another. So since he was broke, he might as well make some cash from what he overheard."

"I see." Jake thought out loud. "So Quistgaard hated the town, hated the people, and needed money. I wonder if extortion might be a part of his repertoire as well as writing a tell-all column."

"That's an interesting theory, but since Quistgaard always claimed that he was hurting for cash, if he *was* blackmailing folks, he was doing a piss-poor job of it."

"Something to consider," Jake agreed, then asked, "So, can I get those back issues of 'The Bend's Buzz'?"

"They're yours if you promise to give me an exclusive when you solve the case." Edwyn's tiny Chiclet-like teeth gleamed.

"I can live with that." Jake shook the editor's hand. "You got a deal."

As he waited for Edwyn to print out copies off his computer, Jake grinned. His heart revved up with the thought that he'd soon be on the trail of a bad guy. Hunting down crooks was what he lived for. Was he seriously contemplating giving it up?

Chapter 19

When Jake walked in my store Tuesday evening at six, I was more than ready to begin our investigation. But even my eagerness to get started didn't stop the tingling in the pit of my stomach as his hand brushed mine when he gave me the stack of printouts from the newspaper. And when he gazed at me with those dark indigo eyes, my heart stuttered and my pulse picked up speed.

I could see the hunger on his face, too, but I throttled back the dizzying current running through me, cleared my throat, and said a little breathlessly, "Did you find out anything from the editor?"

"Edwyn claims that Nadine Underwood was the only one he told about Quistgaard writing 'The Bend's Buzz.'" Jake looked around. "Where do you want to go over the columns? Here at the soda fountain?"

"Sure." I went behind the counter. "Do you want something to eat or drink?"

"Coffee black, if you have it." Jake took a seat on a stool and said, "Did the cops find anything when they processed the store?" I shook my head, and he asked, "Have you gotten any more threats?"

"Nope." I set a steaming mug in front of him, then poured myself a cup and grabbed a plate of pastries left over from the Quilting Queens and the Scrapbooking Scalawags. "No evidence and no threats." I slid the dish next to Jake and added, "But I did find out where we can talk to Yale Gordon tonight." Noah had texted me with the info about an hour ago. I jerked my thumb at the front window. "His jazz band is playing in the gazebo in the town square right across the street at seven."

"Well, that makes it easy." Jake spread out the papers. "I highlighted the really vicious column entries."

"Do the various colors mean anything?" I sat down next to him and examined the pages.

"Items about males are in blue, and references to females are in pink."

I studied the sheets. For every one blue highlight, there were at least ten pink ones. "He really had it in for women, didn't he?"

"Yep." Jake nodded. "I'd say this guy had some real issues with the opposite sex."

"From what I understand, that attitude came out in his poetry, too." I gathered all the columns together and put them aside. "Our best bet, if we want to talk to Yale, is to catch him before his band starts playing, which means we should head over to the square at quarter to seven."

"Okay." Jake glanced at his watch. "That gives us about half an hour."

"We should try to seem as if we just ran into Yale, rather than as if we're interrogating him, so why not make it look like we're there for the performance?" I asked. "We can grab a blanket from the storage room and pick up dinner from Little's Tea Room. It always stays open late on concert nights, and their boxed suppers are famous for their chicken salad sandwiches, handmade potato chips, and lemon tarts."

"That's a good idea. Why don't we do that now and look over the columns when we get back?" Jake suggested. "Since we're short on time, how about I go to the liquor store and get a six-pack of Corona, while you pick up the food?"

"Splitting up is fine, but you'd better get a bottle of merlot and a sleeve of plastic cups rather than the beer, since we won't be able to keep the Corona cold." I tugged Jake toward the door. "Technically alcohol consumption isn't allowed on the village green, but as long as we don't flaunt it, the police won't hassle us. But that means we'll have to hide the booze in my purse. Once wine is poured into the cups, no one can tell it isn't fruit punch."

After we'd secured our provisions, we returned to the dime store and compared the book-club member list that I'd printed out from my computer to "The Bend's Buzz" columns that Jake had obtained. As Gran had mentioned, one of the pieces took a potshot at Ronni. The article claimed that she had gotten the financing for her B & B from a shady source—one that could prove dangerous to her and her guests. Between the lines, I read *Mafia*.

I pointed to the highlighted paragraph and said to Jake, "Looks like we'd better add Ronni Ksiazak to our list of suspects. She was at the book-club meeting, had a run-in with the poet, and this kind of accusation could really hurt her business."

"Yep." Jake took a tiny spiral notebook from his breast pocket.

"And if the information is true"—I rubbed my chin—"Ronni's backers might not have been happy with Quistgaard, either."

"I don't think a stake through the heart is the mob's typical style of execution." Jake grinned. "Now, if he'd been shot at the base of the skull, I'd be more inclined to think it was a hit."

"Good point," I conceded. "I wonder if the way he was murdered means anything."

"I could run it past a profiler I've worked with on some cases, but it will be a few days before I can contact her," Jake offered, then tapped another pink passage. "Here's something about Kiara Howard. Quistgaard claims she left her previous position at a country club in Kansas because she was having an affair with her married boss, and the board forced her to resign."

"Hmm." I flipped through the pages. "I don't

see anything here on Mrs. Zeigler or Zizi Todd, but there is a dig at Zizi's mother."

"Something about Winnie?" Jake leaned over my shoulder to see what I meant. "I don't remember anything about her. How did I miss it?"

"It doesn't mention her by name," I assured him, "but it's pretty obvious he's referring to her, since she's our town's most famous hippie." I read, " 'Which over-the-hill flower child still makes psychedelic trips courtesy of her very own home-grown weed?' " I shook my head in disgust. "If this is true, Winnie could get in real trouble. Chief Kincaid doesn't take marijuana growing lightly, not even for personal use."

"Quistgaard really was a slimeball." Jake pressed his lips into a thin line.

"Of the worst kind." It made me crazy thinking of all the lives the putrid poet might have destroyed with his malicious gossip.

"I see this stuff about Winnie was published only last week," Jake pointed out. "And the item about Kiara was about a month ago."

"The one on Ronni is recent, too." I flipped through the columns with March and April dates. "Look, I bet he's referring to Bryce Grantham here."

"The guy who found the cat for you last month?" Jake asked. "The animal helped you solve the murder that Boone was accused of, right?"

"Uh-huh." I gestured to the printed lines and read, " 'What new Shadow Bend resident is hiding in a closet filled with a skeleton that could cost him custody of his darling little daughter?' "

"But you said Boone won the case for Grantham," Jake reminded me. "His ex-wife had no proof that he was gay or that his life-style was a detriment to the child, so Quistgaard's attack was pointless."

"True." I nodded. Bryce's ex had waited until he'd moved to Shadow Bend before she brought the case to the local court. If she'd done it when he lived in Kansas City, he wouldn't have been so worried about the outcome, but the county court was not exactly a bastion of liberal thinking. "His wife could always try again."

"I suppose."

"You know . . ." An idea popped into my head and I blurted out, "It was almost as if Quistgaard was going after book-club members in particular."

"Maybe he felt the need to be in a superior position when he spoke to them," Jake suggested. "Sort of like picturing your audience naked."

"That could be it." I paused, recalling my brief conversation with the obnoxious man. After a second or two I said, "He did seem to enjoy being in control of others. Almost like he wanted to dominate every interaction."

"A gossip column would be a perfect vehicle for a bully like that." Jake checked the clock.

"Time to go talk to Yale and see if Quistgaard pushed him too far."

"Okay." I stood. "Let me make sure the back door is locked."

As I hurried into the storage room, I checked my cell and found a voice mail from Noah. I held the phone to my ear and played it.

"Dev, Mom's feeling sick again and I'm on the way to the hospital with her." Noah's voice was strained. "I'll call when I have a chance."

I sent a supportive text to Noah, made sure the store's exit was secure, and joined Jake out front.

As he and I strolled across the street to the square, I said, "Noah left me a message. His mother is back in the hospital. Apparently, she had another attack of some kind. She already had a bunch of tests yesterday. I wonder what's wrong with her."

"Hard to say." Jake switched the box supper and the blanket to his left hand and put his right arm around my waist. "Could be a lot of things."

"Poor Noah." I enjoyed the feel of Jake's palm through the thin silk of my top. "Nadine is tough to handle when she's healthy. She must be an awful patient."

"Yep." Jake spread our blanket out near the front of the bandstand among the other early arrivals. "Underwood has my sympathy."

"Look." I nudged Jake with my shoulder. "Over

there, by the pavilion. The guy bending over the instrument case is Yale."

"The guy that looks like a young John Elway?" Jake asked, squinting.

"Who?"

"You don't know who John Elway is?" Jake expression was horrified. "He's a famous quarterback. One of the best." Jake's tone was reverent. "And he's currently the executive vice president of operations for the Denver Broncos."

"Sorry." I shrugged. "I don't follow football." I didn't bother to mention that I wasn't fond of any sports. I had a feeling that wouldn't be a big shock to Jake, but why slap him in the face with my uninterest? Instead, I suggested, "Let's pretend to walk over to the drinking fountain and I'll say hi."

We strolled toward our objective, and when we drew abreast I did a fake double take and said in a bubbly voice, "Hi, Yale. What a surprise to see you here. I didn't know you played in a band."

"Hey, Dev." Yale blushed. "I just started. My buddy put together the group and invited me to join. I haven't really played since college."

"I bet it will be fun for you," I chirped. Yale's blond, clean-cut good looks were that of a typical Midwest farm boy and reminded me of a lot of the guys around Shadow Bend. Gesturing to Jake, I said, "Yale, do you know Jake Del Vecchio?" When he shook his head, I introduced the two men, then said to Yale, "I was sorry to hear that you and Darcie Ann split up. I remember all through high school thinking that you seemed like the perfect couple."

"I thought so, too, but she had other ideas." Yale finished assembling his clarinet and snapped the case closed. "She was tired of small-town life and wanted something more exciting." He paused, then added almost under his breath, "Or maybe *someone* more exciting."

"That's a shame," I commiserated. "And it's a disgrace that 'The Bend's Buzz' printed the whole mess. That was nobody's business but yours."

"Yep." Yale ducked his chin. "That was pretty damn embarrassing."

"I'll bet you could have killed whoever wrote that crap." Jake shoved his hands in his back pockets. "I know I would have wanted to if someone did that to me when I was going through my divorce."

"Hell, yes!" Yale narrowed his pale blue eyes, then grinned. "But it all worked out for the best. Everyone was real sympathetic about Darcie Ann doing me wrong like that with another guy, and now I'm seeing someone who's a lot sweeter and a lot less high maintenance." He twitched his shoulders. "So, in spite of everything, I guess the whole thing was exactly what God had planned."

"Sounds like it," I agreed, then asked, "Did you

hear that the guy who talked to your book club last Friday was killed that night?"

"Sure did." Yale glanced at the bandstand, where the other musicians were starting to assemble. "Right behind your store, right?"

"Uh-huh." I was running out of time. In a few more minutes, he'd need to join his group. "Well, it turns out *he* was the one who wrote 'The Bend's Buzz.' Did you know that?"

"No shit? He was the Buzzard?" Yale's expression was shocked. "How'd you find that out?"

"It came to light once he was dead," I hedged. "A few people overheard him and the *Banner*'s editor talking that night. I guess you weren't one of them, huh?"

"Nah." Yale still looked stunned. "I'm glad I didn't know, or I would have been tempted to punch his lights out. And then I would have been a suspect in his murder." He grimaced. "I did follow Quistgaard out into your store when he left the alcove, just to make sure he didn't cause any trouble there. And I saw him hitting on Kiara Howard—you know that pretty black gal in charge of all the country club's parties and stuff?"

"Right." I nodded encouragingly. "Did you have to intervene?"

"Uh-uh." Yale shook his head. "She didn't appear to need any help. Told him in no uncertain terms to back off or suffer the consequences."

"And did he?" Jake asked. "A lot of men seem

to believe that when a woman says no, she means 'Try again.' "

"Yeah. That appeared to be his way of thinking, all right," Yale answered. "Quistgaard put his hands on Kiara's waist and said something like, 'A high-spirited little filly like you just needs a touch of the riding crop to know who's in charge.' "

"Ew! What a butthead!" I felt my blood pressure shoot up. "What happened?"

"Kiara stomped on his foot with those high heels she always wears and said, 'You couldn't handle me if I came with an instruction booklet and a training video.' " Yale snickered. "Quistgaard hopped backward, howling like a wolf under a full moon. That's when I thought I'd have to step in, because he got a real mean look in his eye and lunged at her."

"And did you have to intercede?" How had I missed all this going on in my own store? In the future, I'd have to keep a better eye on what was happening when I had after-hours groups in the place. The new rule would be, No wandering away from the craft alcove except to use the bathroom.

"Kiara did some sort of fancy judo move on him." Yale smirked. "She got his arm twisted up behind his back and told him that if he ever tried any shit like that again, she'd make sure he was singing soprano for the rest of his miserable little life."

"Good for her." I'd have to give Kiara a high five when we talked to her.

"Hey, I gotta get over to the bandstand." Yale nodded at Jake, then patted my shoulder. "It's been nice talking to you."

After waving good-bye to Yale, Jake and I strolled back to where we'd left our belongings. We sat down on the blue-and-green-plaid blanket, and Jake opened up the white cardboard cartons containing our dinner. I poured merlot into two red plastic cups, then returned the bottle to my oversize purse.

As the first notes of "Moon River" floated toward us, I said, "That was certainly enlightening. Either Yale's a better liar than I would have ever given him credit for, or he's not our man."

"My money says he's telling the truth." Jake took a bite of his sandwich.

"Then I'd say Kiara Howard has moved up to the number one slot on our suspect list." I selected a particularly crispy-looking potato chip. "I wish I could recall if she was around the store when I was asking questions about the murder. I think I would have remembered her, since she's so stunning and is always dressed up."

"Even if she wasn't there, someone could have mentioned it to her." Jake balanced his box on his lap. "Maybe I should talk to her without you."

"Not on your life." I narrowed my eyes,

knowing exactly what Jake was suggesting. There was no way I was letting his protective instinct cover me in bubble wrap and tuck me somewhere safe.

"Just a thought," Jake said with an obvious effort to be patient. Then he drank some wine and added, "You know, divide and conquer."

I ignored his blatant attempt to steer me off course. "We should see if she's at the club now. It's only a little after seven, so we could talk to her and I could still make it home before ten."

"What happens at ten?" Jake asked as he took his cell phone from the holster on his belt and dialed. "Do you lose your glass slipper?"

"Any later and Gran will be in bed." I polished off my croissant. "And I like to check in with her before she goes to sleep."

"Ah." Jake held up a finger and said into the phone, "May I speak to Kiara Howard please?" He listened, then asked, "Is there any way I can reach her?" He listened again. "I understand. But she'll be there tomorrow after four? Fine. Yes. Thank you."

"I take it we're out of luck." I peeled the wax paper from a lemon tart.

"Yep. She has today off, and they wouldn't give me her personal phone number."

"That's frustrating." So much for immediate gratification. "I won't be free until nine tomorrow night."

"No problem. I'll pick you up then and we can head out to the country club. They said she'd be there until at least midnight." Jake reclined on his elbows. "For now, I guess we'll just have to enjoy the concert." He waggled his brows. "Unless you want to go somewhere more private and enjoy something else."

"Down, boy," I ordered. "One step at a time."

Chapter 20

Wednesday morning, Winnie Todd called to tell me that the Blood, Sweat, and Shears sewing circle wouldn't be getting together at the store that night. One of the club's members had won a radio contest and the prize was ten tickets to some big fabric show at the convention center in Kansas City. The whole group had decided to attend, then go out to dinner at a nearby restaurant.

I was a little disappointed, since I'd been hoping to talk to Winnie's daughter, Zizi, during the meeting. I was curious about the conversation that Xylia had mentioned overhearing between Zizi and Bryce after the book club. Now I'd have to track Zizi down to find out what had been said.

But when I realized that if the sewing circle was called off, I could close at six instead of nine, and the cancellation gave me more time to investigate, I decided it was a fair trade. Especially since Zizi wasn't someone who would be hard to find or reluctant to talk to me.

While texting Jake to inform him of the change of plans, I heard the sleigh bells above the entrance jingle. I hurriedly finished the message, stuffed the cell into my jeans pocket, and glanced toward the front of the store. Noah was standing just over the threshold, scanning the shop. When he spotted me at my worktable, behind the front counter, he waved and let the door close behind him.

I waved back, then pushed aside the Mother's Day breakfast-in-bed basket that I'd been assembling and stepped to the counter. As Noah trudged toward me, I saw that he looked awful. His usually perfectly styled hair was sticking straight up, as if he'd repeatedly run his fingers through it, and his face was china-doll pale with deep lines of fatigue etched into his forehead. Clearly, something serious had happened. Had his mother died?

Noah moved as if each of his feet weighed a hundred pounds. My chest tightened with worry when I noticed that his wool suit pants and Perry Ellis linen dress shirt had obviously been slept in, and that his tie had a huge red smudge marring the expensive blue silk. The last time I saw him looking this bad, his fiancée had just been murdered.

I hastily flipped open the hatch so he could join me. As I gave him a hug, the stale odor of hospital miasma that surrounded him nearly made me sneeze, and I wrinkled my nose to stop it.

When Noah staggered, I led him to a stool, gathered the gourmet jellies and syrups that had been occupying its seat into my arms, deposited them on the table, and pushed him down.

Once he was sitting, I said, "Are you okay?" The dazed expression in Noah's eyes worried me. "When's the last time you ate?"

"I'm fine." Noah shoved the hair off his forehead. "I think I had something last night in the hospital cafeteria. I know I went there and ordered some food, but Mom may have called me back to her room before I could actually eat much of it." He slumped against the Formica kitchen table I used as a workbench. "It's all a blur."

"Wait here." I patted his shoulder. "I'll be back in a flash."

Thank goodness the store was empty. I knew Noah wouldn't want anyone seeing him in this state. His reputation as the imperturbable, always-ready-for-duty town doctor would suffer. I just hoped no one popped in anytime soon to buy a spool of thread or an ice cream sundae or any other purchase he or she couldn't live without right that minute.

I hustled over to the soda fountain and poured two cups of coffee, then grabbed some of the pastries I'd purchased for the sewing circle, plopped them on a plate, and scooped up a stack of paper napkins. Too bad I didn't have anything nutritious to offer him, but I figured the sugar-and-caffeine rush would have to do.

As he devoured a cheese Danish, I finally got up the nerve to ask, "How's your mother?"

"Her doctors can't find anything wrong with her." Noah licked frosting from his fingers. "She's had every test for chest pain known to medical science, and a few that I suggested, which aren't usually associated with her complaints, and all the results are negative."

"That has to be frustrating." I sipped my coffee. "What were her symptoms?"

"Discomfort in her left arm, a heavy feeling in her chest, and she claimed she felt as if she could barely move." Noah cradled his mug. "Yesterday, she said every breath was an effort for her, and she was covered in perspiration."

"How awful." I was genuinely sorry to hear of Nadine's health issues. I didn't like the woman, but I hated to hear that she was ill. "So, do you or her doctors have any theory as to what's happening?"

"It could be stress or anxiety causing muscle spasms in her upper body." Noah finished off a cinnamon roll and picked up an apple turnover. "One of her doctors suggested it might even be gas."

"And how did your mom react to that?" I bit back a giggle. No way would Nadine ever admit to having flatulence or a need to burp.

"The poor guy is in the burn ward recovering from her blistering response," Noah joked, smiling for the first time since he'd arrived. "Personally, I think she might be having panic attacks, but since that would imply a mental-health issue and I value my life, I haven't brought up that possibility to her yet."

"Hmm." I raised a skeptical brow. It was difficult to picture Nadine in a state of panic. In a snit, yes; experiencing anxiety, no. "Is she on any medication that could be causing her symptoms? Maybe even something over the counter she hasn't told you about, or some food she's allergic to?"

"She says no." Noah wiped his mouth with a napkin. "And I checked her house. I even looked through her trash to see if she was having some kind of reaction to a substance she might have forgotten to mention."

"Wow." A part of me had wondered if Nadine had deliberately taken something to mimic the signs of a heart attack. She liked attention, and if she felt she was being ignored or neglected, she might decide that appearing ill would be just the thing to get Noah's notice. "Is she still in the hospital, or did they send her home again?"

"I dropped her at her house before coming here." Noah drained his coffee cup. "I hired a health aid to stay with her until we figure out what's happening, but I doubt the poor woman will last long."

"Why?" I gave in to temptation and broke off the corner of caramel twist.

"Mom was already finding fault with the aid before I left." Noah sighed, as if he were to-the-bone exhausted. "If Mom fires her, I don't know what I'll do."

"It sounds as if you have your hands full," I commiserated. "Would you like to hear what's been happening around here, or would you rather just have another cup of coffee in peace?"

"I'll take the coffee, but go ahead and fill me in." Noah's color had improved, and he was sitting straighter. "I want to stay in the loop."

After refilling both our mugs and putting the half-dozen remaining cookies from yesterday's groups on a plate, I brought Noah up to speed on the last few days in my life. When I finished, I said, "So, it really is a shame that you didn't spy on Riyad Oberkircher and see who his mysterious client was. If it's Quistgaard's killer, in all probability, he or she is also the person who put that threatening note on my car."

"Someone pushed you down the stairs?" Noah went back to what he apparently thought was the most important piece of information. "And you're still asking questions about the murder?"

"I'm fine." I leaned across the table and squeezed his arm. "Although the murderer obviously doesn't know it about me, you are well aware that bullying me is not going to make me stop doing anything. I refuse to be intimidated."

"I understand. But I'm worried about you." Noah put his hand over mine and searched my face, his expression thoughtful. "Here's what I'll do. I'm supposed to attend a fund-raiser tonight. I would blow it off, but since it's for one of Riyad's favorite charities—the no-kill animal shelter, Adopt, Don't Shop—I'll go and see if I can wheedle some information from him."

"That would be great." I was touched. I knew how much Noah must hate the thought of trying to trick someone into breaking his or her professional confidentiality. "I'd really appreciate it."

Noah brightened. "Why don't you go with me? It starts at seven thirty, but I know you have the sewing group here on Wednesday nights, so I could pick you up at nine. We could be fashionably late. Riyad will probably have more time as the event winds down than he'll have at the beginning, when he has to host."

I thought fast. Could I interview Kiara with Jake and still make it back to the store in time for Noah to pick me up? Reluctantly, I concluded that I couldn't. At least not without the danger of creating a scene between Noah and Jake. So I said, "Sorry. I already have plans for tonight."

"Sure." Noah nodded, a sad expression stealing into his gray eyes. "In that case, I can go early and try to catch Riyad before the party starts."

He paused. "Actually, maybe I should call him and suggest he meet me for a drink at the bar first."

"That's an excellent idea. And I think you'll have more luck with just the two of you." I beamed at Noah. "A nice, casual chat is perfect."

"You're probably right, but I miss being with you." Noah stood, stepped toward me, and drew me into his arms. "The only thing that's kept me going during the past twenty-four hours has been thinking about doing this." He dipped his head and pressed his lips to mine.

The slight stubble on his chin felt deliciously male against my skin, and when I sighed, he deepened the kiss. He tasted both sweet from the pastries and bitter from the coffee, but as his tongue licked into my mouth, I could no longer tell the difference.

Noah's hands slid under my sweatshirt and into the valley of my spine, and I forgot everything. Just as I was wondering if my workbench could hold our combined weight, the sleigh bells over the entrance rang and we jumped apart.

"I'd better get home and take a shower." Noah traced a finger down my check and winked. "A cold one."

I hugged him good-bye and felt a twinge of guilt when I saw how slowly he walked away. He should be resting tonight, not going to a party to interrogate a friend on my behalf. Resolving to make it up to him the minute we both had some free time, I asked the customer who had just entered the store if she needed any help. When the woman said she wanted to browse, I went back to work on the basket I'd been putting together. Mother's Day was coming fast, and I had several orders to fill.

The rest of the day was quiet, and I had already closed out the register, put the cash drawer in the safe, and phoned Birdie to check on her when I spotted Jake's pickup pulling into a parking spot out front. Grabbing my purse, I hurried out the door, locking it behind me, and hoisted myself into the F250 before he could finish unbuckling his seat belt.

"I guess you really missed me, darlin'." He quirked a brow suggestively. "Maybe we should go find some privacy."

"Maybe we should go to the country club, like we planned." I smacked his biceps. "What I'm anxious to do is talk to Kiara before her event starts, not check into a no-tell motel and jump your bones."

"You keep telling yourself that." Jake put the truck in reverse and backed onto the street. "But sometime real soon we are going to be alone, and then you'll see who the man for you is."

"Right." I forced sarcasm into my voice, but, in truth, I felt a flutter in my chest at his seductive tone. Unfortunately, I'd felt a similar tingle with

Noah earlier in the day. "For now, let's concentrate on finding out who killed Quistgaard."

"If you insist." Jake grinned. "But once we do, we're finding that motel."

"We'll see." I wasn't making any promises.

"Yes." Jake smirked at me. "We will."

I rolled my eyes and changed the subject, telling him about my father's scheduled release date and Birdie's plan for him to move into the rooms over the garage, concluding with, "So I'm a bit worried that Gran will overdo it getting that apartment ready." I didn't add that I was a little relieved that Gran had thought of the apartment for Dad. My gut told me that the three of us not living on top of one another would make his readjustment to home a whole lot smoother.

"Yeah, Uncle Tony's slowing down, too." Jake nodded sympathetically. "And I worry about him working so hard around the ranch."

"When I talked to Gran a few minutes ago, she sounded fine and said she was knocking off for the day." I tucked Jake's comment about his uncle away for later examination. Did it mean Jake was seriously considering taking over for Tony? "But a part of me thinks I should be home with her right now to make sure she's not taking on too much."

"That's a tough call, all right," Jake said, slowing the truck for a family of ducks waddling across the road and into a pond.

"She said she planned to have cereal for supper, since she didn't feel like fixing something just for herself." I chewed my thumbnail. "Which makes me feel guilty, because she'd cook something more substantial for herself if I was home."

"Why don't I call Tony and suggest that he drop by her house with a pizza?" Jake suggested. "I'm sure my uncle would be happy to have an excuse to spend more time with Birdie, and this way neither of them will be sitting around alone, staring at the TV."

"That would be great." I relaxed against the passenger seat. "We just had pizza the other day, but Gran's favorite is sausage with green peppers and onions, and since I hate that combo, she doesn't get to have it often."

The country-club parking lot was only half-full, so Jake found a spot close to the entrance. After shutting off the pickup's motor, he phoned his uncle, then turned to me and said, "It's all set. Birdie's favorite pizza will be delivered by Tony in an hour."

"Perfect." I kissed Jake's cheek after he helped me out of the truck. "Thank you." I took his hand as we walked up the sidewalk.

The country club catered mostly to people who commuted to jobs in Kansas City, so the clubhouse's ultramodern design was no surprise. The newcomers tended to go for contemporary over traditional styles. And they definitely were more attracted to the spectacular than the dignified.

Even I, who preferred vintage buildings with character, had to admire the angled entrance and mahogany double doors, as well as the overhead windows that appeared to hover unsupported over the steps. As we approached the door, I pointed out the impressive architecture to Jake, but he just grunted. Apparently, he wasn't into design as much as I was.

When Jake and I entered the foyer, a gorgeous woman wearing a stunning ice blue sheath looked up from the reception desk and asked, "May I help you?"

"We'd like to speak to Kiara Howard." I smoothed my silk top over my hips, glad I had fixed my hair, put on makeup, and changed from my Devereaux's Dime Store sweatshirt into something nicer. Perfect women like this one always made me a little self-conscious.

"She's busy right now." The receptionist glanced back at her computer, her straight black hair swinging in a satin curtain as she clicked her mouse and asked, "Do you have an appointment?"

"No, we don't." Jake held out his badge. "My name is Jake Del Vecchio. I promise I only need a few minutes of her time." He winked, then drawled, "And I'm sure she'll be happy to see me."

"I sure would be." The woman dimpled up at

him. "Let me check with her." She murmured into the phone, then pointed down a hallway. "Ms. Howard is in her office. Last door on your left."

"Thanks, darlin'." Jake touched the brim of his Stetson and took my elbow. He guided me along the corridor and into an open doorway.

The African-American woman was sitting behind a massive desk. She was dressed in a scrumptious butter yellow dress, holding her cell to one ear and the landline receiver to the other. She nodded in our direction as she concluded both calls; then, gesturing to two wingback chairs, she said, "Please have a seat."

"Hi, Kiara." I settled into the soft tufted leather and said, "I don't know if you remember me. Devereaux Sinclair. I own the dime store where your book club met last Friday night." When she nodded, I added, "And this is my friend, Jake Del Vecchio."

"Nice to meet you. Our receptionist was extremely impressed with your"—her gaze swept Jake from head to foot, and then she raised a brow and finished with—"credentials." It was clear that Kiara wasn't as captivated by Jake as her employee had been. "Is this an official visit regarding the recent murder in town?"

"No." Jake stretched out his long legs. "Just helping a friend."

"I see." Kiara glanced between Jake and me. "What can I do for you?"

245

"I understand that you objected to Mr. Quistgaard speaking at your club." I was counting on Kiara being too well mannered to refuse to answer my questions. After all, someone in the hospitality business couldn't afford to be impolite. "May I ask why you didn't want him there?"

"I'd picked up his book when the used bookstore over in Sparkville hosted a signing for him." Kiara tapped a gold-tipped nail on her desktop. "I found his poetry offensive."

"I see." So she was the member who already owned Quistgaard's book and didn't need to buy one from me. I hadn't remembered that.

"Many of his poems came close to suggesting that a woman should act as a man's slave. I was shocked that Mrs. Zeigler had invited a man like Lance Quistgaard to speak to us."

"From what she said, the sample of his work on his Web site was far different from what was in his book," I reminded her. Then I added, "She was surprised that despite your objection, you showed up for the meeting. Why did you?"

"I enjoy socializing with the other members." Kiara crossed her arms. "And I learned early in life not to back away from a challenge."

"Then I imagine it seriously ticked you off when he made a pass at you later that night," I commented, wanting to see her reaction. "Especially when Quistgaard wouldn't take no for an answer."

"Actually, that was the best part of the evening." Kiara's lips twitched. "It was gratifying to see him cowed and limping after I stomped on his foot with my stiletto and used a little jujitsu on him."

"I'll bet that was a sight worth seeing." I smiled at her, thinking of my own hankering to smack him. "Were you aware that Lance Quistgaard was the columnist who wrote 'The Bend's Buzz'?" I observed her reaction closely.

"No shit!" Kiara squealed, then quickly regained her cool, and *tsk*ed. "Why am I not surprised that a man who wrote such vile poetry also wrote that trash? Now that I know, everything makes perfect sense."

"So you saw the piece he wrote about you?" I asked, realizing that I was getting to the sensitive part of my questioning and that Kiara might end the interview. "The one that claimed you left your former position as an event coordinator because you were having an affair with your married boss. And that as a result of that behavior, the board of that country club forced you to resign."

"Yes, I saw that." Kiara raised a brow. "And I have my attorney looking into a lawsuit, since I can prove that allegation is an absolute lie." She narrowed her dark brown eyes. "And may I ask why you're so interested?"

"Well." I weighed my options and decided there was no harm in telling her the truth. "His body *was* found behind my store, which makes me feel violated."

"I can understand that." Kiara nodded. "But that doesn't seem enough of a reason to get tangled up in the investigation."

"On Monday I was pushed down a flight of stairs and received a threatening note." I smiled without amusement. "Apparently, Quistgaard's killer thinks I know something and is now after me."

For the first time since we'd arrived, Kiara smiled at Jake. "So, you're her bodyguard?"

"In a manner of speaking," he said. "Let's just say I'd be very unhappy if anything happened to Devereaux." His voice dropped to a menacing growl. "And I'd make sure that person was punished."

"Good for you. I wish more law enforcement officers felt that way." Kiara stood. "Now you'll have to excuse me. I have a fund-raiser starting in forty-five minutes, and I need to make sure everything's all set."

We rose to our feet, but before we left, I said, "One more question. Where were you Friday night between nine fifteen and ten?"

"Here." Kiara strode into the hallway. "I got a call as I was leaving the book-club meeting that a set of heirloom glasses for a bridal shower scheduled for Saturday afternoon was missing, so I drove directly here to sort things out." She gestured down the corridor. "Feel free to check with the receptionist on your way out."

As Jake and I walked toward the reception desk, I murmured to him, "That went well. I'm surprised she answered all my questions."

"People with nothing to hide are usually cooperative." Jake curled his lip. "It's the ones with secrets who make things difficult."

"Can you check out Kiara's alibi while I use the bathroom?" All the coffee I'd consumed throughout the day was catching up with me.

"Sure," Jake agreed.

In the foyer, Jake went right and I turned left. After taking care of business, washing my hands, and reapplying a coat of pale pink lip gloss, I found Jake waiting for me outside the restroom door. He put his arm around my waist and we headed back to the parking lot.

As we passed the clubhouse grill, I happened to glance inside. Sitting at the bar talking to Riyad Oberkircher was Noah. At that moment, he looked up and our eyes met. His gaze went to Jake and he scowled; then he lifted his martini glass in my direction and downed the contents.

Chapter 21

Noah felt as if he'd been punched in the gut. Intellectually, he'd accepted that Dev intended to go out with Del Vecchio, but witnessing her on said date was another matter. This open relationship, or whatever the hell you wanted to call it, was turning out to be a lot tougher than he'd imagined.

He was as exasperated with himself as he was with Dev. How did he manage to lose every damn bit of his famous self-discipline whenever he was around her? It was a miracle that he'd been able to regain his cool so quickly and raise his glass to Dev rather than leap off his stool, charge toward the couple, and smash his fist into Del Vecchio's smug face.

Then again—Noah gritted his teeth—maybe he should have followed his instincts and fought for his woman. Would that have helped win Dev's heart? Did she want a man who was willing to let out his inner beast? If that was what it took to win her, he was more than willing to beat the crap out of Deputy Dawg.

Nadine's constant demands since she'd begun to have these mysterious attacks were wearing Noah down, and now this ache at the thought of Dev in another guy's arms was almost too much to take.

He had to get Dev alone, someplace where he could hold her and kiss her and entice her into his bed. He was too old to be making out in a public place like her store or, worse, in his car. If he'd known he had a chance with Dev, he'd have bought an SUV or a minivan instead of the Jag. A vehicle with tinted windows and a roomy backseat.

Noah forced himself to put aside his plans for romancing Dev and concentrate on the matter at hand. Someone had threatened her, and he needed to find out who. Nothing was more important than keeping her safe.

Which was why he'd volunteered to attempt to trick Riyad into revealing the name of his client. As a rule, Noah wouldn't even consider trying to get anyone to break confidentiality; being a doctor, he knew that was a sacrosanct obligation. But at the thought of Dev in danger, all of his high moral standards vanished. In the end, there really was no contest. Saving Dev's life versus maintaining someone's ethics was a no-brainer.

Still, Noah had every intention of protecting Riyad as much as he could. The plan was to make the attorney let slip his client's name, or at least give a hint to his or her identity, without ever realizing he'd done so. How Noah would accomplish that was another matter.

Pasting an interested look on his face, Noah focused on what Riyad was saying. "So, you have to understand how important Adopt, Don't Shop is to the community. A no-kill animal shelter is vital to maintaining a vibrant animal population."

"Of course." Noah realized he'd have to make a donation to the charity to get Riyad's attention away from his cause. "Let me buy you another drink while I write the check." He caught the server's eye and pointed toward their glasses. "You deserve one for all your hard work."

"Terrific." Riyad downed the last of his second martini and put the empty glass on the bar.

"How did that emergency meeting that you mentioned the last time I saw you go?" Noah asked as he reached into his jacket pocket for his checkbook.

"Interesting, to say the least." Riyad slid closer the fresh drink that the bartender had put in front of him. "I can't recall ever being presented with a case like it before."

"Really?" Noah paused with his pen hovering over the amount line. "Was the guy justified in his big hurry? I mean, to make you come in so early?"

"Oh, yeah." Riyad took a gulp of his third martini. "She was right in needing to see me ASAP."

Score! Noah congratulated himself. Now he

knew that Riyad's client was female. "Were you right in thinking that the meeting was about the recent murder?"

"Well . . ." Riyad lowered his right eyelid. "I can't either confirm or deny, but let's say that I'm usually a really good guesser."

"Enough said." Noah wrote down a one and two zeros, then asked, "Theoretically, let's say that the meeting *was* about the murder. Why would that be so interesting? Haven't you handled murders before?"

"A few." Riyad tilted his head, then said with a sly grin, "Sometimes, theoretically speaking, of course, cases are about more than just a single issue."

"And the murder isn't the most important one?" Noah added another zero. "What could be more important than murder?"

"I didn't say *more important*." Riyad hiccupped. "Just more interesting and potentially more lucrative."

"I see." Noah signed the check and tore it free. "Did you take the case?"

"Couldn't turn it down." Riyad's expression grew martyred. "But I'm going to have to split my fee, because I need a co-counsel with experience in the laws concerning copyright and libel." The attorney's eyes widened and he covered his mouth with his hand. "Oops! I shouldn't have said that."

"Said what?" Noah deadpanned, handing over the completed check.

"Thanks." Riyad pocketed the light blue slip of paper, glanced at his watch, and rubbed a hand across the back of his head. "It's getting late. I'd better go splash my face with cold water, then make sure everything's set for the party." He stood and started toward the grill's exit, but stopped and turned back to Noah. "Hey, man. I was just bullshitting you about all that stuff."

"Of course. I didn't believe it for a second." Noah watched the slightly tipsy lawyer walk away.

Deciding to skip the fund-raiser and get some shut-eye, Noah headed home. As he drove, thoughts of Dev and Jake together battled with questions about why the murderer would need an attorney versed in copyright and libel law. Was she going to write a book about her crime?

Chapter 22

I felt awful. Having Noah see me with Jake was something I'd been trying to avoid. There he was in the bar, doing his best to help me out, while another guy was by my side. Although I'd been honest with both men, I didn't want to slap either of them in the face with the evidence of my affection for their rival.

At least Jake hadn't spotted Noah, or if he had, he didn't let on, which was some consolation. I had a feeling Jake wasn't a gracious winner, and I didn't want to have to smack him if he made a snide comment about Noah being date-less.

I was silent as Jake and I climbed back into his pickup, but once we were settled I asked, "Did Kiara's alibi check out?"

"Yep." Jake draped an arm over the back of the seat and turned so that he was facing me. "The Bambi at the desk told me some fancy antique wineglasses went missing Friday night and everyone was in a panic. They called Kiara a little before nine—she remembers the time because of some eBay auction she was bidding on—and Kiara got to the clubhouse about fifteen minutes later. Bambi said it took them until nearly midnight to locate the glasses."

"So another suspect bites the dust." I tapped my fingers on my knee. "Is her name really Bambi?"

"Nah. It's just a tag that the marshals use for a naive young woman whose IQ doesn't match her other . . . uh . . . assets." The tips of Jake's ears turned red, and he busied himself with fastening his seat belt.

"I see." It was obvious he wasn't telling me the whole story about that nickname, but I let the matter drop and said, "It's still early, so we can talk to at least one more person on our list, maybe two. Who should we tackle next: Bryce or Ronni?"

"Do you know where we can find them?" Jake started the motor.

"Bryce is most likely home, since he's a single father and it's a school night," I offered.

"Not necessarily. There's always the local teenage babysitter," Jake pointed out.

"True," I agreed. "Ronni doesn't have a lot of help at her B and B, so she's probably there. But no guarantees for either of them."

"Odds are the B-and-B woman will stay up later, so let's try the guy first," Jake decided. "We don't want to go to his place too late and wake up the kid." He backed out of the parking spot. "Where's he live?"

"Turn left on the main road," I directed, then guided him the rest of the way.

The subdivision where Bryce lived was new by Shadow Bend standards—only fourteen years old. It was built on what had been a forty-five-acre apple orchard a couple of miles outside of town.

When the grove's original owner died, a Kansas City developer persuaded the city council to rezone the tract from agricultural to residential, and then proceeded to outbid any local farmers who were interested in the acreage. Now instead of rows of trees laden with Red Delicious and Jonathan apples, there were 250 houses. I wondered if anyone but me missed the fresh local fruit.

I led Jake to Maplewood Court and had him pull up to the curb. Lights glowed from the windows of the modest two-story house.

We walked up the driveway and I rang the bell, then said, "Let me do the talking."

Before Jake could answer, the door swung open and Bryce said, "Hi, Dev. What's up? Hope you didn't lose Tsar again. Boone would be devastated. He treats that cat better than a lot of people treat their kids."

"Not this time, thank goodness." I studied the thirtysomething-year-old man wearing sharply creased designer jeans, a crisply pressed blue-and-white button-down shirt, and moccasins, then said, "But if you have a minute, we'd like to talk to you about the book club."

"Sure." Bryce glanced curiously at Jake, but stepped back and gestured us both inside. "My daughter's watching a *My Little Pony* DVD, so we have about twenty minutes before I need to put her to bed."

"Great." I introduced the men to each other, and after they exchanged handshakes, Bryce led us into the kitchen. "We won't keep you long. I appreciate your taking the time for us."

"I'm baking cupcakes for my daughter's preschool class." Bryce indicated a couple of stools at the counter. "Sit down and we can talk while I decorate them. Multicolor sprinkles are big this year."

"Thanks." I took a seat. "I understand you were discussing Mr. Quistgaard's book with Zizi Todd while the two of you helped clean up after the meeting." He nodded, and I added, "You two disagreed about the poetry?"

"I just said that Quistgaard's take on small towns wasn't that far off." Bryce took a bowl of icing from the mixing stand and set it in front of him on the counter. "I agreed with Zizi that his portrayal of women was highly offensive." He grabbed a bottle of red food coloring from the cabinet to his right, unscrewed the lid, and squeezed a few drops into the buttercream frosting, then said, "But I was shocked the next morning when I heard he'd been killed." Bryce beat the icing until it turned pink. "The murder was *the* topic of conversation at my daughter's gymnastics class." He paused and looked at me. "Why do you ask?"

"I've been pulled into the investigation," I said, then explained my fall down the stairs and the nasty note, concluding with, "And although I have no idea what the murderer thinks I should keep quiet about, now I have a good motive to want him or her caught."

"I guess you do at that." Bryce raised a brow. "How can I help?" Before I could answer, he picked up a long serrated knife and asked, "Or do you think I'm the killer?"

"Are you?" Jake's tone was light, but his eyes had changed from sapphire to steel blue and his hand inched toward the gun I knew he had strapped to his ankle.

"Whoa there, cowboy." Bryce raised his hands in mock surrender, then lowered them and used the knife to slice a cupcake into two layers. "I had no reason to want that guy dead."

"Where were you between nine fifteen and ten last Friday night, and can you prove it?" Jake asked, his posture relaxing slightly once Bryce laid the knife on the counter.

"My babysitter can testify that I got home at quarter after nine." Bryce swirled frosting on the bottom and top halves of the cupcake before putting the two pieces together. "I walked her out to her car a few minutes later, and after she drove off, the guy next door came over to talk to me about the next neighborhood association meeting. He and I are running for the board, and he wanted to plan our strategy. He stayed for at least an hour or so."

"Thanks for telling us, Bryce." I shot Jake a look that asked "What part of *let me do the talking* don't you understand?" and said, "Of course I didn't think you were the murderer, but I was wondering if you'd heard any rumblings about Quistgaard from the other book-club members. Maybe someone who didn't speak up during the discussion but seemed upset, or who talked about it later?"

"You may not suspect me, but your friend does." Bryce jerked a thumb toward Jake. "So feel free to check with the babysitter and my neighbor." He wiped off his hands and jotted something on a notebook lying by the phone. "Here are their names and numbers." He handed the slip of paper to Jake and turned back to me. "I left right after Zizi and I put away the chairs, and I haven't talked to anyone since, so, sorry, nothing on that front."

"Shoot!" I slumped on the stool. "I was hoping you'd overheard something."

"Nope." Bryce resumed constructing cupcakes. "The only one I really chatted with after the meeting was Zizi." He stopped in midsprinkle. "But now that I think of it, she did say something odd."

"Oh?" I leaned forward, both because I was interested and because the cupcakes smelled amazing. I really hoped I wasn't drooling or that neither man could hear my stomach growling.

"Yeah." Bryce wrinkled his brow. "What was it? Something like Quistgaard's misogyny was evident in all of his writings, not just his poems."

"Well . . ." I started, then paused, deciding not to confront Bryce with the news that Quistgaard was the gossip columnist who had written the vicious piece about him. If he had an alibi and wasn't the killer, why bring up something that would make him feel bad? Instead, I asked, "Did she say what other writing she meant?"

"I think she mentioned that it was a book, but not one of poetry." Bryce twitched his shoulders. "But I could be wrong. I wasn't listening all that closely." His expression was sheepish. "Zizi lectures more than she talks, so I'd sort of tuned out by then."

We'd spent eighteen of our allotted twenty minutes, and I couldn't think of any other questions to ask Bryce, so I glanced at Jake to see if he had anything to add. He shook his head, and I thanked Bryce, then said good-bye. I regretfully declined his offer of a cupcake, having already had enough sugar during the day to fuel a roomful of hyperactive six-year-olds for a twenty-four-hour dance marathon.

Once we had returned to the pickup, Jake phoned the neighbor and the babysitter. Both of them confirmed that Bryce was where he'd claimed to be during the time of the murder. Surprisingly, neither seemed curious as to why we were asking. Maybe it was Jake's official-sounding voice or maybe they just didn't care. Either way, Bryce's alibi was confirmed.

As Jake clicked off his cell, he said, "Why don't we stop by the Dairy Queen for a hamburger before we go over to the B and B?"

"Well, if you're hungry." I pretended indifference, since it seemed that every time I was around Jake, I was starving or stuffing my face. "It isn't even eight yet, so we could spare a half hour."

"I wouldn't mind a bite." Jake cocked his head at me. "And I wouldn't want your friend Ronni to have to shout over your rumbling belly."

"You are so not funny." I smacked his shoulder. "I don't think a second career as a stand-up comedian is in your future." As soon as the words left my mouth, I wondered if Jake had a second career as a rancher in his future, but I didn't ask.

Shadow Bend boasted not just any Dairy Queen, but a Grill and Chill, which meant it served food as well as ice cream. DQ always did a brisk business, but this late on a Wednesday night, I didn't expect it to be crowded.

The nearly empty parking lot proved me right, and in less than ten minutes, we were able to order, get our supper, and settle into a back booth. We spent the next few minutes passing out cardboard containers, squeezing ketchup into the lids, and unwrapping straws.

Once we had taken care of the important stuff, I said, "So, I guess that's another suspect off our list. I'm beginning to think we'll never know who killed Quistgaard or why."

"Unsolved cases do happen," Jake said, picking up his chili cheese hot dog, "but I'm not ready to give up yet. We still have two book-club members to talk to, and I'll stop by the PD tomorrow to see what they've discovered." He winked at me. "Even if the chief isn't willing to bring me up to speed, that dispatcher will be."

"Yes." I swirled a fry through a pool of ketchup. "I'm sure she will." I paused to savor the salty goodness, then commented, "We haven't really taken into consideration the unique way Quistgaard was murdered. Too bad your profiler friend isn't available right away."

"You think the killer might be a vampire hunter?" Jake chuckled. Then, still smiling, he took a swallow of his chocolate shake.

"Right." I snickered. "Maybe we should be looking for Buffy."

"Huh?" Jake's expression was one of pure bewilderment. "Who's Buffy?"

After I explained about the iconic television show, I said, "It still has quite a cult following. Maybe someone got carried away playing the video game and thinks he or she really is the chosen one tasked with slaying all the demonic creatures roaming Shadow Bend."

"Okay." Jake added several syllables to the word, making clear what he thought of my theory.

"Or maybe we should stick to investigating the people we know Quistgaard ticked off." I picked up my Iron Grilled Supreme BLT, tucking stray tomatoes, lettuce, and crisp hickory-smoked bacon into the panini-style bread. "Let's finish eating and go talk to Ronni."

"No need to rush and get indigestion." Jake threw an arm across the back of the booth. "I doubt she goes to bed this early."

I had to agree, especially since I recalled that Ronni had mentioned having insomnia. While Jake and I finished our dinner, the conversation turned to my grandmother, his uncle, and my father's imminent return. When Jake asked if my dad would help me run the store, my throat tightened. I hadn't thought about that. I knew Dad might have problems finding a job at his age and with a criminal record, but the notion of him as my business partner hadn't occurred to me. And I wasn't at all sure how I felt about the idea.

Not wanting to think about my father's work prospects, I asked Jake about his parents. He'd said earlier in our relationship that he didn't like talking about them, but if we were going to have any chance as a couple, I wanted to know why he wasn't close to his folks and what emotional baggage he was carrying around regarding them.

As usual when I brought up the subject, Jake hemmed and hawed without really saying anything about them. Bored, I stared at the gaggle of teenagers who had crowded into the booth across the aisle from us. I couldn't see the cover of the book the girls were passing among themselves, but their giggles and whispers made me curious.

I concentrated as one of the girls read from the novel, " 'He snaps one handcuff over my wrist and the other to the bedpost, and a shiver of fear and something else shoots from my chest down my stomach, and then lower.' "

I frowned. What in the world were they reading? I missed the next girl's recitation, but when a petite blonde grabbed the trade paperback from her friend, I heard her say, " 'He forces me to do things I'd never done with or in front of a man. It feels wonderful to give up all control and know my rightful place as his submissive.' "

I frowned. Something about those words, besides the obvious, made me pause. A glimmer of recognition teased my subconscious, and I tried to lure it to the surface.

Just as I was about to capture the niggling

thought, Jake said, "Are you ready to leave?"

"Sure." I dumped my trash on the red plastic tray and slid out of the booth. "Let's go find out what Ronni knows about our victim."

As I followed Jake toward the exit, I passed by the teenagers' table and discreetly peered at the book they had laid aside in order to dig into their Blizzards. The front showed the back of a naked female torso with bound hands. I squinted at the title. *Ten Colors of Blonde* was scrawled in a bright yellow curlicue font.

So that's what the runaway bestseller everyone was talking about looked like. Although I had ordered a copy for Mrs. Zeigler's basket, it hadn't arrived yet.

Still, that twinge in the back of my mind insisted, Mrs. Z's basket wasn't why what I had just heard was important. There was something else. Something much more significant. I just couldn't figure out what.

Chapter 23

After giving Jake directions to the Ksiazak B & B, I asked myself what a titillating bestseller could possibly have to do with a murder. I was still drawing a blank when Jake parked in the guesthouse's driveway. As we walked toward the entrance, I deliberately set the conundrum aside. Maybe if I didn't think about it, my subconscious would supply the answer.

The B & B was a huge Italianate-style house—a Victorian design that had been popular in the mid-1800s—and I paused to admire it. I'd been there only once before, and I was reminded of how much I loved the cupola in the center of the nearly flat roof, not to mention the ornamental brackets and wraparound porch that suggested a Renaissance villa. For Shadow Bend, the place was delightfully exotic, reminding me; of a mansion that might grace the cover of a gothic novel by Phyllis A. Whitney or Victoria Holt or Mary Stewart.

"All the lights are out." Jake gestured toward the wall of darkened windows facing the street. "Maybe your friend isn't home."

"Terrific." My shoulders sagged. The only other

person on our list to talk to was Zizi Todd, and she was with her sewing group in the city. "Then we might as well head home, because we're out of suspects."

"You'll never be an ace PI if you give up that easy." Jake's lopsided grin did funny things to my insides. "Let's try around back." He put his hand on my waist and steered me toward the rear of the building. "Her living quarters might be in the rear."

"I think you're right." I brightened when we rounded the corner and I saw a golden glow. "That must be the kitchen." I pointed to a set of tall, narrow windows where I could see someone's shadow moving to and fro.

As we approached a small porch with its gabled overhang, raised voices blasted from the partly open back door. At first, I thought it was a television show, but then I heard a male voice say, "Ronni, Ronni, Ronni. Did you really think it was going to be that easy? That I'd just give up?"

I glanced at Jake. He held a finger to his lips and inclined his head, indicating we should listen rather than interrupt.

Ronni's usually laid-back alto sounded heated. "I'm not taking this lying down."

What was going on in there? Before I could decide, there was a loud clatter that might have been a chair overturning, crashing that sounded like breaking dishes, and a string of curses. *Oh, my God!* I started forward, but Jake seized my arm and pulled me back.

The people inside were now silent, and I hissed at Jake, "Let me go. Ronni might be hurt." I tried to move, but he held firm.

He murmured into my ear, "Hold your horses."

"What are we waiting for?" I glared at him, then peered anxiously into the darkness. "That guy yelling at her could be the mafioso that Quistgaard claimed financed the B and B."

Jake opened his mouth to reply, but closed it when we both heard Ronni holler, "Now see what you've done, asshat!" I relaxed. At least she was still alive, albeit in a really bad mood.

I couldn't make out the next few exchanges, but with an obnoxious jeer, the male voice said, "Just pay up and stop your bellyaching. You knew what you were getting into when we started."

"No!" Ronni screamed. "I'd rather die than give you more money."

"That can be arranged."

Jerking my arm from Jake's grasp, I ran for the door, yanked it open, and burst inside. Jake was right behind me, and when I skidded to a stop he slammed into my back, nearly knocking me over.

He grabbed me by the shoulders to steady me; then we both stood frozen and stared at Ronni. She was sitting at an old wooden kitchen table playing Monopoly with a young man who appeared to be in his late teens. The guy was clutching a fistful of brightly colored fake bills in each hand. But the triumphant grin on his face quickly changed to a look of surprise, and he gaped at us as if we'd been transported into the room from the starship *Enterprise*.

Ronni's head swiveled from me to Jake, then back to me. She blinked her blue-gray eyes several times, then finally said, "Is something wrong, Dev?"

"Uh . . . we . . ." I stammered. "I mean, I guess you're okay, huh?"

"Except for him acting like a butthead, yes." She pointed to her opponent. "He was so freaking excited when I landed on Boardwalk with his hotel on it, he jumped up and knocked over his chair, breaking two of my best china plates in the process. Not exactly the picture of good sportsmanship." Ronni ran her fingers through her chocolate brown waves, then seemed to remember our melodramatic arrival and asked, "What did you think was happening?"

I explained that it sounded as if she was about to be murdered. I left out the part where I thought her assassin was a Mafia hit man. By the time I finished my account and introduced Jake, Ronni was laughing so hard, it took her a while to shake his hand.

Finally, she got herself under control and said, "Mr. Destruction here is Cody Gomez. He does odd jobs for me when he isn't at college. And in his spare time, since neither of us has a social life, he comes over and beats the pants off me at board games."

Cody still seemed stunned by our presence, so I asked, "Do you go to the community college near Sparkville?" When he nodded, I said, "My clerk Xylia Locke goes there, too. Do you know her?"

He nodded again, but didn't speak. Apparently, the sight of Jake and me exploding into the kitchen had struck him mute, so I gave up attemptng to carry on a conversation with him. Instead, I turned to Ronni and asked, "Could we talk to you for a few minutes?" I glanced at Cody. "Alone."

"Sure." She gestured to the two empty chairs at the table. "Have a seat. Cody, could you go and look at that parlor door that's sticking?"

He nodded for a third time, got up, and loped away. He seemed like a nervous kid. I hoped we hadn't scarred him for life.

"Can I get you something to drink or maybe a snack?" Ronni offered.

"No, thanks. We just ate." Once we were settled, I decided to plunge right in. "You've heard that the writer who spoke to your book club was murdered and his body was found behind my store, right?"

"Of course." Ronni gathered up tiny green houses and red hotels, putting them into a Ziploc bag. "It's all over town. Everywhere I go, someone is talking about it. Actually, I was surprised it wasn't in 'The Bend's Buzz' today, but the column was missing from this week's paper."

"That's because the guy who wrote it is deceased," Jake drawled.

"Lance Quistgaard was Anonymous?" Ronni yelped. "That supercilious snob wrote that trash? What an SOB! Now I'm glad he's dead."

"I take it you had no idea?" I squirmed, trying to get comfortable on the hard wooden seat. You would think with all the extra padding on my butt it wouldn't be a problem, but it was. "Evidently, Friday night, just before he left the store, a few people from the book club overheard him and the newspaper editor get into a shouting match about his behavior during the meeting, and Quistgaard's secret identity as the Bend's Buzzard was revealed."

"Well, hell." Ronni scowled. "How did I miss that?" She started to say something, then stopped and glared at me. "That's why you thought I was in trouble just now. You read that crap about me getting my financing for the B and B from a shady character. You thought I was about to get rubbed out by the Mob."

As Ronni dissolved into another gale of laughter, I tried to deny her accusation, but eventually admitted that the thought had crossed my mind.

She finally stopped cackling and said, "You

know how that rumor got started?" I shook my head, and she explained, "I was flirting with the cute guy who owns the bakery, and I said that borrowing money from my family for my business was worse than getting it from the Godfather himself, because the emotional interest was so high. Someone must have been eaves-dropping."

"Big surprise." I snickered. "The other day I saw an ad for a T-shirt that read: IF YOU DIDN'T SEE IT WITH YOUR OWN EYES OR HEAR IT WITH YOUR OWN EARS, DON'T INVENT IT WITH YOUR SMALL MIND AND SHARE IT WITH YOUR BIG MOUTH. Everyone in town should be forced to own one of those."

"Definitely." Ronni nodded vigorously. "Especially since whoever overheard me got the story all wrong."

"From what we've been told," Jake said, "Quistgaard seemed to get a lot of the facts wrong."

I explained to Ronni that Jake and I had been trying to help the police figure out who killed the poet by talking to book club members, then told her why I was interested in solving the case.

"Yikes!" Ronni squealed. "Getting shoved down the stairs is bad enough, but then to have that note stuck on your car is really scary." She shivered. "I'm glad I came right back here after the meeting. I wouldn't want the killer to think I saw anything."

"Definitely not." How had I forgotten that Ronni was one of the first to leave? Now I remembered. She'd gulped down a single glass of wine, then apologized for not being able to stay and help clean up, saying she had to be at the bed-and-breakfast to check in a guest who was arriving at nine. I remembered looking at my watch. It had been about eight fifty when she left the craft alcove. "Did you make it to the B and B in time?"

"Barely." Ronni folded the game board. "She pulled into the driveway right behind me."

"Did you hear or see anything odd on your way out the dime-store door?" Jake asked.

"Let me think." Ronni tapped her chin. "When I walked through the shop, Zizi Todd was having some sort of serious conversation by the cash register with someone I couldn't see." Ronni wrinkled her brow. "It looked to me like Zizi was in counseling mode, so I just waved and kept going."

I chatted with Ronni while Jake checked Ronni's alibi with her guest, who, luckily, was still staying at the B & B. Once Ronni's story was confirmed and it was clear she didn't know anything more, we said good-bye. It was now after nine, and I was feeling more and more guilty about neglecting Gran, so I decided to call it a night and asked Jake to take me back to my car.

As we drove the short distance to my store, I

said, "There sure seems to have been a lot going on the night of the book club, but none of it adds up. However, Zizi Todd appears to be in the thick of it. I sure wish I'd gotten to talk to her tonight."

"Yeah." Jake parked next to my BMW. "One thing I learned in my years as a marshal is that witnesses are never around when you need them."

"I hope I can track her down tomorrow." I unbuckled my seat belt and picked up my purse. "The store closes at twelve on Thursday and I should spend the afternoon making baskets, but—"

"I can't get away from the ranch until late afternoon," Jake interrupted. "So you can use the time to fill orders until I come into town."

"I really don't think Zizi is the killer, and I'm certain she would be more apt to confide in me if you aren't with me." Seeing his frown, I added, "But I'll make sure she and I aren't alone."

"I still don't like you seeing her without me." He flipped up the center console.

As I scooted toward the door, I said, "That's too bad." Jake's sapphire eyes were smoldering and I could feel the sparks between us, but this wasn't the place to do anything about them. After the past few times, I'd vowed that there would be no more make-out sessions in any vehicles. "The community college had its finals last week."

"And that's important why?" Jake slid toward me. The intent expression on his face made him look almost predatory, and an excited ping zipped from my chest southward.

"Because"—why did my voice sound so breathy?—"maybe I can get Xylia to come in all day Friday instead of just the afternoon, which would give me more time to work on the basket orders."

"Ah." Jake moved closer to me. "I see you have it all figured out."

"No need to follow me home." I opened the door and jumped from the truck just as he reached for me. "Gran and Tony have been there all night, so there won't be any boogeyman hiding under my bed."

"I'd prefer to make sure." Jake quickly followed me out of the pickup and backed me up against the side of my car. "I'll just watch until you get inside."

"No need." I edged away from him. "I can take care of myself."

"I'm sure you can under normal circumstances." Jake's expression was determined.

When I silently shook my head no, he sighed in exasperation, and then, with a take-no-prisoners smile, he said, "Don't I at least get a good-night kiss?"

I went up on my tiptoes, brushed my lips against his cheek, then slipped hastily into my car.

Revving the motor, I waved and sped down the alley. Glancing into my rearview mirror, I saw that Jake was still standing where I'd left him. I felt a momentary regret, but knew I'd done the right thing in making a quick getaway.

Jake was like the night—dark, seductive, and very possibly dangerous. Dating him and Noah was one thing. Sleeping with either of them until I figured out which one I really loved would be a disaster. So for now, it was best to keep both of them out of my bed.

On my way home, I thought about the past couple of days. I'd been snooping pretty openly and hadn't received any more warnings. The murderer either wasn't aware of my actions or I was so far off the right track, he or she no longer considered me a threat.

Or the killer is waiting to catch me alone. I shivered. Maybe I should have let Jake follow me home. I wasn't sure why I had been so against the idea. Was it because I was used to being on my own and not entirely comfortable needing someone else?

Maybe it was that the only person I felt that I could or should depend on was myself. After all, in the past, anytime I'd depended on someone else I'd been disappointed. Which didn't bode well for a relationship with either Jake or Noah. If I ever really wanted to find my happily-ever-after, I needed to learn how to trust.

Chapter 24

At six a.m. Thursday morning, the strains of Iron Maiden's "Doctor, Doctor" startled me from a deep sleep. When I answered my cell, Noah apologized for the early hour.

I mumbled, "No problem." As I came more fully awake, I asked, "Is something wrong?"

"Mom fired her caregiver, then called me claiming to have chest pains again." Noah sighed. "I'm currently following the ambulance that's taking her to the hospital."

"That's awful," I commiserated. "Do you think she's okay?"

"I think she's fine." Noah sighed again. "But I wasn't willing to take a chance that she wasn't bluffing."

"Hmm." What could I say to that? My bet was that Nadine was crying wolf in order to keep her son's attention focused on her, but I could see Noah's point. How could he ignore the symptoms she claimed to have?

"Anyway, once I get to the hospital I'll have to turn off my cell, and since I've got my Bluetooth, I thought I'd fill you in on my conversation with Riyad."

"Last night when you saw me at the country club with Jake, we had just finished questioning Kiara." Although Noah hadn't brought up spotting me with his rival I felt I had to say something about it. "She was another dead end, so I really appreciate you talking to Riyad."

Noah didn't comment on my explanation. Instead he said, "I didn't get a name, but Riyad did let slip that his client is female. That probably isn't much help, but he did say that she needs both a criminal and a literary attorney—something about copyright and libel. That might be a clue."

"Hmm." I'd have to think about what that might mean.

Before I could come up with anything, Noah, said, "I've got to go. I'll call you when I get back to town."

After thanking him for both the call and the information, I wished him luck with his mother, said good-bye, and closed my eyes. A few minutes later, just as I was dozing off, Bobby Fuller's "I Fought the Law" yanked me from Slumber Land again. This time it was Jake.

"I stopped at the PD after you left last night, and although none of the cops were around, I had a long talk with the dispatcher."

"And what did Nympho Barbie have to say?"

"You sound jealous, darlin'." Jake chuckled.

I rolled my eyes but bit my tongue and kept quiet.

"Barbie, as you call her, reported that the murder investigation is stalled. The cops have talked to everyone who was at the book-club meeting, and anyone else who knew the vic, and now they're going through his personal papers."

"Great." I blew a strand of hair out of my eyes. "So no one is making any progress in finding the killer."

"Barbie also said that it'll take some time to look at all the stuff at Quistgaard's place, since they found an entire room full of documents."

"What kind of documents?" I yawned. Surely Quistgaard hadn't written a note naming the person who was most likely to kill him.

"The dispatcher said it looked as if the vic had printed out and saved every version of every manuscript he ever wrote, dating back to when he was in high school. And the dude must have been damn prolific, since the police checked over a hundred boxes into evidence." Jake's tone was incredulous. "You'd think he'd just burn a computer disk or put it all on a thumb drive."

"Terrific." I groaned. "Any more good news?"

"It appears that someone beat the police to the search, because they found the house ransacked when they arrived, and from empty spots in the dust on the floor, it looked as if at least a couple boxes might be missing." Disgust dripped from Jake's voice. "The LEOs should have secured that location as soon as they identified the body."

"Probably," I agreed. "But since Quistgaard's keys and wallet were missing, the killer most likely went to his house right after the murder."

"Yeah." Jake paused, then said, "Give me a call after you talk to Zizi."

"Okay." I pulled up the covers. "Bye."

Minutes ticked past, and I finally admitted that I wasn't able to go back to sleep. Deciding to make a virtue out of my wakefulness, I got dressed, grabbed a honey-nut cereal bar, and drove into town. With the killer still at large, it was a little scary being at the store by myself, but I made sure both doors were locked, and by seven a.m., I was working on Mrs. Zeigler's anniversary basket. Even though the gift wasn't due for another two weeks, and I was waiting for the delivery of the book that would go in the starring position, I wanted her order to be otherwise ready to go.

Once her basket was done, I turned my attention to the Mother's Day orders. I needed to finish those right away, because they'd be picked up within the next couple of days. We didn't currently deliver, but I'd been getting a lot of requests and was looking into the possibility of providing that service.

At nine, I unlocked the entrance and flipped on the neon OPEN sign. A few minutes later, as I boxed up a dozen strawberry-and-cream truffles for Cyndi Borrows, a member of the Blood, Sweat, and Shears sewing circle, I asked her how the field trip to the fabric show had gone.

"It was a lot of fun." Cyndi took the gold foil carton from me. "I loved getting a peek at the gorgeous new prints and colors."

"I missed seeing you all last night." I moved to the register to ring up her purchase. "Did everyone enjoy themselves?"

"I think so." Cyndi handed me a fifty-dollar bill. "Well, everyone except Zizi. Something was bothering her. Maybe she didn't do well on her finals. She said she took her last one yesterday morning."

"So she's done for the semester?" I counted out Cyndi's change.

"Uh-huh." Cyndi stuffed the money into her purse and headed for the door. "Last night, she said she wasn't getting out of bed for at least a week."

It was a good thing there weren't many customers the rest of the morning. If I'd been busy, heaven only knows what mistakes I'd have made, since I couldn't concentrate. Instead of making baskets or putting out new inventory or even paying bills, all I could do was continually check my watch and think about the murder.

Not wanting to disturb Zizi's rest, I forced myself to wait until eleven-thirty to call her. It was a relief when she answered on the first ring. Although Zizi's tone was curious, and we weren't exactly let's-have-lunch-together kind of friends, she agreed to meet me at Little's Tea Room in forty-five minutes.

At noon, I closed up the shop, texted Xylia to see if she'd be able to come in at ten instead of three the next day, then freshened up. After I combed my hair and put on some lip gloss, I strolled over to the café. It was a beautiful spring day and the short walk helped me focus on what I needed to accomplish during the meal.

The tearoom was in the first floor of a Queen Anne–style house, and I waited for Zizi's arrival in the foyer. Most of the furnishings were original Eastlake-style tables, chairs, and sideboards, and I gingerly sat on a walnut-and-brocade settee. While I loved vintage anything, in the Victorian era people's shapes were generally not as curvy as mine, so I was always a little afraid that I'd break the antique furniture.

Once I was convinced the divan could hold my weight without imminent collapse, I twisted around to admire the floral carvings on the back, then bent to examine the detailed border carved across the bottom. I was running my finger over the tufted upholstery when Zizi came through the brightly painted front door.

I glanced past her and saw that her dented old muscle car with its duct-taped front grille and its spiderweb crack on the windshield was parked in front of the café. Between the primer and the rust, it was hard to determine the vehicle's original paint job, but my guess was cherry red.

Zizi was in her early twenties and had carrot-colored hair, milk-white skin, and an abundance of freckles. Today she sported twin braids and was a dead ringer for the girl on the Wendy's fast-food sign.

Just as Cyndi had mentioned, I immediately noticed that Zizi's usual happy glow was missing. After exchanging hugs and hellos, we moved into the tearoom, where I requested a table in the back. If I wanted Zizi to confide in me, I needed privacy.

Once we were settled and had ordered the special—a pot of tea, a selection of finger sandwiches, cheeses, fruit salad, and tiny cookies—I said, "Thanks for meeting me for lunch, especially on your first day off school. I hope I didn't wake you when I called."

"I wish." Zizi rub her eyes. "I haven't been sleeping well since the murder."

"Are you afraid?" I asked, then frowned, realizing it was strange that no one had mentioned any fear about having a murderer in their midst.

"No, not exactly." Zizi picked up the teapot, poured us each a cup, then added sugar to hers. "Actually, I was happy you reached out to me. I've heard you've been asking around about that night."

"As a matter of fact, I have." Although I was

getting tired of explaining my interest in the case, I repeated what I'd been telling everyone else about my motive for questioning people. As usual, I ended with, "So you see why I want the murderer caught sooner rather than later."

"Oh. My. God!" Zizi yelped when I finished. "Now I really feel guilty."

"Why's that?" I was fairly sure Zizi hadn't just confessed, but I was still glad we were in a public place. Jake would never let me forget it if she tried to kill me after I'd insisted on meeting her without him.

"I know something about Lance Quistgaard that I didn't tell the police." Zizi's sky blue eyes reflected her indecision. "I didn't think it was important, and it put me in a bit of a compromising position, so I didn't bring it up when they questioned me."

"But now you're reconsidering." I wanted to shake her until she told me what she knew, but lucky for her, the server brought our lunch and I regained control of myself.

"Uh-huh." Zizi picked up a miniature cucumber sandwich and popped it into her mouth. When she finally finished chewing and swallowing, she said, "I know you don't participate in Shadow Bend's community sport." When I looked puzzled, she explained, "I mean, I know you don't gossip, so if I tell you, you'll keep your mouth shut."

"Unless it leads to the murderer." I was flattered at my reputation as a nonrumormonger. "Which is, I assume, what you want me to do."

"I guess." Zizi ate a cube of cheddar, then nodded to herself. "Yes. I'll tell you what I know about him, and you decide."

"Okay." I concentrated on appearing relaxed so I didn't scare her. "Shoot."

"You've heard of the book *Ten Colors of Blonde*?"

"Yes," I said, barely stopping myself from shouting, *Not that book again!*

"The author is supposedly a woman named L. L. Charles," Zizi said.

"Right." It took me a second, but I finally put everything together. "Are you saying that Lance Quistgaard is L. L. Charles?"

"Yep." Zizi reached for a tiny round of short-bread. "I was so incensed over the demeaning message that heinous novel is sending about women, and the huge sales it's sucking from more deserving books, I made it my business to find out about the author. It took a little detective work and some questionable computer activity—that's the part I don't want the police to know about—but I discovered that L. L. Charles is the pseudonym for our own Lance Quistgaard."

"Wow!" I was speechless. It floored me that someone who had been so arrogant and condescending about anything he didn't consider true art had written a book that was the total opposite of great literature. Then again, a lot of folks sold out for money, if the amount was high enough.

"Yeah, wow." Zizi shrugged. "It was quite a shocker to learn that the author lived in my hometown, let alone that he was a guy, since the book's written in first-person present tense, from a woman's point of view."

"Did you confront Quistgaard about being L. L. Charles?"

"Yes." Zizi nodded. "I followed him when he stormed out of the book-club meeting."

"What did he say when you told him you knew he was the author?"

"He denied it, of course." Zizi smiled meanly. "But I didn't care. I knew, and he knew that I knew, and that was what I wanted."

"Did you intend to make that knowledge public?" I asked, then held back a grin and added, "Maybe take it to the *Banner*?" Wouldn't Quistgaard have been shocked to find gossip about himself in the paper where he wrote his own malicious column?

"I hadn't decided what to do." Zizi smirked. "Since Quistgaard wouldn't admit he was L. L. Charles, he couldn't exactly ask me, could he?"

"Quistgaard didn't attack you, did he?" I suddenly had a horrible vision of him going after Zizi, and of her defending herself with the fence post. "Because if he did, you know that would be self-defense."

"No!" Zizi looked at me, horrified. "You can't think I killed him."

"Well . . ." I hesitated, then realized I had to ask, "Do you have an alibi for between nine fifteen and ten?"

"Yes." Zizi nodded. "Yale Gordon is dating one of my friends. He and I went to Gossip Central after the book-club meeting to wait for her to get off work. She's one of the weekend waitresses there, and her shift ends at eleven."

"Great." I hadn't had a chance to ask Yale about his whereabouts, but now I could clear him, too. I excused myself, ducked into the washroom, and called Poppy. She put me on hold, consulted with her bartender, and verified that both Zizi and Yale came into her bar about a quarter after nine and didn't leave until eleven.

When I returned from the bathroom, Zizi asked, "Do you think Quistgaard's second career is important?" She wiped her fingers on her napkin. "I can't see how it would be a motive for murder."

"I can't, either," I agreed, then paused. There was something else I'd intended to ask Zizi, but her shocking news about Quistgaard had sent it out of my head. I'd have to call her when I remembered. "But if I do figure out how the two are connected, I'll tell Chief Kincaid that I got an anonymous tip and leave your name out of it."

"Thank you!" Zizi leapt from her chair and hugged me. "I knew you'd know what to do."

"Actually"—a thought popped into my head—"the cops will probably figure it out on their own. They're going through Quistgaard's personal papers, so I imagine they'll find the manuscript or a contract or something that links him to that book, which means you won't have to worry about it."

"Phew! That's a relief."

We split the check and said good-bye at the door. I waved as Zizi roared away in her Pontiac GTO, then headed back to my store to check something on the Internet and get some cash from the safe. When I had mentioned that the police were examining Quistgaard's documents, I'd remembered about his pawned laptop. It had given me an idea, and there was a good chance that I'd need more than the twenty bucks I currently had in my wallet to execute it.

Shadow Bend Pawn Shop and Jewelry was located on the edge of town, not far from the highway's entrance and exit ramps. As I pulled into the empty lot, I was glad to see that there were no other customers. What I had to do was best accomplished without witnesses.

The three floor-to-ceiling windows that faced the road were outlined in blue neon lights with the words BUY, SELL, PAWN in red. A yellow OPEN sign blinked on and off as I pushed through the glass door, and I immediately noticed on the back wall behind the register a poster listing electronics, jewelry, guns, musical instruments, sporting goods, tools, and lawn equipment as items that were pawnable.

Although a buzzer had sounded when I'd entered, Addie was nowhere in sight. While I waited for him to appear, I wandered around the huge space. A wide-ranging array of items, from an Elvis costume to a complete set of antique china, was on display, including a Wurlitzer Vintage 850 Peacock jukebox that made my heart go pitter-pat. Too bad the ten-thousand-dollar price tag nearly gave me a coronary.

Having called out Addie's name two or three times while I browsed, I realized several minutes had gone by and there was still no sign of him. Had he fallen asleep? Or had something happened to him? I shivered. Maybe Quistgaard's killer had had the same idea as I'd had, and come for the author's laptop.

I dug my cell from my purse and punched in 911; then, with my thumb ready to complete the call, I yelled, "Addie, are you here?"

Silence.

I moved toward a passage leading to what I assumed was a back room and raised my voice. "Addie, it's Dev Sinclair. Are you okay?"

This time I heard a thump, then what sounded like the squeaking wheels of an office chair. As I edged a little closer to the hallway, I wished I had a Taser in my hand instead of a cell phone.

Deciding to try one more time before I got the hell out of there, I shouted, "I've called the police, and they're on their way." As I backed toward the entrance, I hit a table full of Calphalon pans. The sound of clanking metal rang through the shop like the clapping of the amplified cymbals of an acid-rock band.

"What the f—" a deep voice roared, and my heart stopped.

"Damn it!" Addie lumbered out of the corridor. "What's going on out here?" Old-fashioned earphones hung around his neck, and he scrubbed his eyes with his fist. Clearly, I'd woken him from a nap.

Once my breathing was back under control and I'd checked to make sure my undies were still dry, I said, "Sorry. Did I wake you?"

"I thought I'd locked that door." Addie didn't bother to answer my question.

"Nope." I took a step away from him, briefly wondering how Addie's anger-management classes were going. "Maybe I should come back later."

"Nah." Addie's posture relaxed and he pasted what might have been a smile on his face. "My meditation is all gone to hell now. That yoga shit is harder than it looks. I should go back to lifting weights." He patted his stomach. "Especially since my six-pack is now hiding behind my keg."

"You look fine." What else could I say? I wasn't exactly a poster girl for *Hot Bod* magazine myself.

"Thanks." Addie ducked his head, then asked, "So what can I do for you?"

"Last time I saw you, you said you had Quistgaard's laptop. Did you mention that to the police?"

"Nope." Addie raised a pierced brow. "They didn't ask, and I didn't tell."

"Because they would have confiscated it and you'd be out whatever you gave Lance for it?" Knowing Addie's fondness for profit was similar to my own, I had figured that he'd kept quiet about the computer.

"Yep." Addie didn't seem at all uncomfortable with my allegation.

"How much do you want for it?" I had done a quick search on Bing back at the store and I knew a used laptop wasn't worth much. Depending on the model it could be anywhere from sixty dollars to four hundred.

"Three bills and it's yours." Addie went behind the register.

"What kind is it?"

Addie flipped through a stack of papers. "Dell Latitude D600."

"I'll give you a hundred bucks, assuming it works." I reached into my purse, grabbed five twenties, and fanned them out on the countertop.

"Two C-notes, and I'm only doing it because you're a friend."

"One twenty." I added another Jackson to the stack. "And if I don't end up turning it over to the police when I'm through, I'll give it back to you for free."

"Deal." Addie's huge paw engulfed the money on the counter, shoved it in the register, and handed me the Dell. "Don't tell the cops where you got it," he ordered.

I bobbed my head noncommittally, then made a hasty exit. When I slid into the car, I noticed a scene from Bosch's triptych *The Garden of Earthly Delights* on the computer's lid, and snickered. How apropos for a man who had written a book about sex.

After a quick call to Jake to tell him I was safe and heading home to spend the rest of the afternoon and evening with Birdie, I put the BMW into gear and pulled out of the parking lot.

As I drove, I wondered if the answer to the mystery of who had killed Lance Quistgaard was waiting inside the laptop right beside me.

Chapter 25

Gran kept me busy for the rest of Thursday afternoon, helping her get the garage apartment ready for my father's return. When the rooms were up to her standards, she asked me to drive her over to the county seat so she could buy new sheets and towels for him at Walmart. It was really too bad that no one in town sold linens.

I'd considered stocking them at the dime store, but I didn't have enough space. Maybe I should open up a bed-and-bath department in the unused upstairs rooms. I'd have to crunch some numbers and see if the profits from the additional merchandise would justify the added costs.

After we finished shopping, Gran decided she wanted to see a movie and go to dinner. Since I'd been neglecting her recently, my guilty conscience badgered me into agreeing to all her demands—even if it meant yawning through the latest slasher flick and consuming truck-stop food.

We didn't get back home until ten, and by then I was too pooped to do more than take a quick look at the laptop. When I saw that the computer was password protected, I gave up and went to bed.

At 6:05 the next day, the ping of a text coming into my phone roused me from the Land of Nod. According to Noah's message, the doctors had kept Nadine overnight but still couldn't find anything wrong with her, so they were sending her home. Noah was heading into his clinic to take the morning shift, and he'd stop by the store when he got off work.

I frowned. How long could the poor guy dance attendance to his mother, see all his scheduled patients, and not collapse? His mom may not be having a coronary, but she might give him one.

I wasn't pleased with Noah's new habit of waking me at the butt crack of dawn, but I had to admit that I liked what I could accomplish with an early start. After a quick shower and a hurried breakfast with Gran, I arrived at the dime store at seven thirty.

Xylia had sent me a text agreeing to come in at ten and stay until we closed, so I was hoping to spend most of the day creating baskets. Once I finished the Mother's Day orders, my next priority were thank-you baskets for my biggest client, Oakley Panigrahi, a Kansas City real-estate tycoon who sold luxury properties.

Noah had hooked me up with Oakley six weeks ago, and I was working on his second order of twenty baskets. He demanded that the gifts to his buyers be filled with unique items customized to their tastes, which took a lot of research and inspiration. I was willing to put in the extra effort to get everything just right, because if he continued to order baskets from me, his business alone could potentially keep me in the black.

At nine, I greeted Hannah and opened the store. She and I dealt with the morning shoppers until Xylia arrived. I told them I'd be at my worktable if there were any questions or problems, and left them to handle the front of the shop on their own. By twelve, when Hannah left to attend her after-noon high school classes, I'd made good progress on the baskets and decided to let Xylia take a break.

As usual, lunch-hour business was slow, and in between the infrequent customers, I was able to finish up the rest of my orders by the time Xylia returned. Turning the register back over to her, I grabbed a cup of coffee and a bagel, went into the storage room, and opened up Quistgaard's laptop.

Now that I wasn't so tired, it took me only a few minutes to find a blog that told me how to get into a password-protected computer. It instructed me to press the CTRL, ALT, and DELETE buttons simultaneously, then put the word *administrator* under the user name and leave the password box blank. The blogger explained that this method worked because there is a secret administrator's account in every computer.

I was congratulating myself for getting in when I ran into a second wall of protection. The poet had password protected his files. *Shoot!* I knew accessing those wouldn't be as easy.

Most people used fairly common words or phrases for their passwords, such as their name or the name of their spouse or child. I tried LANCE and QUISTGAARD with no luck, and, as far as I knew, he didn't have a wife or any offspring—at least none he acknowledged.

Next, I typed PASSWORD. Nope, not that either. According to his Web site, he didn't have a pet, but it did say he'd attended the University of Missouri at St. Louis, so I keyed in several variations of that. His site said he was a Valentine's Day baby, so I tried his birthdate with several guesses as to the year, but, again, nothing.

I was getting frustrated, but counted myself fortunate that at least the password program didn't lock me out after so many attempts. That annoying feature would have made the search much more difficult, as I knew after forgetting my username on eBay so often.

After trying GOD, DEVIL, LOVE, LETMEIN, MONEY, WELCOME, and the title of both Quistgaard's books and his column, I was stymied. Getting up, I stretched and checked my watch. It was a few minutes until three. Time for the after-school rush.

Exasperated, I returned the laptop to my desk,

locked the drawer, and took my place behind the soda fountain. Hannah had lined up all the supplies before she left, so with Xylia manning the candy case, we were ready for the onslaught. She and I worked steadily until four thirty, when most of the kids left to go home for supper, and by five the store was empty.

As I'd made sundaes, shakes, and root-beer floats, I'd been thinking about my problem. I'd put in a call to Chief Kincaid yesterday afternoon and he still hadn't returned it. Once he did, I'd have to turn the laptop over to the police.

With that in mind, I retrieved the computer from my desk drawer and set up Operation Get the Hell into Lance's Files at the soda fountain.

I tried every shred of information from Quistgaard's Web site, any word related to "The Bend's Buzz" that popped into my head, and all the famous poets I could either think of or find on the Internet. Then, as I was running out of ideas, it hit me. Holding my breath, I typed in LLCHARLES, and, like magic, I was in.

Most of his files were manuscripts, poems, and gossip columns. I opened a spreadsheet labeled MONEY and whistled noiselessly. Although his advance for *Ten Colors of Blonde* was only five thousand dollars, he was waiting for his first big royalty payment, and he estimated that check would be in the high six figures. Who knew that there was that kind of cash in authoring soft-core porn? At those prices, if I had a shred of writing talent, I'd sure give it a try.

Curious about all the fuss the novel had garnered, I clicked on a file labeled TEN COLORS OF BLONDE and started scanning the document. Within the first few pages, I learned that the point-of-view character was Xanthia Luce, a twenty-year-old accounting major attending a small Midwest college and working part-time as a clerk in a dollar store. She had mousy blond hair and dressed like she was teaching at a parochial school.

The next chapter began with the line, *I stare at myself in the mirror. My only unique feature is a heart-shaped birthmark high on my right cheek, which I find myself touching when I'm nervous.*

Why did that sound so familiar? A second later, my gaze flew to Xylia, who was dusting a display in front of me. Our eyes met and I glanced quickly away. *Oh. My. God!* Xanthia Luce was Xylia Locke.

Suddenly I remembered what I had wanted to ask Zizi. I had never found out whom Ronni had seen her talking to after the book club. Of course, now I didn't have to ask. It had to have been Xylia. Had Zizi recognized her as the woman from Quistgaard's book and asked her about it? Most people wouldn't have mentioned it, but Zizi wasn't most people. She clearly had a bee in her bonnet about the novel, and she would have considered it her duty to confront Xylia about her role in it. Why hadn't Zizi mentioned that to me? I bet Xylia had pleaded with her to keep her identity a secret, probably playing on Zizi's social-worker instinct to keep what people told her confidential.

I opened a file labeled XANTHIA. It contained notes and a video link. I muted the sound, then clicked. When the recording started right up, I was glad I'd sprung for the highest-speed Wi-Fi connection. As I watched Lance Quistgaard and my straitlaced clerk having some extremely unstraightlaced sex, I swallowed a gasp. If the handcuffs and spanking were any indication, Xylia had been an extremely naughty girl. It was time to shut down the peep show. I had already seen more than I ever wanted to witness of my employee's love life.

Oh, shit! Had Xylia murdered Quistgaard because of her role in his book? A shiver ran down my spine. Would she off me if she found out I suspected her?

Before I could hit the little *x* in the corner that would close the window, an arm slammed around my throat and Xylia whined, "I warned you, Ms. Sinclair. Why didn't you stop snooping?"

I clawed at her sweater-sheathed arm, wishing for the long nails I used to have before I quit my city job. "I. Can't. Breathe." What kind of person was willing to kill me, but not call me by my first name?

Xylia loosened her grip but replaced her arm with a hand holding a jumbo box cutter that seemed suspiciously similar to the one I used to open big cartons. So nice that I could provide her with a ready weapon. No need to bring a gun when a handy, everyday item will do.

"How did you get his laptop?" Xylia demanded. "I couldn't believe my eyes when I saw that decal on the cover and realized it was Lance's."

I opened my mouth to answer her, but the sharp corner of the razor poked into the delicate skin covering my jugular vein as she muttered to herself, "I went through everything at his house and made sure I destroyed any trace of that awful book."

"But it's published." I eased a fraction of an inch away from the blade.

"Without him or his notes, no one could prove the woman in that novel was me." Xylia used her free hand to pull her cardigan together, almost as if she were chilly or maybe covering her breasts.

"But Zizi knows," I blurted out, then mentally kicked myself for putting my friend in danger. I needed to focus and figure a way out of this rather than throw other people under the bus.

"With Lance dead, there's no one for her to pillory, so Zizi won't pursue the matter." Xylia licked her lips nervously. "If she does, I'll appeal to her woman to woman. She'll protect my name. I told her how badly Lance abused me. I showed her the marks on my wrists and ankles from the handcuffs." Xylia straightened her shoulders. "I've got an attorney investigating whether there's any way to stop further publication of the book. He says we might be able to threaten the publisher with libel, but that it's hard to prove."

Well, that explained Riyad's disclosure that the killer also needed a literary lawyer. I doubted she could stop the distribution of such a megabestselling novel and wondered if she realized that a lawsuit would expose her identity to a lot more people than Zizi ever could.

"You had no idea he was basing Xanthia on you?" I asked, trying to keep her talking until I could think of a way to overpower her.

"Of course not," Xylia snapped. "Before I overheard him on Friday night, I had no idea he wrote 'The Bend's Buzz.' Then later, when Zizi told me about that book, I was in shock. He always claimed he didn't care about material wealth or fame. He said he was a poet, not a merchant."

"I guess even artists have to eat and pay the rent," I said. Then, when Xylia frowned, I quickly changed the subject. "So, Friday night after Zizi told you about the book, you decided to kill

Lance?" I thought about the timeline, then asked, "But he'd already left the store by then. How did you lure him back here?"

"One of his fantasies was sex in a forbidden place." Xylia noticed I had moved away from the box cutter, and she adjusted her aim. "He ordered me to hide in the store after everyone left, and let him in the back."

"Ah." I *knew* I'd locked that door. "So he walked right into your trap?" Why hadn't I ever asked Xylia for her alibi? Oh, yeah, there was nothing to connect her to the victim. She wasn't mentioned in the "Buzz," she hadn't challenged the poet when he spoke at the book club, and she'd said she didn't know Quistgaard when I'd asked her about him Friday afternoon. No. Wait. She'd hedged and never answered my question.

"That isn't how it happened at all." Xylia shook her head so violently, she nicked me.

"Ouch!" I winced, staring at the red droplet that fell to the front of my sweatshirt.

"I never meant to kill him. It was an accident." Xylia seemed unaffected by the sight of my blood. "We were in the May flowers display, and he wanted me to sit on the table while he, you know, did me. But I confronted him about the book, and about him exploiting our relationship for profit."

"That must have been very painful for you to find out about," I soothed.

303

"It was." Xylia sniffed. "When he first asked me to be his submissive, I . . . I was so inexperienced and so insecure, I actually thought I liked having him tie me up and beat me. He was so sweet to me afterward, and he made me feel attractive and desirable. But gradually his demands got kinkier. Even then, I was so in love with him, I just kept giving in."

"Giving up on someone you think you love is always hard," I said.

"Eventually, though, the whole situation got scary and I wanted to stop being with him. But he said he owned me, and the times I didn't show up at his house when he ordered me to, he came and dragged me out of my apartment. He was really hurting me, and I could barely cover the bruises." Xylia wiped a tear from her cheek with the back of her hand. "Then he told me I had to turn over my valuables to him. When I said no, I ended up having to go to the emergency room for stitches. After that I was so afraid, I gave him what he wanted, but it was never enough."

"The time you went to the ER, was that when you told me you'd hit your head on an open cupboard door?" I asked, feeling guilty. How could I have not noticed that my clerk was being abused?

"Yes. The other stuff I could keep hidden with my clothes, but that time he hit me in the face."

"What happened Friday night?" I asked, intent

on distracting her as much as I could while I looked for a way to escape.

"When I called him a sellout and said I'd make sure everyone in town and in the literary world knew exactly who and what he was, he grabbed me by the hair." Xylia took a ragged breath. "And as he was dragging me toward the back room, I snagged a fence post. Then when he got me outside and tried to strangle me, I stabbed him in the chest."

"That makes it self-defense." I smiled reassuringly at her. "You won't get in trouble for that. I'll go with you to the police and help you explain. I'm sure Chief Kincaid will understand."

"I still have bruises on my throat." Xylia fingered the silk around her neck. "That's why I've been wearing scarves this week."

"See, you have proof," I cajoled. "There's no way you'll have to go to jail."

"Actually," Xylia sighed, "Mr. Oberkircher said he wasn't sure if the prosecutor would take a deal because she might think the bruises were from consensual sex. You know, because of how Lance portrayed me in the book."

"Still." I was pleading for my life and wasn't giving up that easily. "No jury around here would convict you. At least one juror wouldn't believe that anyone enjoyed that kind of sex."

"I can't go to trial." Xylia bit her lip. "Everyone will find out the character in that book is me. I can't have that happen."

"But . . ." I stalled, gathering my strength to tackle her and knowing I'd most likely be stabbed in the process. "No one will care what you do in your private life. It's okay to blow off a little steam."

"That depends on what's making the water boil." Above her cute little upturned nose, Xylia's eyes had turned into reptilian slits. "Now it's time for me to tidy up one last loose end."

Hell! I shrank back from the slowly advancing blade. This had turned into my farewell party, and it looked as if I would be the balloon that got popped.

"That's not necessary. I promise to keep quiet," I pleaded while I desperately tried to gauge the best angle to spring at her. As I tensed my thigh muscles to leap, I heard a chorus of angels singing. Actually, it was the jingle of the sleigh bells above the front door, but it sounded like a heavenly choir to me.

Xylia swung her head toward the entrance, and I launched all of my not-inconsiderable weight at her. We both toppled to the floor, but she was stronger than she looked. She pushed me off, grabbed the box cutter that had flown from her hand, and crawled toward me, a furious expression on her face.

I scuttled backward, searching frantically for

any kind of weapon to use to defend myself. My fingers closed around the shepherd's-hook plant hanger in the display, and I swung it at Xylia's head.

She ducked and kept coming. I wound up for a second try, but Xylia grunted and lunged at me. I pointed the shepherd's hook at her, hoping she'd impale herself on the end, but before she could shish kebab herself, a pair of large masculine hands wrapped around her waist, lifted her up, and threw her to the side.

I stared, stunned, at the sight of Noah kicking the box cutter from Xylia's grasp, then seizing her by both wrists and holding her captive. When had Noah gotten so strong and learned those kinds of Bruce Lee moves?

As I contemplated that question, another pair of hands scooped me up and into a warm embrace, holding me as if they'd never let me go. I lifted my head and gazed into the bright green eyes of . . . my father.

"Are you okay, Pumpkin?" he demanded, running his fingers over the small puncture wound on my throat.

"I'm fine. That's only a scratch," I assured him, vaguely aware of Noah talking on his cell to the police. I laid my cheek against my father's chest and held on to him, feeling completely safe for the first time I could remember since he went to prison. "How did you get here?"

Dad had changed very little since the last time I'd seem him nearly thirteen years ago. Yes, he'd aged since he'd been away, but his tall, lean frame was still as erect as it had been the day they led him out of the courtroom. His auburn hair had a few strands of gray, and there were lines in his face that hadn't been there before. But I could tell by the expression in his eyes that his genial personality remained the same.

"The warden decided to release me early so I could spend the weekend with my family." His voice was muffled against my hair. "My lawyer dropped me off."

"At Noah's?" I was confused.

"No. Here." Dad cupped my cheek. "Noah was just pulling up when I arrived."

"Oh." I had forgotten what it felt like to be held in a parent's loving embrace, and the distraction of the experience made it hard to think. "Well, you two are certainly my white knights."

"Always happy to ride to your rescue, sweetheart." Dad chuckled. "But it looked as if you had things under control. Another second and that woman would have been a chick satay." He frowned and finally blurted out the question that he must have been dying to ask from the beginning. "Why was she attacking you?"

While I explained what had been happening in Shadow Bend during the past week, the police arrived and took charge of Xylia.

Chief Kincaid exchanged affectionate greetings with my father. Then he had me relate the events of the past half hour, several times, until he was finally satisfied. He confiscated Quistgaard's laptop, told me to come into the PD the next day to make my statement, and left with his prisoner.

I kissed and hugged Noah, promising to call him; then I locked up the store and drove my father home.

We were both quiet during the short ride. Fighting for my life had exhausted me. But when I stopped the car in front of our house, I put my hand over my father's and said, "Welcome home, Dad."

Epilogue

Apparently, my existence was just one giant Möbius strip, because the two men in my life were once again sitting shoulder to shoulder, glaring at me. This time they were seated at a picnic table, but it was still way too much déjà vu for my liking.

We were all at my father's Get Out of Jail Free party, which, due to the unusually warm weather, was being held by the duck pond on our property. Coward that I am, I remained at my dad's side instead of joining the disgruntled duo on the bench. Dad and I were chatting with Chief Kincaid. It was two days after Xylia had tried to kill me for discovering her dirty little secret, and I hadn't heard what had happened to her since she'd been incarcerated.

Even though Xylia had tried to slit my throat with a box cutter, I still felt sorry for her. I hoped she would be treated okay while she was locked behind bars. On the bright side, having viewed the video of her and her lover, I knew that wearing handcuffs wouldn't be a problem for her.

Snickering at my own wit, I turned my attention to the chief. But before I could ask about

Xylia, Dad said, "Mr. Bourne has offered me my old job back."

"Oh." I was surprised. Mr. Bourne owned Shadow Bend Savings and Guaranty Bank, and Dad had been its vice president. "That was nice of him. Are you going to take it?"

"I'm not sure yet. He feels guilty for believing what Robinson said about me." Dad shrugged. "But I don't blame him."

"Robinson fooled us all," Chief Kincaid said, shaking his head. "If that man ever stopped lying, he'd be mute."

For a few seconds I contemplated my own guilt for not believing in my father's innocence. Then I said to the chief, "What do you think will happen with Xylia?"

"Her attorney and the county prosecutor are working on a deal. It looks as if they'll agree to self-defense in the case of Quistgaard's death, and allow Xylia to plead out to attempted murder and assault for her attack on you."

"Oh." I glanced at my dad, silently asking him if he was comfortable with the subject, considering his own recent imprisonment. When he nodded, I asked, "How long will she get for that?"

"Probably ten years, but it could be as much as twenty-seven." The chief took a swig of his beer.

It was odd seeing him in civilian clothing, relaxed and partying. Although I'd known the chief all my life, we didn't socialize, and it was extremely rare to see him in civvies. Even as a teenager when I'd hung out with Poppy at his house, he almost always wore his uniform.

He and my father had had a long talk, and from what I could tell, their friendship resumed where it had left off thirteen years ago. I was happy for them. Chief Kincaid seemed to have few true friends, and who knew how people would treat my dad? Both men could use a pal.

"So the lawyers have hashed things out," I commented, then asked the chief, "Are you satisfied that she stabbed Quistgaard in self-defense?"

"I am." Chief Kincaid nodded. "Between the photos her lawyer produced showing the bruising on her neck, her neighbors confirming that Quistgaard used to drag her screaming from her apartment, and—"

I interrupted, appalled, "Why didn't her neighbors do something?"

"They didn't want to get involved. They claimed Quistgaard threatened to kill them if they interfered." Chief Kincaid shrugged, then said, "From what Xylia's told us about how her relationship with Quistgaard had changed from consensual to abusive, I'm convinced she feared for her life the night she killed him."

"You believe her story that she'd become fearful of him and wanted to stop the kinky sex and not be his submissive anymore?" I still couldn't quite wrap my mind around my prim-and-proper clerk's twisted bedroom activities. "I mean, isn't what she describes pretty much the essence of S and M?"

"I'm not getting into that discussion, but Quistgaard's abusive treatment of Ms. Locke went beyond anything that could be considered role-play, no matter how extreme your definition of S and M may be." The chief's mouth tightened. "When she tried to end the relationship, he forced her to sign what little property she owned over to him, and he beat the crap out of her when he found out she had withheld some family jewelry." Chief Kincaid crossed his arms. "We found the contracts he made her sign in his safety-deposit box, and we obtained the ER report of her injury."

"The ring and locket he pawned were hers?" I guessed.

"Correct." Chief Kincaid frowned in my direction. He'd already yelled at me for not informing him immediately about Quistgaard's laptop. I'd pointed out that I had put in a call to him to do that very thing, and it wasn't my fault he hadn't gotten back to me straightaway. He sighed and continued. "Lucky for Ms. Locke, Quistgaard kept meticulous notes and videos on his computer about *all* their interactions."

"It's a shame Xylia didn't turn herself in right after she killed him," I mused.

"Most criminals would be better off if they did that. Or not commit the crime in the first place." Chief Kincaid turned abruptly to my father and said, "I've got something for you in my car. Care to take a little walk with me?"

As my dad and the chief wandered off, I looked around for another excuse to avoid Jake and Noah, but Boone, who had gotten back from his cruise yesterday, was in a deep conversation with Miss Ophelia, Shadow Bend's foremost authority on etiquette, and I wasn't quite up to hearing about the latest trends in excruciatingly correct behavior. It surprised me that Boone was so interested, unless they were talking about fashion rather than manners.

Poppy, Tony Del Vecchio, and Gran were laughing together, and I was afraid to find out what that trio was plotting. Especially since they kept directing inquiring little peeps my way.

Okay. Instead of mingling, I'd eat. Gran had made her famous hummingbird cake, and if I didn't nab a slice soon, it would be all gone. I took a paper plate from the pile, cut myself a generous piece of sugary goodness, and settled on a blanket that had been spread in the shade of a towering elm tree.

I had just forked a bite into my mouth and was savoring the pineapple, banana, and cinnamon yumminess when two tall shadows fell across my face. When I inhaled sharply, a pecan fragment got stuck in my throat. While I was trying to get my breath back, Noah and Jake surrounded me, each taking one side of the blanket.

Before either one could speak, I said hastily to Jake, "So, did you give Grant Edwyn the exclusive story from your inside point of view for the *Banner*, like you promised him?"

"Of course." Jake shot Noah a lofty look. "Unlike a lot of men, I always keep my word."

Dead-ending on that topic, I turned to Noah and asked, "How's your mother?"

"She hasn't demanded to be taken to the hospital in two days, so that's a plus." Noah kneaded the back of his neck. "On the other hand, she's rejected every health aid that I've tried to hire."

"You know, I have an idea about that." I leaned forward. "I bet all the ones you've selected have been female, right?" Noah nodded, and I went on. "The problem with your choices is that Nadine doesn't like women—other than herself, that is."

"True." Noah nodded again. "She feels either threatened by them or superior to them."

"So hire a man." I put my hand on Noah's knee. "Preferably a young and attractive one."

"Ew." Noah wrinkled his nose. "That's just, just . . ."

"I know it's gross, and I'm not suggesting she's going to . . . You know she wouldn't dream of having an affair with the hired help." I patted Noah's leg. "But if you find the right guy, she'll flirt with him and enjoy having him around."

"And not fire him." Noah smiled and kissed me. "You're a genius."

Jake growled, and I felt his hand on my shoulder, pulling me away from Noah. I allowed him to separate us, not wanting to upset either man by seeming to favor one over the other. This rivalry between them was getting worse. Could I really keep seeing them both?

As I contemplated what I had gotten myself into, I heard a deep voice bark, "Del Vecchio, why the hell aren't you answering your phone?"

A wiry man dressed in tight black jeans and an even tighter black T-shirt stomped up to where we were sitting.

"What are you doing here, Glen?" Jake stiffened, then rose smoothly to his feet. "And how did you find me?"

"I tracked your cell," Glen snapped. "Why aren't you answering it?"

"I don't work for you anymore." Jake shrugged. "I put in my resignation yesterday."

"We'll discuss that later." The man's eyes narrowed. "Right now, you need to come with me."

"Why?" Jake's posture was rigid. "I quit, remember?"

"The Doll Maker escaped as he was being

escorted back to prison from his appeals trial." Glen put his hand on Jake's arm. "He kidnapped Meg and he says he'll make her his next sculpture if you don't show up at the foot of the Gateway Arch at midnight tonight."

"Son of a bitch!" Jake swore, than turned to me and said, "The Doll Maker is a serial killer who carves women's faces and bodies into what he considers to be the ideal form."

I gasped, speechless.

Jake drew a deep breath. "Meg and I are the ones who originally captured him."

I finally managed to ask, "Is there anything I can do?"

"Wait for me." Jake pressed a hard kiss to my lips. Then with a farewell caress to my cheek so gentle it nearly broke something inside of me, he and the other man sprinted toward the driveway.

I stood frozen as I heard Jake's truck roar to life, followed by another engine starting. Noah got up and put his arm around me. He didn't say anything, and neither did I. My feelings were too mixed. Fear for Meg, joy that Jake had resigned from the Marshal Service, and another emotion— one I wasn't proud of and couldn't bring myself to name.

Of course, Jake had to go try to save Meg, but a part of me, a part I didn't want to admit existed, wondered if he'd gone not because it was the right thing to do, but because he still loved his ex-wife.

I thought about Xylia, a classic case of a vulnerable woman who had sought love in the very worst place. Was that me, too? After all, Noah had let me down once. Maybe he'd do it again. Furthermore, I'd had no inkling that Xylia was involved in such a kinky, and, eventually, abusive relationship. Which made me wonder, How much did I really know about Jake?

I didn't want to be one of those people who clung to their emotional baggage as if it were a floatation device, but I still hadn't gotten over all the betrayals in my life. What if Jake always felt compelled to run to Meg's rescue? What if Noah was never able to free himself from his mother's control? Could I handle either of those scenarios? Did I want to have to try?